Books by Megan Slayer

Anthologies

Out of Bounds
Aim High
Brothers in Arms

Single Titles

Wild Card
We Belong Together

WE BELONG TOGETHER

MEGAN SLAYER

Dedication

For all of us who believe in second chances.
CD & MS thanks for pushing me to finish.
SAM it's great to be working with you again.
JPZ – we do belong together

Prologue

"I'm not leaving without her." Daryl Evans paced in front of the entryway to the security checkpoint at the airport. He couldn't go yet. Couldn't. He groaned. His girlfriend, Sarah Morrison, wasn't the type to arrive late to anything. She kept him in line and forced him to be early. Except today. She wasn't behaving according to her norms. He glanced at their mutual friend, Lyndy. "Think she got caught up in traffic?"

"She's not here so that's a possibility." Lyndy folded her arms. Her ample chest strained the thin fabric of her T-shirt. "Or she decided to dump you. I told you she wouldn't arrive." She shrugged. "You put too much time into the relationship with her. You're leaving and she doesn't want to be here. She'd rather not watch you go than have to face the reality that you're moving on."

"That makes no sense." He stopped walking and frowned. "Lyn, she's rock solid." Sarah wasn't the type to shy away from responsibility. She saw things through. How could she not be there? She was supposed to be leaving on the plane with him.

"Right." Lyndy rolled her eyes. "Which is why you're here at the airport and she's not."

"She could be running late." He stuffed his hands into his pockets. The hum of conversation in the airport as well as the hustle of people aggravated him. Maybe he was just moody. In the next few hours, he'd leave the safety of his college home and family for the chance to work in the movie industry. He had no guarantee he'd even hit the big time. For all he knew, Hollywood would reject him. Sarah should've been there with him. She'd been his strength through so many rocky moments. He checked his watch. *Shit.* Almost time to go through the checkpoint.

Where is Sarah?

"She's not coming." Lyndy sighed. "Traffic isn't that bad this time of the day to hold her up. She's chickening out on you."

Maybe she was, but he doubted it. He forced his attention to the doorway once more. *Please, God, let Sarah show.* He needed her.

The doors opened and Sarah ventured into the lobby. His heartbeat sped up but he relaxed. *Sarah.* "Babe." He rushed up to her. Instead of dragging along her suitcase, she'd brought nothing along — not even her purse. "Did you drop your things off at the counter?"

"My things?" Her voice dropped an octave and her shoulders trembled. "We need to talk."

"About what?" He rubbed her upper arms. "Are you scared? We can be scared together. I'm freaking out about going to California. It's a huge step, but we're doing it together." Christ, he'd become redundant. "You and me against the world. We got this."

"No." She placed her hand on his chest. "I'm not done."

"What?" Nothing made sense. Besides, they had to get into line. "I don't understand."

"I tried to tell you last night, but you were so busy."

"We had dinner with my folks. It was good. Things were..." He couldn't exactly ignore the sinking feeling in the pit of his stomach. "Then talk." The faster they got through this conversation, the better.

"I got my final grades and I didn't have enough credits to graduate yet." She scratched her nails on his chest. "Meaning I need to stick around for another semester."

"Fine. You can join me when you're done. We can work with it." If her needing a credit or two was the only issue, then there wasn't a problem. He'd wait.

She drew in a deep breath and let it out slowly. "It's more

than that."

"More? How?" Anger rose within him. "Sarah, we'll work things out."

"We can't." She grasped his shoulders. "Listen to me. You're meant for greater things than Kenton. This town and all of what you've learned has prepared you for your future. You've got bigger and better experiences ahead of you."

"And you'll be right beside me."

She shook her head. Her green eyes sparkled and tears shimmered in her lashes but she didn't cry. "I'm an anchor. You'll be so much better off without me. Go to California and be the star I know you are."

"Sarah." She couldn't be saying these things. They'd been through so much together. How could she back out now? *An anchor? What in the hell?* "You're not bringing me down. You're the one who buoys me. I'm better when I know you're in the audience. I can handle six months apart. Hell, it'll be a great Christmas present to have you with me again."

"I *can't*."

"What are you saying?" He couldn't process everything. His head swam.

"I'm saying, you need your freedom. You need the chance to be the actor you know you should be. The world is waiting for Daryl Evans to burst onto the scene and make women lick the screen. I bet you'll have a new girlfriend within a month and you'll have six within the next year. Women want you and men want to be you." She straightened her shoulders and pulled her hand away. "I apologized to your parents last night. They said they understood and your mother looked relieved."

He swayed on his feet. The woman he loved was leaving him. She was pushing him away to let him have the life he'd thought he wanted. He opened his mouth to protest but the words never materialized. She wasn't allowed to leave him. She was his best friend, his partner and the best cheering section ever.

"I'll give Lyndy my ticket. She's always wanted to go to California." She met his gaze and smiled, but the emotion never reached her eyes. "Good luck and knock 'em dead out there. I know you can and will."

Sarah didn't cry or waver. "This is in your name, not mine." Instead, she pulled the ticket from her pocket and offered the piece of paper to Lyndy, then walked away.

"Sarah. Wait. We can work this out." He reached for her, but grasped the air. "Sarah." She wasn't stopping or looking back. "Sarah."

She walked straight out of the terminal and disappeared around the corner. Lyndy slugged his shoulder. "I know you want to run after her, but you dumped too much money into these tickets and we have to move. The line at the security check is getting longer. We'll miss our flight."

He balled his hand and gritted his teeth. Sarah had made her choice. *Damn it.* Now Lyndy, the one woman he didn't want to be with, would be right beside him for the flight. Chasing Sarah wouldn't do him any good. She wasn't coming back. Part of him understood. She saw more for him than he'd achieve in town. Maybe she was right, but that didn't make him feel any better. She'd given him his freedom. He didn't want to be away from her, but he doubted he'd be able to change her mind.

"I'll do it," he muttered. "I'll become what you think I can be and I will get you back."

"Hey." Lyndy clapped his shoulder again. "Daryl? I told you this would happen." She linked her arm with his and grasped his hand. "We're going to rock California."

He hated to admit Sarah was right. She'd made him into a strong man but there was more work to be done. Leaving him didn't feel like the right answer, but if he was going to promote himself the way he should, then he'd change his behavior to make her happy. Being a star meant making himself happy and doing what the public wanted.

Still, he hated knowing he'd have Lyndy with him. She'd

only showed up to increase her profile. She wanted to be with someone famous…the opposite of Sarah. He shook his head and made his way through the security checkpoints. *Fuck it.* He'd become famous. He'd do it and make Sarah proud. But he'd come back for her. Damn it. She was the one he loved and he wasn't about to walk away from her for good. Not a chance.

Chapter One

Seventeen years later

"Are you sure this will be fun?" Sarah wobbled on the stool. The daiquiri dribbled over the glass and while the fruity drink had seemed like a good idea, now she didn't want the alcohol. She surveyed the crowd in the dance club. So many bodies...so many people at least a dozen years younger than her thirty-eight. She didn't belong there, or in Las Vegas for that matter. She wasn't the party girl type or a drinker.

Mischa Delbonne fluttered her hand. "You're fine. We'll have lots of fun. Guys are already checking us out."

Us? Sarah snorted. The men around her weren't watching her. They only saw Mischa. Long blonde hair with teal and purple streaks, an ample bosom and such a tiny waist. She reminded Sarah of a model...or a porn star. Sarah massaged her forehead. The throbbing of the bass music along with the pulsing lights in the club were giving her the start of a headache. The scent of cologne and sweat hung in the air. *So many damp bodies...* She shuddered. Noise and large groups of people weren't her thing. Then again, the high heels and short dress weren't her best choices for the night, either.

"What's wrong?" Mischa toyed with her glass of wine. "Had too much at the buffet?" She snorted, then tipped her head back and laughed. "I'm kidding. You're gorgeous."

Sarah forced her attention anywhere but at her promotions expert. Writing took up so much of her time and having someone to get her name out as well as book appointments and such was a tremendous help. Normally, she would've allowed her friend Addie to assist, but Addie hated social media. Having an online presence wasn't easy if one hated the different media outlets.

"Aren't you going to dance? You love to bump and grind at the house." Mischa cocked one eyebrow and the corner of her mouth kinked in what she called a smile. Sarah referred to the look as Mischa's shit-eating grin.

"That's private. There's too many people here." She'd come out to Vegas for a combination of a girls' weekend and a book signing. So far, she'd spent most of her time at the bookstores. Besides, if she tried to toddle out in the middle of the throng of dancers, not only would she probably fall down, she'd embarrass herself with her lack of coordination. Give her a computer and a plot and she'd be fine. Put her in public and everything went to hell.

"I'm going to refresh my wine. Want anything? That daiquiri is probably enough, though. You have to think of your waist." Mischa slid off her stool and strolled away before Sarah could answer.

She groaned. Trust Mischa to jab without sounding like a complete jerk. Most of the time, the things Mischa said weren't too awful but sometimes she went overboard. Heaven help the person who called Mischa on the carpet for her comments. Sarah had learned not to challenge Mischa early in the pairing. She'd prefer a snarky Mischa than Mischa angry.

Sarah folded her arms on the table and surveyed the crowd again. She'd heard stories of people running into celebrities at such places. Maybe someone famous was in amongst the dancers. Then again, how would she know? She spotted one man. He kind of looked like the actor Liam Turner. She'd never met him in person but the guy appeared to be the right height and had the same cleft in his chin—well, kind of. The scruff on his cheeks and chin sort of covered the divot. He wore dark-rimmed glasses too. A disguise? *Is he smiling at me?* Her blood heated and her nerve endings tingled. Even if the guy wasn't Liam Turner, he seemed to be gazing in her direction. She grinned and lowered her arms. Maybe if she bunched her breasts, she'd catch his eye?

Embarrassment washed over her. What in the hell was she doing? Trying to be sexy to snag a man? *Good Lord.* She was too old to be flirting in a club with a guy she didn't know. She had a kid. Grown women with children didn't act so...loose. Still, as he strolled toward her, her heart skipped a beat.

What should she say? Be coy? Tell him her name? Ask him if he'd had a good night so far? She clenched her teeth and continued to smile to hide her awkwardness. Coming on to guys wasn't her forte.

The man approached her table. Sarah opened her mouth to speak, but instead of stopping the guy kept going. Realization washed over her. He hadn't been making eyes at her. She glanced over her shoulder. Sure enough, a stunning woman with tawny hair sat over at the bar.

She'd made a fool of herself and knew when to retreat. She scooted off her stool and smoothed her dress into place as best she could.

"What's wrong?" Mischa brought a fresh glass of wine to the table. "What happened?"

"Nothing." She considered downing her drink but thought better of the idea. "There was a guy...he resembled Liam Turner. I thought he smiled at me."

"At you? For real? He's here. The word at the bar is a couple of actors stopped in." Mischa downed half of the wine. "Could be just gossip."

"Could be." The tips of her ears burned. She'd mistaken someone for an actor. Thank goodness she hadn't opened her mouth and spoken to him.

"I mean, if he's truly here I don't know that he'd stop, but it's possible," Mischa said. She sipped more of the wine.

"I'm cute." Passable...at least she cleaned up well.

"Uh-huh." Mischa didn't look at her. She bobbed her head to the music and her boobs jiggled in her tight dress.

"Anyway, the guy kept going. Turns out he'd zeroed in on someone behind me." She twisted the wristband around. She wanted to leave...the club? *How about Vegas, too.* "We should head to the room. I'm worn out."

"Already?" Mischa whined. "We just got here. I want to dance." She frowned, knotting her eyebrows. "Why don't you go and I'll stay? I've got my phone, credit card, ID and some cash. I'll be fine."

"No. I can't leave you here alone. You've been drinking and anything could happen." She gripped the back of the stool. *Shit.* She'd never get out of the club.

"Our room is downstairs. I'll be fine." Mischa finished the last of the wine. "I came to Vegas to have fun. I'm going to do so."

"Then I'm staying." She flexed her fingers on the stool. Now she had to figure out how to get back onto the seat. *Shit.*

"Oh my God." Mischa's eyes lit up and a wide grin spread across her face. "No way."

"What?" She never could figure out what excited Mischa. She'd squeal over a pair of designer shoes or a fancy handbag as much as she did over people.

Mischa pursed her lips and dragged the edge of the wine glass across her mouth. "I believe Dare Evans is here."

Sarah froze. She hadn't heard that name in forever. "Who?" She knew who Dare was, but she hadn't disclosed such information to Mischa.

"Dare Evans. You know...the walking wet dream. He's been in all the magazines. He won the hottest man alive a few times." Mischa didn't meet Sarah's gaze. "A birdie told me you knew him."

What the hell? A birdie? The only person who knew about her past with Dare was Addie and Addie hated Mischa. Back when she'd known him, he'd been called Daryl. "Kind of."

"Well, he's right behind you." Mischa grinned. "Dare Evans? Would you like to dance?"

"What?" Sarah closed her eyes. Dare...Daryl Evans couldn't be behind her. He wouldn't be in a club in Vegas. Not in a place she could get into. No, he'd be in an exclusive club with women on each arm. He was a true celebrity, not a commoner like her. She opened her eyes and hoped any mention of Daryl was part of her imagination.

"Hi." Mischa batted her lashes. "The music is great tonight."

"What are you doing?" Sarah bit back a groan. So much for wishing him away. The scent of his cologne wrapped around her and memories flooded her brain. *He still wears the same scent after all of these years?* Butterflies swarmed in her belly. She balled her hands. Maybe someone else had the same cologne?

"Sarah?" Daryl eased up beside her. "You're...I'm... wow. You're really here." He blocked her view of Mischa. His blue eyes sparkled and his mouth kinked into a smile.

She met his gaze and a shiver ran the length of her spine. Dear God, the man could still make her wet with just a grin. She fought to catch her breath. "I'm here." Not that she sounded intelligent, but who cared?

"Good." He eased his arm around her. "You're my date."

"Me?" she squeaked. "How? Don't you have one?"

"I do now." His breath tickled her ear.

"How about we?" Mischa asked. "I'm single. You could have the both of us."

Daryl laughed. His grip on Sarah tightened. "My friend Dom is single, too. I'll get him." He disengaged from Sarah long enough to twiddle with his cell phone.

Sarah swept her gaze over Daryl. He'd grown more handsome over time. The rugged look worked for him. He'd honed his muscles and bulked up a bit. The creases around his eyes added to his appeal. She longed to run her fingers over his chest and feel his breath on her skin once more.

"There." Daryl tucked his phone into his pants pocket. "He'll be over." He turned his attention to Sarah. "I've missed you."

"I missed you, too," she blurted. More than she'd ever realized, she'd missed him.

He tugged her into his arms — so strong, but tender. "Let's dance." He didn't give her a chance to protest, but rather led her deep into the throng of people. No one seemed to bother him as he moved around. He held her close and patted her ass. Instead of moving to the quick beat of the techno song, he moved slower and swayed. His breath warmed her neck and ear. She shivered again.

"God, you're still beautiful," he said. "Gorgeous."

"I'm okay." She'd never win a beauty contest, but she did just fine with her assets.

"Nah. You're better than okay." He nibbled her earlobe. "You still fit perfectly in my arms."

"So does every eligible female in Hollywood." She paused. *Shit.* She hadn't meant to say that out loud.

"*Touché.*" He grinned again and rested his forehead against hers. "Those women aren't like you. You're different...unique."

"I'm plump." She had curves and not in all the right places.

He swatted her ass. "Don't you dare cut on yourself. I won't allow it."

Who was he to tell her how to feel? He didn't own her. The frustrating man… "Daryl."

He moved with her out of the knot of people to the edge of the room. Instead of letting go, he continued to a wall of curtains. He pulled one of the sheer panels of fabric aside and nudged her into the new space. The music wasn't as loud.

"Going to chew me out in private?" She toyed with the sequins on her dress. "I've already heard it all, so don't bother. Just let me go. Okay?"

Daryl shook his head then enfolded her in his arms again. "Don't start. You're beautiful and you're going home with me. If I have to spank your ass to make you understand, I'll do it."

She shivered. She hadn't played such games in years and only with him. She paused. *Going home with him?* "Wait, I am?"

"Yes."

"I have a room at this hotel." She wasn't sure why she'd said that. "I don't need to go home with you." What in the hell was she doing? Turning him down? Why?

"Good to know. I've got one in this hotel as well." He smoothed his palm across the back of her neck and threaded his fingers into her hair. He tipped her head. "I'm in the penthouse."

"I'm sharing a room with Mischa," she blurted. "In the peon section."

He bumped noses with her. "Let me get Liam and check in with Dom, then we'll go." He brushed his lips across hers, then pulled away. He toyed with his phone. "Liam will be right back."

She peeked through the curtains. Leaving Mischa alone wasn't smart. Mischa had access to her bags and things. If she felt she'd been abandoned, she'd have a fit. Sarah spotted her assistant, but Mischa wasn't alone. "Is your friend Dom tall with black hair, dark eyes and a beard... kind of?"

"Yeah. You see him?" Daryl eased up behind her.

"You set him up with my assistant. They're over by the bar." She leaned in to Daryl. He'd situated the bulge in his pants between her ass cheeks. More memories popped into her head. Nights spent tucked up tight against him, making love to Daryl so many times and the taste of his kiss...

"Good. Then he can babysit her." He nibbled her neck. "If you're ready, we'll head out."

"No." She wasn't sure she wanted to leave the privacy of the curtained-off room. The rational part of her brain still hadn't come to terms with him actually being there or touching her.

"I meant Liam." Daryl kissed her neck, just behind her

ear. "He finally got away from the redhead."

A man—the one who looked remarkably like Liam Turner—stood on the other side of the little room. He smiled and folded his arms. "I'm ready."

"Let's go." Daryl kept her tight to his side and escorted her out of the curtained space. He hustled through the club and said something to one of the bouncers.

Before she knew what had hit her, she stood in an elevator with the guy who resembled Liam on one side and Daryl on the other. "What are we doing?" she asked.

"Going to the penthouse." Daryl palmed her butt. "I'd rather have the privacy of our room over the club."

The bellman kept his back to them. When the car stopped, he moved aside. "Your floor."

"Thanks, Ben. Got the tip, Li?" Daryl asked. He shuffled forward, nudging her out of the elevator. She stood in the middle of a tiny foyer with three doors in front of her.

Sarah glanced back at the other two men. The bellman grinned and accepted the money, then the elevator doors closed again.

"Do you want to go upstairs with us? I want to be sure you want to. I won't pressure you and neither will Liam."

If she got to spend the night with Daryl for one more shot at what they'd once shared as well as a chance to be with Liam, one of the stars of her fantasies...then yes, she wanted to join them But Jesus. This was her first threesome. She'd never done anything like this before. Fear crept into her brain, but so did excitement. How was this—being with these two guys—happening to her? *Her!* What if she embarrassed herself? What if...*fucking hell*. The fear won out. "Guys..."

"Before we head into the room, I should show I have manners. This is Liam. You might have heard of him—Liam Turner?" Daryl let go of her and leaned against the frame of the middle door. "Liam, I give you Sarah Morrison."

"The one that got away?" Liam smiled and slipped her hand into his. He kissed her knuckles. "It's a pleasure to meet you."

Holy hell. He really *was* Liam Turner. She'd watched the movie *Kaleidoscope* a hundred times because he showed his naked ass and was so sweet to the heroine. She'd pictured herself in the heroine's place during nearly each viewing. "I loved you in *Kaleidoscope* and *Patchwork*. I felt like I knew you in both roles." *Christ, why am I so nervous?*

"I didn't do much acting according to my directors. They felt like I'd either melted into the roles or I was being myself. I say being myself. Daryl helped me prep for both." Liam grinned. "He's good at helping."

"Oh." *Interesting.* A tinge of jealousy hit her. She remembered being the one who ran through lines with Daryl. She'd been replaced. "He's good at getting into a role. I bet he rubbed off on you."

"He did."

She folded her arms to stave off the chill. Awkwardness filled her brain. Because they were hot? Because Daryl was her ex? She wasn't sure. "So…you've got girlfriends." She knew that much from her cursory glances at the tabloid papers at the supermarket. And why shouldn't Daryl and Liam have girlfriends? Maybe because they'd invited her upstairs. "Am I here for one more night with the ex? You want to get me out of your system, right?"

"Not at all." Daryl hesitated in the hallway. "I'm not sure it's possible."

"I've never been with you, so how could I get you out of my system when you've never been in it?" Liam frowned, then shook his head. "Somewhere what I said made sense." He opened the door. "After you."

"Thanks." Liam had a point. Daryl…not so much. "What are you two doing in Vegas?" The question was a little silly, but she didn't care. She crossed the room and put some distance between her and the handsome men.

"We knew you were here." Daryl eased up to her and toyed with a hank of her hair. "I've wanted to see you again for the last seventeen years."

He had? "Why didn't you?" she asked.

"Because I was ashamed." Daryl curled the chunk of her hair around his fingers. "I didn't make it big like you said I would. Not right away and I was ashamed. I couldn't come back and proclaim my triumph in California when there wasn't any. I thought you'd laugh or say you'd told me so. God knows Lyndy did."

Of course. Her former friend had only wanted Daryl because she thought he'd be rich and she wanted money. Sarah had to be honest with him. "I wouldn't have thought less of you." She rested her head against his chest. "I missed you." She winced. By admitting that, she'd opened the wound up again. Christ, she was sad...but they were together. Even if only for a short time, she had a second chance with the man she'd once loved.

Daryl wound his arms around her. "I missed you too and I truly couldn't get you out of my system." He tipped her chin, forcing her to look him in the eye. "You're one in a million, Sarah." He brushed his lips over hers.

Tingles shot around her body. She'd missed the passion in his gaze and the tenderness in his touch. She sucked on his tongue. Holy hell, the man was intoxicating.

Daryl broke away first. "I need you," he murmured. "Always have."

She nodded. Common sense said she should leave and keep her heart from being hurt again. But she'd missed Daryl too much. The old feelings hadn't died. They'd just been buried deep in her soul. A thought occurred to her. "What about Liam?"

Her pussy clenched. Part of her wanted to be with just Daryl, but the rest of her wanted the attention of both men. She'd never slept with two men at one time. She trusted Daryl to be tender and swore her gut feeling about Liam being the same was right. Good God. She had to be crazy. Not having sex in the last year must've messed with her judgment.

"He won't touch you if you don't want him to," Daryl

said. He caressed her cheek. "We want to make you happy. To make you fly."

"What if I want him to? I want both of you to...make me fly." *Oh boy.* She'd voiced her desires. She'd done it.

Liam eased her away from Daryl and helped her to the couch. He sat beside her. "Only if you're sure. I'm dying to kiss you, but I refuse to push."

"I want to be pushed." She wanted to feel desired, needed...important. When Daryl sat on her other side, something within her relaxed.

Neither man spoke. Instead, Daryl kissed her again. Liam eased his fingers around her arm and kissed her bare shoulder. Tongues of fire touched her from within. She pressed her knees together. Her clit throbbed. *Oh goodness.* When she shifted her hips, her panties stuck against her labia. These men did this to her...they made her so wet. A needy desire filled her. She wanted to caress them in return, but she wasn't sure what to do.

"Like that?" Liam asked. His warm breath tickled her neck.

She broke away from Daryl and panted. "I do." Daryl and Liam muddled her thoughts.

Daryl patted his lap. "Come here." He helped her onto his thighs and rested her back against his chest. He shifted her enough to resume kissing her and nipped her bottom lip. This time, he sucked on her tongue. She spread her legs, using his knees as leverage.

The tingles increased in her veins. She moaned and clasped Daryl's hand to her breast. She loved feeling so free and wicked but cherished.

Liam settled between her knees and eased her shoes from her feet. He nudged her skirt up. Leaving a trail of fire, he kissed his way along her inner thigh. "Damn," he said against her skin. "Delicious."

Daryl slid his arm around her waist. He didn't need to hold her down—she didn't want to run away. Not now. Being with him and Liam excited her. She scooted down on

Daryl's lap enough to push the fabric up around her hips. At the same time, Daryl massaged her breast through her cocktail dress. He pinched and rolled her nipple between his fingers. She moaned. The feelings for Daryl—love, devotion and passion—came back and she could've sworn they had never gone.

Liam nosed her panties, touching her but not giving her satisfaction. The tease. He'd managed to kick her desire up a few notches. When he pushed the flimsy material aside and bared her pussy to his gaze, she whimpered. She slid her fingers into Liam's hair. Freedom and delight washed over her.

Liam dragged his tongue along her labia. A fresh wave of sizzles hit and she tugged Liam's hair. She tried not to yank on him. Christ, she had to keep her wits about her, but he knew how to kiss her pussy to make her feel alive. With each lick and nip, he nudged her closer to coming apart. She couldn't breathe. Once he slid his finger into her channel, she whimpered again. He sucked on her clit and pumped his digit within her and the combination of sensations turned her senses inside out.

She shivered. "Oh." She fought the urge to cry out more. She'd learned to remain quiet and keep her pleasure to herself. Making noise during sex hadn't been wanted. She pressed her lips together and gritted her teeth.

"So beautiful," Daryl whispered. "You're into this."

"Yeah." She rested her head on Daryl's shoulder and shivered. "Daryl."

"Let go." He kissed her neck. "You're on the edge. Relax."

Liam pumped his finger in and out of her cunt while he continued to nip and flick his tongue across her clit.

"Oh…" She released her grasp on Liam's hair and closed her eyes. She writhed on Daryl's lap and pressed her pussy tighter to Liam's face. "Fuck." Her thoughts blurred even more. How could she think or make rational statements when he had her right at the edge of climax? Easy. She couldn't. If she was going to experience this—being with them both and having the time of her life — then Daryl and Liam were the right men for her.

Sarah gave in to the orgasm. Her legs trembled as ecstasy washed over her. Her knees wobbled and she sagged against Daryl. Liam licked a few more times. When she opened her eyes, the room seemed to spin. She panted until she gathered her bearings.

Liam sat back on his heels. His chin shone with her juices. He grinned. "Delicious."

"I want a taste." Daryl chuckled. "My turn. Soon."

Sarah whimpered. Yeah, she wanted him to have a chance, too. She might not be able to walk when he and Liam were done with her, but she didn't regret a moment of their time together.

"I want to make love to you," Daryl murmured. "May I?"

He'd asked. Even when they'd been together so long ago, he'd never taken the time to vocalize his desire in such a manner. She turned her head to look at him. Even if she'd wanted to prevent him from being with her, she wouldn't. "Yes." She closed her hand around his wrist. "Both of you." Doing so was a crazy notion, but she wanted both Liam and Daryl.

"You're sure?" Daryl petted her hair. "We won't push. Honest."

"I *want* to be pushed." She wanted them surrounding her again. She reached for Liam. If they were offering then she'd take them up on the opportunity. Could she be about to be taken advantage of? Possibly, but she doubted they'd be so callous with her.

"Sarah." Liam wiped his chin. His eyes widened but his gaze didn't shift. "We'll be gentle."

A twinge of doubt hit her. She probably shouldn't trust Liam. She'd just met him. But he was friends with Daryl. She couldn't be sure Daryl hadn't changed with time, but the man she knew wasn't the type to mind fuck anyone. He hadn't played the role of pushy celebrity or even acted like a jerk.

"We will treat you with respect." Daryl nuzzled her neck. "I love you."

She bit back a snort. Loved her. Good Lord. There was the celebrity portion of him. Loved her… He probably said that to all his conquests.

Daryl's smile fell, but he didn't speak.

Was he upset? Too bad. Once the night ended, he and Liam would forget all about her. She eased off Daryl's lap and smoothed her dress back into place. She needed a moment to think. How was it possible for these two men to play her body so well? She made her way across the room to the bedroom portion of the suite. Instead of finding two beds or maybe two bedrooms, a single king-sized bed hulked against one wall.

She sighed. *In for a penny…* She unzipped and shrugged out of the garment. It landed in a heap around her ankles. Chilly air wrapped around her and her nipples beaded.

"Holy shit," Daryl said.

She kept her back to him. For the first time since she'd gone to the suite with him, she worried about her figure. She had flaws. Plenty of them. Hell, she had curves to spare. What would he say when he saw her naked? She breathed in the scent of his cologne — sexy, masculine and spicy. He eased his arms around her and held her to his chest.

"I've wanted to do this for so long." He kissed her shoulder. "Seems like forever since I've held you."

"Was just a moment." She gasped and parted her lips. "I've missed you, too."

Liam strode around her and Daryl. He stopped before her and yanked open his shirt. Buttons sailed across the floor.

She groaned. Seeing Liam on the big screen didn't compare to being confronted with the real deal. He was more toned than she'd expected. She trailed her fingers over his pecs. Fire lit in his eyes. He eased up to her and kissed her. She didn't see him open his jeans, but she heard the *snick* as he popped the catch.

"Yeah," Daryl said. "Hot."

Was Daryl encouraging Liam? Or was he just caught up in the moment? She brushed off the feeling of confusion and focused on the way Daryl and Liam made her feel—desired.

Liam broke the kiss and eased away from her enough to shove his pants to the floor. She'd expected to see his underwear, but instead, she drank in the image of his dick. He wasn't lacking in the bedroom department. His cock was long, thick and with a thatch of dark curls around the base. The trail of hairs stretched in a thin line up to his belly button. Her mouth watered. She'd loved him in so many movies and ogled his ass plenty of times, but she'd never seen all of him. Now she had and loved the view.

"Do what your heart desires," Daryl said. He let go of her.

Is he talking to me or Liam?

Sarah shoved her damp panties down around her knees until the garment landed on the floor. No turning back now. She picked up one of the condoms on the nightstand. She tore open the wrapper then draped her arms around Liam's neck. He brushed his lips over hers then nipped her. His cock jabbed into her lower belly. She sucked on his tongue, simulating sex. The taste of mint, cola and her own juices filled her mouth. She brushed her breasts against his chest. Electrical zaps attacked her from within. She moaned and he swallowed the sound.

"Damn, that's hot." Daryl palmed her ass. "Beautiful."

She couldn't see him but she heard the *snick* of his pants opening. She shivered against Liam. Being with both men was going to happen. *Holy shit.*

Daryl eased up behind her again and resumed kissing her neck. He situated his cock between her ass cheeks.

Warmth from Daryl and Liam enveloped her. For the first time in a long while, she felt safe and needed. She leaned in to Daryl but kept her arms around Liam. Sarah whimpered and allowed her men to walk her to the bed. She held the condom, still in the wrapper, in her hand. In a tangle of arms and legs, she landed on top of Liam. He laughed and brushed her hair from her face.

"Hi," Liam said. He grinned. "Fancy meeting you here." He palmed her cheek. "Ride me."

She nodded and freed herself of Daryl, then rolled the condom over Liam's cock. When he gasped, power surged in her veins. She'd forgotten how it felt to please a man.

"Come here." Liam reached for her. "I want to be inside you."

She wanted him there, too.

Chapter Two

Sarah straddled Liam's lap. She'd never been this free with her body in her life, but the thrill of being with both men turned her on. Although her heart wanted her to rush and please herself, she followed her brain and moved with caution. She eased down onto his cock until he filled her to the brim. Damn, he stretched her. Her nipples ached and the breath wrenched from her. Her hair slipped in front of her face when she tilted her head to meet Liam's gaze.

Liam grasped her hips. "So sweet. You fit me perfectly." He tugged her to his chest and kissed her while he rocked his hips.

She trembled in his arms and tried to relax, but how? She was in the middle of making love to Liam Turner. She bit his bottom lip then moaned into his mouth. Being with him was so out of her element, but she loved what she was doing.

"I craved this." Liam threaded his fingers through her hair and held her close. "Keep your eyes on me and relax. I know it's hard."

She almost asked him why she was supposed to focus on him, but stopped short. He wanted her to be calm because of Daryl. Soon, he'd be inside her, too. Her heart hammered and goosebumps spread across her arms. *Both men...at once...holy shit. This is really happening.* She cuddled against Liam and tried to only watch him.

"Babe." Daryl swatted her ass. "Forgot how lovely your butt is. It's perfect for my hands and such a pretty pink."

She suppressed a yelp. She'd forgotten how much she liked it when he swatted her. He'd been the only man to touch her in such a manner. She trusted him—unlike others.

Daryl added three more swats then caressed her fevered skin. Her nerve endings sizzled and she wound her arms around Liam's shoulders. The combination of pain from the spanks and pleasure from Liam being inside her almost overwhelmed her.

"Ready?" Daryl asked. Something cool slid between her ass cheeks. She shivered. The lube helped to calm some of the fever in her body, but fear crept into her brain. So many dicks. *Will they both fit? And why am I thinking about this now?*

"Look at me," Liam murmured. Had he noticed her worry? He smiled and cupped her cheek. "Focus on me and breathe. We'll do our best not to hurt you."

She stared into his eyes and studied the gray and green flecks in amongst the blue. She didn't have to speak as Daryl toyed with her asshole. No words worked anyway. She gasped and winced as streaks of pain bounced around within her. Daryl pushed one finger into her hole. Dear God, she was so full. Her thoughts turned to mush and she tightened her grasp on Liam. She was truly surrounded by these two handsome men. She blew out a long breath and reminded herself they were trying to be gentle.

Liam brushed his thumb across the apple of her cheek. His soft touch eased some of the tension within her. The pain switched to pleasure and she forced herself to breathe. She could do this. The fullness wasn't gone, but she could handle it. She whimpered. As much as she worried about being with them, she summoned her inner strength. She liked them both using her. Hell, with a little more practice, she could see herself preferring the ménage over being with one man. She buried her face against Liam's neck and trembled. She had to be crazy loving the feel of two guys in her body, but she did and wanted more from them.

"I've got you," Liam whispered. "Always."

His words comforted her and for a split second she believed he might always be there. She relaxed a bit more and kissed his neck. The scent of his cologne, spicy and tangy, comforted her on another level. She panted and rocked into Daryl's touch.

"Sarah." Daryl eased his finger from her ass. "Mine."

She couldn't see what he was doing, but she certainly felt the blunt head of his erection bump against her hole. She turned her head to breathe more easily and bore down on him as he entered her. "Fuck," she gasped. "Liam." Her strangled cry echoed in her ears.

"I've got you." He trailed his fingers along her spine. "Breathe, sweetheart. Relax."

Easy for him to say. She closed her eyes and willed herself to calm down. She opened her asshole as much as possible and breathed.

Daryl moved deep within her and paused. "Oh fuck." His words rumbled in the room. "Damn." He swatted her rump again. "Yeah."

He spanked her a second time, but if he'd spanked her to help her relax, his plan was working. Still, she yelped. She allowed him farther into her asshole and marveled at the fullness. She rocked on his dick.

Liam continued to stroke her back. "You're doing so well. So sexy and wonderful. Love this."

"Thanks," she murmured. More than she'd wanted to admit, she loved this too.

Daryl's thrusts started slow. He eased deep into her, then pulled most of the way out before starting over again. When he filled her to the hilt, he swatted her. His groans and grunts rumbled in the bedroom.

She calmed as he increased the speed of his plunges into her ass. Part of her wanted Liam to move within her, too, but she doubted he could since he was pinned beneath her.

"Holy shit, that's beautiful." Daryl smoothed his palm over her butt and caressed her abused skin. "Yes." The sound of his hips colliding with her rump sounded almost as loud as his groans.

She eased up enough to look Liam in the eye again. The pain-filled pleasure threatened to sweep her over the edge.

She moaned and rested her forehead on Liam's. He'd become a rock to her and she appreciated his ability to relax her.

Daryl tightened his grasp on her hips and his nails bit into her skin. He swatted her once more, hard. He shoved fully within her and the pressure increased. He shivered. "Damn." He panted. "My knees are weak." Another grunt escaped his throat. "Fuck me, I'm coming." His cock throbbed within her ass and his pubic hair tickled her sensitive skin. He added a few more thrusts before he stopped again and leaned over her. "I never forgot that or you." He kissed between her shoulders then eased out of her ass. He collapsed next to Liam on the bed and scrubbed both hands over his face.

She allowed herself to breathe. Liam grinned. "So pretty," he murmured.

Daryl patted her butt. "Not letting you go."

He still cared for her? Or was his declaration just pillow talk? She couldn't be certain, but he sounded genuine. Hope blossomed in her heart. She doubted they'd be together, but a girl could dream.

"Sweetheart?" Liam asked. "May I make love to you?" The tenderness in Liam's voice curled around her heart.

Without thinking twice, she answered him. "Yes." She scooted off his lap and shoved her hair out of her eyes, then settled between him and Daryl on the bed.

Liam pinned her beneath his strong body. He kissed her and swiped his tongue along the seam of her mouth. Where Daryl moved with force and got right down to business, Liam took a slower pace. He eased his cock along her labia and toyed with her clit. His eyes sparkled as he cradled her in his arms.

She held him in her embrace. She liked being teased. The simple act of caressing her labia kicked her desire up a few more notches. She opened her legs and accepted him into her body once more.

"That's so hot." Daryl smoothed his palm over her forearm

then grasped her hand. "You're beautiful together."

She bit back a snort. Liam was the pretty one. He moved with fluid grace. She gasped as he began to push into her body. He filled her like Daryl had, but with a different kind of pressure. She rode the wave of pleasure. Her synapses misfired and she clutched Liam as well as Daryl's hand. Like she had with Daryl, she met Liam thrust for thrust. She shuddered beneath him.

Liam sat up and folded her legs to her chest. The change in position sent him deeper into her pussy.

She clenched her legs around him and moaned. She felt the ripples of his dick in her cunt. Her thoughts fuzzed again. How did these two men do this to her? How did they manage to keep her wondering what they'd do next while making her want more? She grasped Daryl's hand and placed his palm on her breast. When he tweaked her nipple and sent a new wave of pain through her body, she yelped. The sting added to her desire.

She trembled and held on as the orgasm continued to roll through her. "Liam." She tried to say more, but the words evaporated. Her resistance shattered and the orgasm swept through her. She clung to Liam. Her limbs felt loose and her thoughts swam. For a few moments, the room seemed to spin. She focused on Liam. He'd blown her mind.

Liam continued to push into her and tilted his head back. He groaned. "Shit," he said and met her gaze. "I'm. Coming." He slammed deep into her pussy. The lines around his eyes and in his forehead crinkled. His lips parted and he shuddered. His hair slid over his forehead and the ring of blue in his irises thinned. A lazy smile curled on his lips as he slumped forward. He sighed. "Gorgeous."

"You took the words right out of my mouth," Daryl said. He rolled onto his side and trailed the back of his knuckles across her cheek.

Her face and the tips of her ears burned. She'd heard the words but still didn't believe Daryl. He knew how to say the right thing to get what he wanted. He also knew how to build others up, but sometimes wasn't as genuine as he wanted people to believe. She didn't want to accept that this could be one of those times, but still. She had to keep some of her guard up. She'd bared everything else to him and Liam.

Liam eased out of her and removed the condom, then settled beside her. "Fucking balls, that was good."

"You've got such a way with words," she managed. She blew out a long breath and closed her eyes. She couldn't deny the headiness of being with two celebrities. So she knew Daryl and had dated him before he'd become famous...he was a different person now. She'd never get this opportunity again. They'd move on and leave her behind. She opened her eyes. At least the experience had been worth the hassle.

Daryl yanked the comforter over their naked bodies. He kept her tight between him and Liam. "Christ, I'm getting old. I'm worn out."

"Me, too." Liam snuggled up to her and tangled his legs with hers—as if she'd been sleeping with him for years.

"You're a dream come true," Daryl whispered. He closed his eyes and eased onto his back. "Love you." Within moments, his breathing evened out as he fell asleep.

She rolled her eyes. Of course he'd tell her loved her. He probably felt obligated to tell her what he thought she wanted to hear.

"Uh-huh. Me, too," Liam said. He nodded off to sleep just after Daryl.

Sarah stared at the ceiling. Tiredness filled her body but her brain refused to shut down. She had too much to think about. She'd slept with two movie stars. Liam Turner, the man who'd turned out to be much sweeter and more tender than she'd expected. His sex appeal on the big screen translated right over into real life—as if he truly cared about her. Then there was Daryl. He'd been much of the same man she'd remembered. Maybe he had a few more lines around his eyes and his voice had grown deeper, but he still reminded her of the handsome man she'd fallen for years before. She'd shared the greatest night of her life with them both.

But like all good things, this night had to end.

Sarah remained still until she knew Liam and Daryl were fully asleep. She had to go. She'd done what she'd come to do and needed to leave before she had her heart broken. She refused to be dumped in the morning or shown out the door shortly before dawn. No, she'd go on her own terms. She scooted up onto the pillows and eased out from between Daryl and Liam. When Daryl shifted, she moved the middle pillow into the space she'd vacated.

Thank goodness no one had bothered to turn the lights off. She snatched her dress from the floor. Where were her panties? She cast a cursory glance around the floor, but abandoned her search when Liam sighed. She had to keep moving. The panties were nice, but not so valuable that she needed them right now.

She slipped into her dress and yanked the zipper into place. She'd forgotten about the bracelet snapped onto her wrist, but now she appreciated the thing. Instead of having to keep a key card with her, she could wave the barcode on the bracelet over the reader on her door to enter her modest suite. She snatched her shoes from the floor and glanced back at Liam and Daryl.

"I'm sorry, but I'm not sorry," she murmured and blew them a kiss. Sarah straightened her shoulders and left the bedroom. Once she escaped into the silent starkness of the hallway, she put her shoes back on and summoned the elevator. Leaving Daryl and Liam sucked. They'd been great together, but the fairy tale had to end. She needed to get back to Ohio, to her job and her son. Life might wait for celebrities but she wasn't famous and she still had commitments.

The bell dinged and the doors opened. The bellman smiled but said nothing. Without looking back, she stepped into the elevator car and left her fantasy behind.

"Fourth floor, please." She clasped her hands together at the small of her back and nodded. "Thank you."

And thanks to Liam and Daryl for a night I'll never forget.

* * * *

The next morning, Daryl rolled over and patted the bed. Instead of finding Sarah beside him, he palmed Liam's hip and something soft. *A pillow?* He didn't open his eyes. There wasn't any point. She'd left. He should've known. He hadn't slept this well in ages and now she'd gone. He'd probably snored his way through her escape. *Shit.*

He settled onto his back and opened his eyes. The patterns on the ceiling weren't that interesting, but he couldn't bring himself to gaze at her empty spot on the bed. From the moment he'd spotted Sarah at the club, he'd wanted her. She made his heart beat again. He felt like himself, not the hyped celebrity. She managed to ground him. Only Liam had been able to do that and now he wasn't sure Liam was enough.

"You're thinking about her, aren't you?" Liam didn't roll over. He tugged the blanket across his shoulders. "I can feel the heat from your brain working too hard."

Ah, Liam. He should've known his partner would have him figured out. Daryl moved the extra pillow out of the way. He eased up behind Liam and draped his arm over his lover's hip. He kissed Liam's neck. Liam kept him sane, too. But with Liam, things were different. He loved Liam so much. Liam helped to bring out the human side of him while making him stronger.

"Start talking." Liam laced his fingers with Daryl's. "I'm listening."

"I'm thinking about her." He kissed Liam's shoulder. "I made a mistake inviting her upstairs so fast. We should've romanced her more. Taken her to dinner. Dancing. Anything to keep her between us where she belongs."

"And here I thought you were going to say you had

second thoughts because you don't really want someone else in our bed." Liam shifted around until he faced Daryl. "You need her so much. I used to be that for you."

"Li." *Shit.* He couldn't lose Liam. The rift between them had already become too wide. He had to save the situation. Adding Sarah into the equation balanced him, but he hadn't discussed things with Liam enough to be sure Liam agreed. He'd dealt with this situation like every other one and foisted his decision onto Liam without giving a damn about his lover's feelings.

Liam propped himself up on his elbow. "Who do you want?"

"You," he replied. "…and her." He couldn't lie.

"If I told you I don't want to share you again, would you be okay with that?" Liam asked. "Don't sugar coat."

"I married you for a reason. You're my other half." He refused to look away from Liam's gaze. "But she's very important to me. I thought I could leave her behind. Thought I could have a life and she'd be just a memory, but I'm not so sure any longer."

"That's what I suspected."

"Li." His skin prickled and his stomach soured. Honesty was usually the best policy, but he doubted the validity of that thought.

"Before you lose your shit, I'm not going anywhere."

"No?"

"No, but tell me your plan." He grabbed Daryl's hand and twined their fingers together. "Be honest. What do you want?"

He could do this. "I want Sarah."

"That's not a plan."

True. He dragged a long breath into his lungs and let it out. "I've never been able to get her out of my mind. I love you, but I love her, too. Things between us have been strained. We're always apart and when we're together we're fighting. You think I'm cheating. I think you are. It's a mess. I don't know how, but I thought she'd be the glue to keep us together. If we had her in the middle and everywhere else, maybe she'd help us to see we make each other happy."

"Still not a plan." Liam let go of him and sat up. He rested his elbows on his knees. "We don't trust each other. Even when we say we do, we don't."

"I know." Saying those words out loud broke his heart. "It's not the whole truth. I trust you more than you realize. I wouldn't have entered into this marriage if I didn't believe you'd keep the secret. I wouldn't have explored my feelings for you if I didn't feel safe in your arms. I know you won't cheat on me and that I have no desire to cheat on you — except with Sarah."

"You'd throw away what we have in order to have her?" Liam's eyes widened.

"No." Not a chance. Liam meant too much to him. He couldn't see life without him.

"Then what? Something changed the moment we stepped into the club tonight. What?"

He had to bare his heart and his emotions. Liam deserved no less. Daryl squeezed Liam's hand. "When I found out she'd be in Vegas...I thought if I saw her, I'd either want her or be able to move on. As soon as I held her in my arms, I couldn't let her go. I can't let you go either and I didn't want to choose, so in my head I planned for us to live together as a threesome and have lots of sex while we grow old together."

"Were you going to tell her that?" Liam asked. He stared at Daryl. "She can't read your mind. God knows I can't."

"Don't be so sure. You're on my wavelength a whole lot more than you realize." Daryl chuckled. "With Sarah, I'd thought about it. I had this idea that this morning, while we shared breakfast and another round of sex...I'd explain the situation." Truth be told, he hadn't given the situation much consideration beyond fucking a lot and whisking her back to the townhouse he shared with Liam in California.

Liam scrubbed both hands over his face. He didn't speak

for a long moment. Daryl's heart hammered. He wanted Liam to say something. Chew him out, scream, agree… anything.

"I must be losing my mind." Liam left the bed and strode nude across the bedroom. His ass flexed with each step.

"How?" This time, Daryl sat up. His mouth watered. As much as he worried about losing Liam, he couldn't help but ogle his butt. The hours at the gym was reflected in Liam's toned physique.

"I like her." Liam faced him and rested his hands on his hips. The muscles in his chest flexed with each breath. "The thing is, I can see the three of us working. I know you and me. We might be happy with the pole, but we love pussy when we've got the chance to be with one hell of a woman. She's gorgeous. I can see why you'd be taken with her. Hell, I've been more than a little in love with her since you first showed me her photo. I never said anything because I thought you'd be angry. Maybe you'd be jealous. I don't know."

"Unless she chose you over me, I wouldn't be jealous. But there's got to be more to the story." He liked what he'd heard, but he didn't believe everything could be going so well. There had to be a few wrinkles.

"But you're assuming she wants you back. For all you know, this was a one-time thing. She might have a family or a husband back in Ohio. She might have used us as a fling. You know, to say she'd fucked a celebrity." Liam shook his head. "I don't believe that, but I've been fooled before."

Daryl nodded. He knew Liam's past all too well. The poor guy had been married when they'd met and Liam's wife had lied about her fidelity. She'd embarrassed him in the tabloids when she'd hooked up with a record producer. She'd broken his heart and tossed him out like garbage, but through the media. When she'd decided to divorce him, she'd gone through her legal team rather than facing Liam. After she'd devastated Liam, he'd closed himself off and had focused on his acting. Getting Liam to not only open up after the divorce but to let Daryl in as more than a friend had been almost impossible. But he'd convinced Liam to give their connection a try.

"So what are you thinking?" He leaned against the headboard and crossed his ankles. "It won't work? Or do you want out? You said you weren't leaving. Is that true?"

"I've done a lot of hiding for you. I've lied and kept so many secrets. I'm not sure I can do it again." Liam folded his arms. "Are you absolutely sure you want her in our marriage?"

"I am." He also felt like a jerk for insisting. Liam was right. The whole partnership was just a friendship, according to the tabloids. No one knew about them being a couple other than the justice of the peace who had married them. Strike that—Liam's mother knew and so did his brother, Keith. He doubted now that anyone would care if he and Liam came out of the closet, but still. They were supposed to be the hottest single men in Hollywood. He'd used that angle to garner better roles in some of his movies. Would he still be offered plum jobs if he admitted his bisexuality?

"If we have a threesome with Sarah, then we go public. We tell the truth. I'm tired of being a secret. I'm not just your best friend," Liam said. "I'm your husband and I want to touch you in public. I want to be able to kiss you and tell everyone I'm the luckiest man alive because I finally found the love of a lifetime."

"I agree. Even if she doesn't want to be with us, we can't lie any longer." He'd been scared to death to admit that truth before, but now his attitude was different. Hiding wasn't an option. Liam deserved more. "Then what do we do?"

"We should first call Mischa, since you don't have Sarah's number. Once we get it, we should connect with Sarah and at least talk about what happened last night." Liam grabbed a pair of boxer briefs from his suitcase and donned them. "Next, we set up a plan. I'm very fond of her, even after one night. I'm game to try, despite the little voice in my head screaming this is nuts. Once we have a plan, we romance her and give her time to come around or tell us to get lost."

He sagged against the headboard. "What about us?"

"What are you talking about?" Liam crossed the room and crawled onto the mattress. He sat beside Daryl. "I love you. Always will. You're my partner, my husband and my best friend. We're in this together."

"You're not having second thoughts? I want to make our marriage a threesome."

"I know." Liam grinned. "My head is swimming. Part of me isn't sure, but the rest of me...I can't think of anything else more logical. When we were together, things felt right. We worked in harmony."

"We did." He reached for Liam and cupped the back of his husband's head. "I love you."

"Then call Mischa."

"What about a text?" He hated using the phone for actual calls unless he truly wanted to speak to someone. Getting Sarah's number was important, but he couldn't stand Mischa.

"Your decision. I'm taking a shower." Liam kissed Daryl then left the bed. He wandered into the bathroom. Within seconds, the whoosh of running water filled the air and steam billowed into the suite.

Daryl snatched his cell phone from the nightstand then hesitated. *Dear God. You want her. Just do it.* He hated having to give himself a pep talk, but Christ—this could kill him. He'd faced plenty of difficult moments. Why did connecting with Sarah on her turf seem so damn scary? Because she could turn him down. He didn't want another abandonment.

He pressed the buttons and composed the text.

Hey Mischa. How is Dom? Bet he's happy and sleepy.

Stupid for a text, but he had to be sweet to get what he wanted.

He's beside me. Yep, sleeping. What's up?

He blew out a long breath. He could do this.

What's Sarah's number? We forgot to exchange digits.

Within seconds, Mischa replied. *She usually doesn't share. Srry.*

A moment later, another message from Mischa arrived. *BTW, she left 4 home this AM. Srry. Guess she wasn't that n2u.*

Damn it. He still had to be a gentleman.

Thanks.

Daryl stared at the open bathroom door. Mischa hadn't been any help. He scrubbed the back of his hand across his mouth. Who could help him? The Internet wasn't a person, but he might find info about her there. He typed her name into the search engine on his phone. Results returned for plenty of women named Sarah, but not his. He scrolled through the links. At one time, she'd sworn she wanted to teach at their alma mater. Could she be at Kenton University? Anything was possible. He searched for the college, then her name. Four women named Sarah and all professors. *Hmm...* Some of the names were hyperlinked. He clicked on the first one, then the second. No dice. Maybe he was wrong. He'd come to dead ends hunting for her before. He tapped the third link and his breath lodged in his throat.

"Sarah," he murmured. She'd changed her name. Not Morrison, but Nelson. She'd gotten married? He scanned through her bio and learned pretty much nothing about her personal life other than that she had a cat. Still, he had a lead.

"Did she cough up the number?" With a towel around his hips and water splotched on his chest, Liam strode up to the bed.

"No. She wouldn't." He gripped the phone. "But I found Sarah. She's a Nelson now and teaching at our old college."

"Smart and pretty. I like." Liam folded his arms. "So?"

"I can't go to her." He sagged back against the headboard and stared at Liam. "I've found her, lost her, convinced you to go along with my fucked-up plan and found her again, but I can't accompany you to Ohio. I've got to be on set in two days. I'll be stuck in California for at least three weeks."

"Okay." Liam shrugged. "I'll go."

He opened his mouth but didn't speak. He needed a few seconds to think things through. If Liam went to Ohio, he might be able to convince her to open up. He'd always been the softer and sweeter of the two. Liam understood finesse.

"I'm due for a nice, long break," Liam said. "I've made three movies in the last year and a half. The movie-going public will be so tired of me when the films come out."

"They'll see fantastic work and appreciate what you've done. They will love the movies." Daryl nodded and tossed the phone onto the blankets between his knees. "As for Sarah, you're right. You should go. I'll make a mess of the situation. She's probably hurting, angry and she'll want answers."

"I want them, too," Liam said. "But are you sure she'll believe me? If I poof into Ohio and find her, she might not be so receptive."

"She will. She likes you, too. I could see it in her eyes." He'd missed that look and warmth from her. He remembered she tended to wear her heart on her sleeve. He'd known from the first time he'd spoken to her that she liked him and couldn't wait to see her again. Now he had the chance to reconnect with her for more than a night. Liam was the bridge and his best chance. If nothing else, he'd have Liam when everything else fell apart.

"Then I'm heading to Ohio." Liam grinned. "I've never been there. Pennsylvania…Indiana but not the buckeye state. I'm excited." He paused. "I need a plane ticket."

"Yeah." A calm swept over Daryl. He didn't doubt his decision other than wanting to be with Liam on the trip. Still, he had a good feeling about Sarah and Liam. They were his missing pieces and once they were all together again and could talk...he'd have his heart's desire.

Chapter Three

That evening at midnight, Liam crossed through the Cleveland airport terminal. When he'd hopped on the plane, he'd forgotten about the time change. *Damn.* Bone-deep weariness washed over him. He needed sleep and food, but not necessarily in that order. He made his way down to the baggage claim and picked up his suitcase, then tucked his carry-on bag on top. He stopped at the first information desk he could find.

The woman behind the counter grinned at him. "May I help you?"

"You sure can. I need a hotel. Is there one close?" He wasn't sure if there were any within a short drive. Maybe checking on the lodgings before he left would've been smart. *Too late now.*

"We have the Cardinal Suites just beyond the parking garage. There's a shuttle leaving every half hour to take passengers to and from the hotel. Go out to the passenger pick up area and the shuttle should be by shortly."

"Thank you." He gripped his bag and glanced around the baggage claim level for a sign board. The airport wasn't that big. He should be able to find where he needed to be without too much trouble.

"I don't know if anyone has ever told you this, but you look a lot like my sister's favorite actor, Liam Turner." The woman smiled and laced her fingers together. The move bunched her breasts together beneath her uniform shirt. She pursed her lips. "We don't get many celebrities through here."

He'd seen this sort of thing before—people hoping to

meet someone famous and trying too hard to impress him. He bowed his head and leaned in close. "I'm not him, but I get that a lot. The guy is certainly hot. Hell, I'd do him." He'd pushed his luck a little by admitting he was attracted to men, but he doubted he'd ever see the lady again.

"Oh." Her eyes widened. "I'll...tell her you aren't him." She nodded. "Well, have a good night and I hope you enjoy your time in Cleveland."

"Me, too. Night and thank you. You've been a lot of help." He winked, then strolled away from her toward the escalator. He shouldn't have lied, but he also didn't feel like dealing with a possible fan at midnight. He wasn't at his best. Call him vain, but he'd rather be primped and pressed before going into public as the celebrity. Right now, he was just William.

He rode the escalator up to the ground floor. There, he wandered out to the covered drop-off area. Sure enough, a shuttle with the name of the hotel waited in a labelled parking spot. He strode up to the mini bus and waved.

The driver opened the door. "Going to the hotel?"

"Sure am," Liam said. "What would you like me to do with my bags?"

"We'll put them here behind the front seat. You're my only rider and I'm due at the hotel in a few minutes." The driver left his post and helped Liam with the suitcase. "Won't be long." He sat back behind the wheel and closed the door.

Liam settled in his seat and held onto his carry-on bag. He'd be able to rest soon. He shook his head, getting Sarah and the conversation with Daryl out of his brain. He'd fallen hard for Sarah. She'd been scared and unsure about being with them, but once they'd all gotten together, she'd asserted herself. She'd directed what she wanted and hadn't given them the chance to be celebrities. She'd acted as if she wanted the real guys. Then there was Daryl. He'd practically decided from the first he wanted her in their marriage. Daryl was that type—he made his choices and stuck to them. Good or bad, he held to his decisions.

Normally, Liam didn't care. He trusted Daryl's judgment. But sometimes he wished Daryl would ask before he moved. Sarah was one of the few catches. He liked the way they had worked together and the way she had felt in his arms. He could see a future with her and Daryl.

But what if she didn't want them? She'd left them high and dry in the morning. Here he was in Ohio ready and willing to chase her. *It could be a good move or it could be the silliest thing I've ever done.*

Once the shuttle pulled to a stop in front of the hotel, the driver waved to Liam. "Here you go. Enjoy your stay in Cleveland."

He offered the driver a five-dollar bill, then hefted his suitcase into the lobby. He wandered up to the counter. A man in a suit looked up from the computer. "Welcome to the Cardinal Suites. How can I help you?"

"I need a room and I'd love something to eat." He rested the suitcase next to his hip. "A king-sized bed would be perfect. Two nights, please." He needed time not only to find Sarah, but to plan out what he'd do once he located her. Rushing in and professing his attraction to her probably wasn't the smartest bet.

"Well, the best I've got is one of the suites on the top floor. We've normally got more open rooms than this, but tonight we're nearly full. The kitchen is open until one, so if you've got an idea of what you'd like, you'd be best off to place the order as soon as possible."

"Then that's what I'll do. The suite will be fine." He didn't care if it was the biggest room or not. He wanted a bed. He'd prefer Sarah and Daryl there with him, but beggars couldn't be choosers. He offered up his credit card and held his breath. This card bore his real name. Hopefully, the man wouldn't figure out Liam's identity. Few people knew him as William Walsh. He worked way too hard to keep up the Liam Turner persona.

"Perfect." The man gave Liam back his card, then slid the key cards across the counter. "You're in room eight-one-two on the eighth floor. Swipe those in front of the sensor and you're good to go. Have a good night."

"Thank you." He tugged his suitcase down the hall to the elevators and waited for the car to open. Within a few moments, he ended up on the eighth floor. He located his room and once inside, he collapsed onto the bed. He scrubbed both hands over his face. According to the attendant at the counter, he needed to hurry up and order if he wanted food. *Well, shit.* He swiped the menu from the nightstand and made his selections. Once he'd phoned in the order, he flopped onto the bed again. His feet ached. His back hurt and he regretted his decision to catch the first flight to Ohio. Damn, he hated the time changes.

Twenty minutes later, the bellman arrived with Liam's burger and fries. Liam devoured his food and downed the soda in what seemed like two gulps. He hadn't realized just how hungry he was until he smelled the hamburger.

He turned on his laptop and inputted the Wi-Fi code. While he ate, he searched for Sarah. Her name brought back a couple of dozen results. He switched to the photos. Ever since he'd been a child, he'd loved looking at photographs. Most of the images weren't her, but a handful were. His skin sizzled all over again. Her smile warmed him and memories of Sarah filled his mind. He could almost taste her kiss on his lips.

Among the photos of her were two of a guy Liam didn't know. How should he know the man? He barely knew Sarah.

His phone buzzed. *Shit.* He'd forgotten to switch it back to the ringtone. Daryl's face lit up the screen. At least it was Daryl on the other end, not their agent. He answered. "Hi, babe."

"You made it?" Daryl asked.

"I did. I'm at the Cardinal Suites trying to get used to it being almost one in the morning." He stretched out on the bed. "How'd it go with Samuels?"

Daryl snorted. "Awful. That director is out to get me."

Liam chuckled and crossed his ankles. "How?" Daryl could be so overly dramatic — and not just in front of the cameras. He tended to worry about his performances and hated to read reviews. Not that Liam enjoyed having his work on screen critiqued, but still. Daryl needed more of a support system than some actors and Liam didn't mind being that strong man. Besides, Daryl probably just needed to vent. He worried too much for his own good, too.

"The bastard wants a whole bunch of retakes. The sets have been destroyed. They were taken down pretty much the day after we shot the love scenes. I don't know how it'll match up. I'm sure we won't get the same look, but he's convinced the passion wasn't there between me and Ariane. Well, no shit, it wasn't. I can't stand her."

Liam smothered a laugh behind his hand. He'd known from the moment he'd met the actress that she wasn't a good fit for Daryl. She was the type to fall for her co-stars and Daryl didn't. If she thought she'd use him to up her importance in Hollywood, she'd been mistaken. She'd even made a pass at Liam — not that he'd been interested either. He composed himself. If he kept quiet for too long, Daryl would think he'd dropped the call. "You'll be fine," Liam said. "You'll kiss her, pretend to fuck her and it'll be over. Think about me when you're kissing her, or me and Sarah."

"I'll be hard the whole damn time and she'll think I'm really into her."

"I don't know what to tell you," Liam said. "How many days will you be in Nevada?" He needed to plan his course of action for the rest of the week.

"Three, I believe. But given Samuels' attitude, it could be two weeks," Daryl complained.

"You'll live." Liam kicked out of his running shoes. If he rested on the bed for too much longer, he'd fall asleep. He had to focus. "I found Sarah. Kind of."

"And?"

Now he had Daryl's full attention. "I'll spend tomorrow making sure it's her and how to get to where she is, but

I'm pretty sure she's in Kenton. Possibly a professor at the college there. Just like we thought. It's got to be her."

"It's been years since I saw her," Daryl said. "I don't want to think of her as being with anyone else, though. She's *ours*."

"Slow down. She was *ours* for one night. That doesn't mean she'll want to do it again." He blew out a long breath. He should've known Daryl would be overly anxious to find Sarah. Once he got his mind set on something or someone, he didn't stop. Good thing Liam wanted to see her just as much as Daryl. "When I meet up with her, I'll let you know," Liam said. "Promise."

"Good deal." Daryl paused. "Li?"

"I'm here." Not like he'd be anywhere else. "I'm getting tired. The flight was rough from turbulence and the woman next to me spent most of the time staring at me."

"I wish I was there with you. I love you, Li. More than anyone. Even Sarah."

"I know you do." He smiled, even though he knew Daryl couldn't see him. "I love you, too." He hadn't expected Daryl to say *more than Sarah*. Hope filled his heart. Maybe they could get this threesome thing to work—if Sarah was open to being with the both of them again.

Daryl's voice dropped an octave. "Thanks for going on this crazy wild goose chase with me. I can't do it without you and I wouldn't want to."

"Same here." Damn, he wished Daryl was there. He wanted to hold his husband as he slept. "I miss you."

"Miss you too. I have to go. You've got a long day and I've got an early morning. I'll call you tomorrow and text when I'm on my way to Ohio."

"I'll have my phone on. Night, D." Liam closed his eyes. He couldn't wait for Daryl to finish the retakes and come to Ohio. They hadn't had time to themselves since the short respite in Vegas and the week between Daryl's latest films. Liam appreciated his decision to take six months off for family time, but wished Daryl could, too.

"Night, Li. Love you." Daryl hung up, leaving Liam in silence.

Liam left the phone beside him on the bed and got up long enough to ensure the door was locked before he collapsed again. He buried his face in the pillow. Sleep overtook him in no time. He didn't even dream. The tiredness was too much for his body. For the first time in a long while, without Daryl beside him, he succumbed to a decent night's sleep.

* * * *

Liam slept long into the next day. He spent his waking time in his boxer shorts and a T-shirt. He ordered in food and showered late that night. By the time he woke the next morning, he'd not only located Sarah and knew for certain she was the one he'd been looking for, but had also booked a rental car and a room at one of the hotels in Kenton.

Wednesday morning, he packed up and headed to Kenton. He marveled at the splashes of color along the way. He'd forgotten the beauty of the leaves changing in late September. He'd gotten used to palm trees and elaborate landscaping. Once he left the buildings and urban area around the airport, farmland stretched out on either side of the highway. The scent of corn hung heavy in the air. He missed the serenity of the farms and open spaces.

Liam drove an hour and a half across the state to Kenton. Once he reached the sleepy college town, he understood why Sarah would want to live there. Tall oak trees lined the roadway. The buildings seemed to be integrated into the landscape rather than dominating it. Students milled around the common areas, in and out of the café, coffee shops and a water bar. He wondered what a water bar might be and would have to check it out later. First, he wanted to find the hotel.

Once he drove to the south end of campus, he located his lodgings for the night. The hotel reminded him more of a dormitory than anything. The five story, red brick Walters

Hotel reminded him of every other building on campus, but at least it had a sign in front. He parked and made his way into the hotel without a problem.

Leaving posed an issue. A young man bumped into him. "Hey, watch it," he snapped.

"Sorry." Liam smiled and patted his pockets to ensure he still had his wallet, keys and phone. Call him crazy, but living in urban areas and moving around the movie lots had taught him to keep his possessions close at hand.

"Who do you think you are?" the guy asked. "Someone special?"

"I wasn't watching where I was going. Simple mistake. I'm sorry." If he'd been Daryl, he'd have disclosed his celebrity status. Good thing Daryl was still in Nevada.

The young man rolled his eyes and strode off.

"Welcome to college life," Liam muttered. He stepped up to the first map of the campus he could find and hunted for the Leonard building. According to the course offerings, Sarah should be in the middle of a class on creative writing. He pointed to the building, gathered his bearings and set off. The campus appeared bigger in the photographs online. He managed to cross over to the Leonard building on the far side of the campus in about five minutes.

Liam wandered into the building. He needed to find room one-o-two. Unlike most offices he'd visited in California, this one didn't have numbers on the doors. *Well, shit.*

"Are you lost?" A girl, probably around nineteen or twenty, stopped him. She grinned. "Got separated from a tour group? Parents lag all the time. You stop and look and before you know it, they've moved on. Where are you going?"

"Room one-o-two." He smiled to hide his embarrassment. *Parents.* Did he look that old? Sure, he was thirty-seven, but he wasn't quite old enough to have a college student as his child. Could he? Maybe if he'd started young...*nah.* Right now, he needed to find a good lie to cover his mild humiliation. "My son wanted to sit in on one of the creative

49

writing classes. I stopped to use the bathroom and now I'm not sure where to go."

"Oh, you want Professor Morrison's class." She pointed to a set of double doors. "In there."

"No, I'm looking for Sarah Nelson's class," he corrected.

She frowned. "She hasn't been Nelson in a couple of years." The girl nodded to the doors. "Her class is in there." She snickered and clutched her books as she walked away.

So much for having tact and composure. First, the girl thought he was a parent and now she'd had to correct him on Sarah's name. Boy, he was a mess. He gripped the handle and waited a beat before heading into the room. Without windows in the doors, he wasn't sure what kind of situation he'd be walking into.

Liam didn't have to worry much. The entryway led to the back of a lecture hall. No one seemed to notice him as he eased into the room. *Good.* He wanted to be inconspicuous and observe her.

Sarah stood in the front of the space and pointed to a chalkboard. "Goal, motivation, conflict. That's what you need in this assignment."

He eased onto one of the empty chairs at the back of the room and listened to her speak. She had a way with the students—she knew how to answer questions without seeming to talk down to them. Hell, he wanted to find a piece of paper and pen something for her—and writing wasn't his forte. He folded his arms and watched her move around the small stage area. She answered a few more questions, then offered up an exercise.

"You're stuck, right?" She gripped her pen. "You're not sure what they'll do next. One thing you can do is put them into a situation that seems innocuous. Like, you've got buddies, right? And they're living through the zombie apocalypse. Plunk them down in the middle of department store. How would they act? Would they get along and shop together? Argue? Let them tell you how they'd deal with being there while there's the threat of zombies at any time.

Then you'll get to the root of the characters and you'll know how to handle the next part of the tale."

Another student asked a question, but Liam didn't pay attention. Sarah held his focus. He couldn't wait for the class to end so he could talk to her. His body warmed and he longed to hold her in his arms again.

A timer behind Sarah pinged. She clapped her hands then turned off the ringing. "That's it for today. Bring your outlines back on Friday. I'm grading them on whether you've done them or not, so be prepared."

Liam waited for the students to file out of the room. Once alone with Sarah, he approached. His heart hammered. He hadn't been this out of sorts since the day he'd met Daryl. He hooked his thumbs into his belt loops to hide the trembling.

Sarah gathered her papers then glanced up. When she saw him, she wobbled backward against the table. "You?"

"Me." Liam smiled. "Remember me?"

"How could I forget?" She blushed from her hairline to the collar of her blouse. She clutched the papers to her chest. "What…what are you doing here? Why?"

"Why not?" He tilted his head and met her gaze. "I wanted to see you. When we woke up and you weren't there, you stung us. Daryl hasn't stopped talking about you."

"Hush." She left the table and ducked behind the podium. "I know we're alone, but you never know who will walk in here."

"No one for now." He stood tall. The scent of her perfume wrapped around him. He'd rather have her in his arms, but he'd accept being in the same room as her.

"Are you planning on heading back to college?" She tucked her papers into her messenger bag. "You want to bone up on creative writing? My friend, Walter Tate, has a great class you can sit in on. He's fantastic."

"I came here to see you." He rounded the podium and stilled her hands. "I'd even like to give you my assignment. My goal is to have another date with you. We had a hot night and the start of a strong romance. The motivation? We had one hell of a great night and Daryl wants you as much as I do. The conflict is that we're not sure we can convince you to give us another try."

Her eyes widened. "One night doesn't mean much. You're reading too far into this."

"I disagree. That night meant a lot to me and Daryl both." He rubbed his thumbs across the back of her knuckles.

"You're nuts."

"Maybe." He'd been told as much plenty of times.

"How…how'd you get around the people? You haven't been noticed, have you?" She narrowed her eyes. "No, I bet you have and basked in the celebrity status."

"You wound me." He left her alone behind the podium and took a seat in the front row. "I was recognized once. I told the woman I wasn't him and was mistaken for him often. She believed me. Otherwise, I've been ignored. Well, no. The girl who told me where to find this room…she recognized me." He paused. "She thought I was a parent who'd been separated from a tour group." He shrugged.

She shook her head and rolled her eyes.

"I must look like a parent." He stretched out his legs. "But seriously, can I take you to lunch? Somewhere here on campus?"

"Are you crazy? People will see you." She finished putting her papers and notebook in her bag, then clutched her keys. "They'll mob you."

"I doubt they'll do that. They might see me, but I don't care."

"Right. You want to be seen." She stepped up to him. "I get it. I'm fine and you don't have to do this. Go on your merry way. There are a hundred or so girls out there right now who will love to see you."

"Who said I want them to see me? I haven't been honest about my identity for a reason—I don't want to be interrupted. I came here to see you." *I came here to touch, caress and taste her kiss again.*

"What about Daryl?" She paused and held tightly to the strap of her bag.

"What about him?"

"He never does anything without a master plan. He sent you, didn't he? You're here to seek me out, feel me out and report back to him." She held her hands up. "I'm not... Look, it was one night. I got caught up in the mood and the memories. Okay? I did something out of character and although I liked it...*it* won't happen again."

The hell it won't. "Why?" He blocked her from leaving. "Are you sure you'd never do *that* again?"

"Yes," she snapped and sidestepped him. "Positive."

"I see." He stuffed his hands into his pockets and followed her up the aisle. He had to convince her that she might enjoy another night or two or even ten with him and Daryl. "How about just lunch? We get something from the student center and go somewhere quiet to eat? What about your office?"

"No." She didn't turn around, but she held the door for him.

"No dinner or no office?" He followed her through the lobby of the building and out into the sunshine on the sidewalk.

"No office." She stopped by the stone wall ringing the landscaping along the walkway. Her lips curled into a small smile. "You're determined."

"I try." He wanted to touch her. He missed the softness of her skin and the way she'd whimpered when they'd made love. She made him feel so much—happiness, love and a completion he'd thought was only possible with Daryl. He wanted her more than she realized. "So...lunch?"

"There's an Italian place in the student center. We can get sandwiches there and take them out to the hill. It's not too private, but it's quiet." She nodded. "Will that work?"

He fell into step beside her and shook his head. He insisted on taking care of his dates and she was more than just a lunch companion. "Deal...but I'm buying. No questions asked."

"Fine. Thanks." She half-smiled. "That's the first time you've asserted yourself and acted like a hoity-toity celebrity."

"I treat my partner with dignity. I offered to buy you lunch. How could I not pay for it?" He rested his hand on the small of her back. "Besides, you don't have to sound like you hate me."

"I don't." She didn't pull away from him, but didn't tuck in tight to him either. "This way." She pointed to a large pale brick building. Instead of speaking, she kept quiet.

He'd expected her to argue or at least give him hell for being pushy. The silence unnerved him. In the past when he'd had to deal with the gaps in conversation, he'd assumed he hadn't pleased his partner. Daryl hardly ever stopped talking and when he did it was because he was angry. *Is she angry and playing coy? Fuck.* "Do you go to the student center often?" *What a great question.* He sounded as if he didn't know what to talk about. Well, he didn't.

"No, usually I bring food and eat on the hill." She shrugged. "I have a class at four, so I use the time to work on the lessons and answer emails while I eat. When it's cold or snowing, I find a quiet spot in the staff building, but there tends not to be much quiet in there. I like the hill better."

"Then we'll go there. What is your next class?" He held the door for her. "You first."

"The same." She paused. "Sorry, thank you."

"Don't tell me no one ever held the door for you. If Daryl didn't, I will set him straight." He waited for her to enter the building, then followed behind.

"He used to." She stuck to his side now. Too many kids seemed to be milling around the large room. "It's complicated."

"What? How?" He needed to know. If she had a boyfriend or husband, then he and Daryl were wasting their time.

A few students waved, but no one paid him any mind. Liam appreciated the blessed anonymity. He didn't have to please anyone but Sarah. He stayed with her as she approached the short line for the Italian restaurant window. A red and white checkerboard ringed the large counter.

"What would you like?" she asked.

"Whatever you're getting, make it two." He rubbed her back. "I'm easy."

"Don't say that too loud. Someone will get the wrong idea and you'll get propositioned." She smiled. "I'm shocked you'd give me that much power. What if I order something you don't like?"

"First, I'm old enough to be the father of a bunch of these students. That's a little too old to mess around with any of them. Second, I trust you." He met her gaze. "Give yourself a little credit. You're a smart woman. Unless you feed me anchovies and pineapple together, I'm good. I've got great company and I'm not going anywhere." He wasn't sure why he'd admitted all of that, but whatever.

"Two regular calzones and two bottles of water," she said when they reached the counter. "Extra napkins."

Liam paid the bill and accepted the bag of food. Sarah picked up the waters. With her beside him, he headed back out of the student center to the fresh air outside.

"That was nice." She chuckled and bumped shoulders with him.

He couldn't quite read her expression. "What?" He wasn't sure what she meant.

"Do you work this hard for every girl you want to sleep with?"

"No."

"We'll go over here. There's more sunshine and fewer people." She led him to the hill and hiked about halfway up. "I wish I'd have brought a blanket. We'll have muddy butts."

"Nah. But I think your butt is sexy, mud or not."

She plopped onto the grass and stretched her legs, then placed the bag by her hip. "One question. Why me?"

He eased down beside her and paused. "Why not you?"

"I'm nobody. You're somebody," she said and dropped

her voice to a whisper. "You could have a hundred girls on this campus alone—most of them much prettier than me. You'd be dripping with women."

"Doubtful."

She offered up his calzone, then stared at him. "I was too easy, wasn't I?"

What in the hell did she mean? "No, you weren't." He watched her. She sat beside him, so composed and with class. *So she seemed a little unsure on the inside...* He liked her mix of strength and fragility. He could listen to her forever and now he understood why Daryl hadn't gotten over her.

"Are you okay?"

"Fine," he said. "Why?"

"You're staring at me." She took a bite from her calzone and a little of the sauce remained at the corner of her mouth.

He fought the urge to lick her clean. "I'm listening to you." He folded his legs up underneath himself and rested his lunch on his lap. "You're not easy. Challenging is more like it, but in a good way." He opened his calzone. "I'm not backing down, no matter how much you try to push me away. So, since you're stuck with me for a while, tell me about you." He had a question burning into his brain and needed an answer. "Why'd you leave us?"

Chapter Four

Liam ate his calzone and waited for her answer. He'd pushed her and hated himself for making her uncomfortable, but he needed an answer. If she wasn't interested in being with them then he needed closure.

Sarah crossed her ankles and held her calzone in both hands. "It's complicated."

"You've mentioned that," he said between bites. "How? I'm listening."

"You don't want my kind of chaos in your life." She polished off the calzone, then blushed. "Sorry. I was hungry."

"You don't have to apologize for eating. I'd rather you be yourself and eat if you need to than starve yourself." He peeled the foil down on his calzone. "Tell me why you're chaotic. I'm not seeing why the perfectly beautiful woman beside me is still single and can't accept a compliment."

Her eyes widened. "You think I'm pretty?"

"Stunning. I wouldn't compliment you if I didn't." If he was nothing else, he was honest with his partners. He refused to lie to Daryl and would treat Sarah the same way.

"You need your eyes checked." She opened her bottle of water. "I'm decent at best."

"Oh, I probably should take a trip to the eye doctor, but that's not important. You're stalling." He grinned. "What do you want to know about me, since you're apprehensive about talking to me? We can trade off." He finished his calzone as he waited for her to speak.

She stared at him for a moment and narrowed her eyes. "In *Maritime*, you broke the fourth wall. It completely fit with the story, but it also felt improvised. Why'd you do it?"

She'd seen his work. He shouldn't have felt so flattered, but he did. She also hadn't brought up his appearance in the film like most might have done and the papers did. *Nice.* And as a bonus, she'd picked up on a nuance in his performance. He knew he liked her for a reason. "The initial idea was for the movie audience to be part of the crew. We were all supposed to do that—break the fourth wall. But time and costs forced us to make a bunch of cuts. My speech to the audience was kept in because the director said it was moving."

"I don't think I would've liked the movie as much with everyone breaking that wall, though." She gripped her water bottle. "It was good the way they left it."

"I like the finished product, too." He tossed his foil into the bag and collected up her foil as well. "My turn. Why'd you ditch us?"

She swallowed her water and sighed. "That whole weekend was out of my comfort zone. I'm not a party girl and I had no business being in Vegas. I'm the one who goes to a party and makes friends with the dog. I had a miniscule book signing at one of the smaller bookstores off the strip, but really, the trip was all Mischa's idea. I should've stayed home, but I'd just gotten into an argument with my other half, so I went."

His heart dropped. "You're married?" Shit. No. She couldn't be.

"No, not for thirteen years."

"Oh." He still wasn't relieved. "You've got a boyfriend?"

"Nope. My best friend Addie and I argued over Mischa. She hates Mischa because she thinks Mischa isn't promoting my books, but rather invading my life. I don't know. Sometimes I think Addie's right. Mischa doesn't do much promotion, but then Mischa can be charming and misleading. The thing is, when Addie doesn't like someone, she's normally spot on. I should've listened, but I also sort of wanted a change of pace. I wanted to feel…wanted. I ate too much and allowed Mischa to con me into buying that dress. I looked…horrible and squeezed into it."

"I disagree. You were and are gorgeous."

She rolled her eyes. "You're too generous. Anyway, the booze got the better of me and when I thought I saw you smiling at me, I decided to smile back."

"I was and I'm glad you did." The moment he'd seen her was seared into his memory. He'd never seen anyone so captivating and the sparkly red dress had accentuated her curves. He covered his crotch with his folded hands to keep from embarrassing himself. "Daryl called me off and the blonde swooped in before I could explain."

"That happens a lot, being swooped in on?" she asked. She finished the bottle of water then shifted to face him. "I bet you don't get much privacy."

"Depends on the situation." He brushed her hair from her cheek. As much as he liked listening to her and most certainly touching her, he could tell her ploy from a mile away. "Stop stalling."

"I'm not…intentionally." She bowed her head. "I've never…had a threesome before."

He wished he'd known that ahead of time. He'd have moved with more tenderness and taken more time to ensure she was comfortable. "You seemed okay with it, but I wish you'd have clued me in."

"At the time, I thought I was brave. I enjoyed myself." She met his gaze. "For being the first time, you were great. It hurt, which I expected, but not as bad as it could've. Besides, I trusted Daryl. If he decided you were fine, then I could trust you, too."

"I'm honored." And pleased to the core. He'd hoped she'd enjoyed herself. He couldn't wait to be with her again.

"But then you both fell asleep and my fears got the better of me. I had to go. I retreated so you wouldn't have time to break my heart. Was I a coward? Sure. I didn't want to face you in the morning and chance being left before I could go first." She shrugged. "I don't regret what I did."

"I do. I wanted to see you and wake up next to you." He'd looked forward to holding her in the morning for another leisurely fuck.

"It was for the best." She balled her hands. "Trust me."

"Why?" She'd piqued his interest. Leaving them was not for the best.

"Do we have to go through this?"

"Yeah." He needed to know. "Did we do something? Don't you like us? Please?"

She groaned. "I had to get home to my son."

He paused as he realized what she'd said. *Holy fuck. A son?* "You're a mom?" he blurted.

"Yes and I shouldn't have acted the way I did. I was...it was wrong." She hugged her knees. "I'm a mom. I should've been in my mom frame of mind."

He had to think and say something intelligent. "Just because you have a kid doesn't mean you can't have a good time."

She laced her fingers together across her forehead. "He's seventeen. I should be setting a good example. Instead... I slept with two men very much out of my league and my circle of understanding. I aimed for the sun and got burned, even though I tried not to."

"I don't think so."

She hadn't been screwed over by them. Hell, she'd hosed them to a degree by leaving without telling them goodbye, but he'd decided to patch the wounds. He'd make up for her hurts.

"Of course you don't think so. You got sex out of it," she snapped.

"We weren't there to fuck you." He unlaced her fingers and held her hand. "Sarah, we were there because Daryl missed you."

Sarah stared at him. Her jaw slackened and confusion cluttered her brain. Daryl missed her? Of course he'd said that during sex, but still. How was that possible? "We were an item in college, but he's moved on. He missed the friendship. That's it."

"No." Liam chuckled. "He's got a photo of you that he keeps in his wallet. You're standing with him by a tree. It's in black and white."

Memories hit her hard. She remembered that picture. He'd told her he wanted her to pose with him, but he hadn't mentioned the photographer would be capturing them both. He'd pulled her close at the last minute and whispered in her ear to make her smile.

"He loves that one. It's on the wall at the house as well as his wallet." Liam kissed her knuckles. "I love it, too."

"Good Lord. It's so old." She flipped her hair over her shoulder. "Why would you both love it so much?"

"He won't say. I like it because you look happy and beautiful."

"You're both nuts." She checked the clock on her phone. *Shit.* If she didn't get moving, she'd never get her lessons in order before her next class. "I have to run. I've got class in half an hour, then I'm heading to the park to pick up Todd."

"Your…boyfriend?" His eyes widened.

"Son." She patted his thigh and bit back a moan. Damn, she'd forgotten how strong he was or how he must've spent time in the gym. "My son. He's on the cross-country team and his car is in the shop. I have to pick him up so we can get the car."

"Cool. Does he enjoy running?"

"Yeah." She shrugged, then stood and dusted off her ass. "He's not the fastest, but he doesn't care. He's probably the least competitive kid out there, but he works hard to do his best." She offered her hand. "Thank you for lunch. It was great to see you. Are you heading back to…Vegas? Hollywood?" She sounded awkward, but how else was she going to walk away from him? Everything was so messed up.

"California." He smiled and swept his gaze over her.

"Oh. Nice. When?" Soon, she hoped, so she could close this chapter of her life.

"Not sure. I'm in between projects." He grasped her hand again and started down the hill with her. "I told my agent I needed six months of not working so I could have some family time and just exist. I've got a picture in the works for next spring. The sequel to *Maritime*, actually."

"Oh." She'd said that already, but she wasn't sure what else to say. She'd assumed he had worked lined up for the next few years.

"I did a couple of independent films and wanted some free time. You'd be surprised how time can get away from you."

"I see." She stepped onto the sidewalk. "So you came to see me?"

"I have and I'll be around until Daryl joins me."

Joins him? She stopped short, yanking his arm. "Are you two…together? I've seen stories on the celebrity shows. If you are, that's fine. None of my business." Although she'd feel really silly if they were a couple. She'd intruded on their relationship. Good Lord. Maybe they'd kept their relationship a secret. Or there wasn't one to hide.

"We tried twice and realized we liked women too much."

She frowned. He hadn't said they weren't together, but hadn't said they were. "Who is your lucky lady? I saw you split from Agatha Vero. She seemed nice."

"She had her moments, but it was more of studio set-up than a romance." He shrugged and continued walking with her.

"I saw your name in the papers linked with Della Dubois, too." *Please, God, don't let him be with someone.* She'd feel like shit for splitting them up.

He shook his head. "No. We did a horror flick together and that was more than enough. She's nice on film, but scary as fuck in person. Besides, the papers always get those things wrong."

"How? They seem to have spies everywhere." She

stopped outside the Leonard building. "For all we know, we're being watched right now."

"I doubt it. No one knows I'm here." He grasped her other hand. "The thing with the papers is they expect celebrities to couple up. When they don't cooperate, the writers tend to put us together." He met her gaze. "I'd like to start seeing you."

She opened her mouth to speak but the words melted away. *Seeing me? Me?* He'd lost his mind. "You're crazy."

"It's been mentioned. What's wrong with dating you?" He curled his fingers under her chin. "I know who I like and who I want. You happen to be at the top of that list."

"Because Daryl probably put you up to it." She'd jumped to a huge conclusion. Daryl would be joining him. For all she knew, he was just keeping her warm for Daryl. Or they wanted another go 'round before they walked away, on their terms. Christ, she didn't trust anyone.

"I admitted I love that photo of you." He brushed his thumb across her bottom lip. "Daryl knows I'm here and he wants us to get together…but he wants you, too."

He'd wrenched the words from her a second time. Both wanted her? She should've seen this coming. "I can't juggle two guys." She dropped her voice to a whisper. If her students heard, she'd never get beyond the embarrassment. "I'm a mom," she snapped. "It's ridiculous."

"Life stops because you have kids?" He leaned in closer. "I don't think so."

"No, but—"

He kissed her, stealing her breath and blowing her mind. He licked the seam of her mouth then nipped her bottom lip. Just like the night in Vegas, he moved with tenderness and pushed without being too aggressive. He eased his arms around her waist and held her close. Her knees weakened and she sagged into him

Liam broke the kiss first. "Life doesn't have to stop with kids. It should start there."

"Uh-huh." She couldn't form a rational sentence. Not

now. Every cell in her brain screamed for her to kiss him again. Her heart wanted him, but Daryl, too. God, she was fucked up.

"Why are you afraid of me?" He kept her in his embrace. "I'm not a bad guy."

"I'm betting you're not." Her heart hammered and her nipples tightened. Liam managed to create within her the first flutters of attraction and excitement. She could have a connection with this man and not just a one-night stand. With Liam, things would be different and deeper.

"But?" he asked.

She looked him in the eye. She had to be honest. Being a mom was her first priority and her career at the college was second. Dating was a distant third place. "I'm not in a position to date anyone. I'm Mom. I have to think about my son and I need to be stable for him. I can't introduce a new person into my life."

"Even me?"

"Yes. I can't introduce you and expect him to be okay with it." She knew Todd. He'd be crushed.

"Because I'm an actor? Or otherwise?"

"You're famous. You can do better than me and I know it because I've seen the women you've dated." The last thing she needed was to fall for him only to have him leave her for one of his co-stars. She didn't want the heartbreak.

"I'm a guy. Daryl is a guy. When we pick a partner, we're devoted. You know that. You know Daryl. You, Daryl and I had something special once and it can be again." He brushed his mouth over hers. "I know that's possible."

Shit. So much for no complications. She flattened her hand on his chest. Liam smelled so good and felt like heaven under her touch. She had to be losing her mind, but she couldn't do this. "I can't. We'll never work out." She checked her phone again. She had fifteen minutes until class started. "I need to go. Thank you for lunch and I hope you enjoy your time in Kenton without getting mobbed." She shrugged out of his grasp and darted toward the Leonard building.

"Sarah." Liam caught up to her, but didn't touch her. "Are you sure?"

"I am." Not completely, but still. He didn't need to know the truth. "Tell Daryl I said hi." Good God, she sounded cheesy. She waved, then walked away from him again. She held her head high and straightened her shoulders. *I'm putting distance between me and what could be a once-in-a-lifetime love. Yeah, no pressure.*

"Sarah?"

She swallowed hard and stopped again. When she glanced over her shoulder, Liam hadn't moved.

"Give us a chance. We'll do everything in our power to make you happy." Liam tipped his head and smiled, then stuffed his hands into his pockets. He turned on his heel and walked away.

She brushed her hair from her face. She felt like the first time she'd met Daryl, back in college—overwhelmed and certain the fall was coming but unable to stop it.

* * * *

After class, Sarah drove to the horse park. Despite her best intentions, she couldn't get Liam and that kiss out of her brain. She still tingled all over. He wanted to see her. Daryl supposedly wanted her. What were they thinking? She wanted to be the woman in the middle of the man sandwich. What was *she* thinking? She still loved Daryl more than she'd ever let on.

When she pulled into the parking lot at the equestrian center, she noticed Addie's car. *Well, shit.* She'd left Ohio on bad terms with her best friend and now she had little choice but to talk to her. She dreaded facing Addie. Because she'd been a jerk. She'd ignored the advice of someone she trusted to have a good time in a place she didn't belong. Yeah, Addie should be kicking her ass right about now.

Sarah parked next to Addie and turned off the engine.

You can do this. She's your best friend. She summoned her courage and left her vehicle, then rounded the fender to sit on the front bumper. Addie strolled over to the cars and stuffed her hands into her back pockets.

"Hi," Sarah said. "How's practice going?"

"It's going. The kids are running well. Todd broke his personal record Saturday. I'm sure he told you."

"He did and I'm sorry I missed it."

"You had other things to do." Addie settled onto the bumper of Sarah's car. "You're not with Mischa? Come on. You're best buds. Tight and stuff."

Sarah groaned. "I deserve that. I'm sorry."

"You cut me deep."

"I know. It was stupid." She forced herself to look at Addie. "I'm sorry. Really."

"She's not much more fun than I am." Addie didn't meet her gaze. Instead she seemed to watch the runners sprinting across the field.

"You're right. The trip wasn't what I expected." In so many ways. She had baggage now she didn't how to deal with and experiences she'd never forget. *Was it worth the trouble?* Yes and no.

"You're home now." Addie still didn't look at her.

"Forgive me? Please? I'm sorry." God, how many times did she have to apologize?

"You know I can stay mad forever, right?"

She scrubbed both hands over her face. "I do." She hoped she hadn't damaged the friendship beyond repair.

"But you're my best friend and you're allowed a couple of lapses in judgment." Addie faced Sarah. "But just a couple. Don't do that again."

"I'm done with jacked-up judgment." She snorted. "I had some fun, yeah, but I've got a whole lot of regret going on."

"First I want to know why you regret whatever happened, but I doubt you're done with making mistakes. We all do." Addie bumped shoulders with Sarah. "So...what'd you do? Does it have anything to do with the photos I saw on television?"

Sarah stared at Addie. *Photos?* "What are you talking about? I didn't take any photos." The last thing she knew, Mischa hadn't photographed her, but she couldn't trust the woman to be truthful. "Is something on social media?" What shitstorm did she have to ride out now?

"You're all over the television and the Internet." Addie tugged her phone from her back pocket. She twiddled with the screen and turned it to show Sarah. "See? I thought you knew."

Sarah flipped though the images. Her leaving with Daryl. Her with Liam. A couple of shots of the three of them together. One of them entering the elevator. Her knees buckled. *Oh shit.* "Who...who all has seen these?"

"Everyone, I'd imagine. I've gotten pins, tweets, emails and texts about you. I keep telling them you just look like the woman, but they figured it out. They wouldn't ask if it wasn't obvious. Your damn blue streaks gave you away." Addie laughed. "Honey, it's silly, but it's not. I hope they aren't what you regret. I'd give Matt's left nut to sleep with Liam Turner."

Sarah winced. She didn't want to think of her best friend giving her brother's left nut away for anything. Matt was her gay best friend and one of the few men she trusted. "No, no, no." She sagged on the bumper. "Does Todd know?" *Dear God. Does my ex-husband know?*

"Yeah. Kennedy saw them first and showed me, then she told Todd. He thinks it's a joke." Addie shrugged. "You can't keep it from him. Not in this day and age."

"I knew as soon as I got onto that plane I'd regret the trip." She'd made a mistake. She'd missed Todd's best run. Mixed him up in her private drama and made said drama public.

"Slow down," Addie said. "You needed a break. Anyone would've jumped at the chance to go to Vegas. So, you tangled yourself up with a couple of movie stars. It doesn't happen to everyone, but hey, it did to you. Don't knock it. Besides, if I didn't hate Mischa as much as I do, I might have gone along."

"It wasn't my best decision. Rest or not." Her stomach soured and she wanted to throw up...just not in front of her son and his cross-country team.

"You thought she was normal. We all did at first. Well, no, you all did. I saw through her a month after she moved into town." Addie shrugged. "But you can't beat yourself up over this."

"I know, but I doubt it's possible to let everything go."

Addie rubbed Sarah's back. "Oh, honey. Did you like them? I remember Daryl. Rather, I remember how long it took you to get over him the first time." She crossed her ankles and continued to rub Sarah. "You had a fling with him. Are you considering reconnecting for a longer-term situation?"

"No." Not now. She'd done way too much damage by having a one-nighter with him.

"What about Liam? He's cute and very lickable."

"No." But he was tasty. "I need to think about Todd and my job. What I did was impulsive and crazy. I never should've gotten involved with them."

"It was one night. No one says you have to do it again—unless you want to. The photos will fade and give it another few days before the next big scandal hits. You'll be yesterday's news. People will forget. They always do."

She faced Addie. "Then why didn't I forget Daryl?" Why'd she think about him almost every day since they'd split in college? Why couldn't she get him or Liam out of her brain now?

"Or Liam? I saw the sparks. I only saw pictures on the Internet, but I could feel the connection between you."

"Well? Why can't I get over him?" Or over them?

"Because they're both flippin' hot? I like Liam and I'm married." Addie shrugged. "Dix would flip, but oh well. Liam is...I keep thinking of him in *Maritime*. I so wanted to lick the screen."

She wanted to lick him too. But she had to think about more than her libido. Part of her still wanted space, but the rest of her wanted Liam and Daryl. "I'm a mess."

"Who isn't?"

"I seem to draw drama like flies." She leaned on her friend and rested her head on Addie's shoulder. "I made mistakes. Again."

"You're fine. Your ex-husband was the crazeballs one." Addie hugged her. "You can't measure every man by that stick."

"Don't remind me."

Addie sighed. "All I'm saying is we have all done things we regret. You happened to make your mistake—if that's what you want to call it—on a grand scale. So what? Own it and move on. You had a good time with two hot men. I'm jealous." She paused. "And I'm done talking about it because our kids are coming over."

Todd jogged up to Sarah and Addie. "Hey Mrs. Marshall. Mom." He threw his sweaty arms around Sarah's shoulders and hugged her. "You had a good time in Vegas?"

"I did." She shook her head. "More than I should've."

"Don't you know the fun you have in Vegas is supposed to *stay* in Vegas?" Todd grinned. The perspiration in his hair brought out his curls. "I gotta do a cool down run, stretch and pick up my meet sheet, but once I do all of that, I'll be ready to go." He waved, then jogged away.

"Kennedy kept him company while you were gone." Addie folded her arms. "I hope you're ready to shell out for homecoming. He asked her to go with him."

"He's got to pay off his car, first." She couldn't afford both. Not right now. "I need to get my next book going."

"You've got fodder for it." Addie smiled and clapped Sarah's shoulder. "We'll get you through this. Promise."

Sarah opened her mouth to argue with Addie, but her phone rang and interrupted her. She recognized the ringtone and groaned.

"Ding, dong. Parasite's on the phone." Addie stood and

shoved her hands into her back pockets again. "What's she want?"

"I don't know and I'm not asking. I'm letting it go to voicemail. She hooked up with a guy in Vegas, too. One of Daryl's friends, I guess. Dom someone or another. She and her sister left me at the airport. They were going to have a hot time together and needed another day in Vegas." Sarah rubbed her temples. "I don't know what her game was while she was out there, but I don't want to play any longer."

"Good for you."

"That's why I'm ignoring her calls." She tucked her phone back into her pocket. "Out of sight. Out of mind."

"I don't think you've got much choice." Addie nodded. "She's coming over. Like right now."

"What?" She turned to look where Addie signaled. Sure enough, Mischa had left her sports car and crossed the lot to where Sarah and Addie stood. "Fuck," Sarah murmured.

"How?" Mischa asked. She widened her stance and her tank top strained against her breasts.

"What are you talking about?" Sarah asked. She hated cryptic people.

"How'd you do it?" Mischa folded her arms. "I slept with a movie star, too, but there hasn't been a peep in the news about me. You...you're everywhere."

"It wasn't by choice," Sarah confessed. "We thought we'd sneaked off."

"Well shit. You're better at promotions than I am. What dirt do you have on Daryl? A secret baby? Secret wedding? You're related?" Mischa asked. "Give."

"I got nothing." She shifted and stood beside Addie for support. The uncomfortable discussion weighed on her.

"Look, Daryl called me trying to get your number. I passed it along to him, but I'm going to say this. When you're done with him, let me know. I'm interested." Mischa grinned. "*Very* interested."

"In him or the notoriety?" Addie snapped.

"Hmm…" Mischa's grin widened. "Him, of course." She waved. "My friend Lisa asked me to pick up her son, Dyllon. Sarah, I'll see you at the college, you crazy girl."

Sarah waited for Mischa to leave before she spoke. "So much for wanting it to all go away."

"Did he remember?" Addie asked.

"What? Me? Us?" Sarah fumbled. Memories rushed into her brain. "Yeah, he did. It was like old times, but with Liam added in." She missed him. Missed both of them. "But it's over."

"You're not giving him over to Mischa? I'll kick your ass if you do that." Addie cocked her hip. "Seriously."

"Not on her life," Sarah said. "I like him and while he and Liam drive me crazy, I'd never do that to them."

"Good." Addie elbowed her. "Let's not fight again, okay?"

"Deal." Relief swept over Sarah. One part of her life was back to normal.

"Next time you talk to Daryl, be honest with him," Addie said. "I remember the split. He came back to Kenton that one weekend and you ignored him. I know why, but still. He invited me over and played *She's Gone* over and over on the CD player. He…the breakup crawled under his skin and I don't think he ever got over you."

"He survived." Hell, he'd thrived. She'd seen the tabloids, too.

"Surviving doesn't mean it didn't hurt." Addie nodded once.

"We've both moved on. He went to Hollywood, found a girlfriend and became famous. I'm a footnote in his story. As for Liam, he's going to California. I don't matter to him, either." *Liar.* "I'm — going to be okay."

"Do you want to go with that or do you want to be honest with me and yourself?" Addie asked. "Talk to him."

"Later. Practice is over and I need to go home." Sarah didn't want to see or hear from Daryl. Just thinking about him was too painful. The night she'd thought she'd get closure had only stirred up old feelings. She'd never forgotten him. He'd been her true love, but he'd gone to Hollywood with another woman — because she'd pushed him away.

With Todd in tow, Sarah headed back to her car and blinked back tears. She wasn't a crier, but Daryl and Liam seemed to bring out her deep emotions. She dragged a long breath into her lungs, then exhaled. *Time to really move on.*

Chapter Five

Daryl stared at the tablet screen. He hadn't been back to the set in Nevada for more than a few hours when the photographs had hit the Internet. So many pictures and so much information in the wrong hands. He liked seeing Sarah with him and Liam and looking so happy, but he couldn't hide his irritation. He had an agreement with the paparazzi. No photos and no questions. In return, he'd do whatever interviews they wanted, but on his terms.

He massaged his temples. He'd wrapped Sarah up in his personal disaster. He should've known she wouldn't get through unscathed. He couldn't get out of the Nevada desert and to Sarah and Liam fast enough. Although he'd spoken to Liam the night before, he wanted an update. Had Liam made progress with her? Maybe smoothed things over and convinced her to give them another try?

Daryl turned off the tablet and stuffed the device into his knapsack. He had to see Sarah and explain the situation. Hell, he had to get her back. She was the missing piece in his marriage to Liam. With her, things would be better. They'd be perfect.

"Fuck it." Daryl shook his head. He'd wasted enough time on retakes that weren't necessary. He gathered up his things and deposited his bags in his car.

"Where are you going?" Griffin Talcot chased after Daryl. "We're not done."

"You've shot enough footage of my hands that you should know them better than I do." Daryl squared his shoulders. "You don't need me. Nothing we've done truly required me. I'm leaving because I need a break. Not just a couple days, but a few weeks' break."

He checked his trailer once more for the rest of his things, then climbed behind the wheel of his car. He'd drop off his bags at the townhouse, then off to Ohio. He'd wasted more than enough time.

* * * *

Six hours later, Daryl strolled through the terminal of the Cleveland airport to the pick-up lanes outside of the building. As he passed through the sliding doors, he noticed Liam waiting on him in a black coupé. He grinned and brought his suitcase over to the vehicle.

"Long time, no see." Liam opened the passenger door. "Hurry up. I've been spotted and we've had enough photos taken for a while."

"No shit." He shoved the suitcase into the backseat, then collapsed onto the passenger one. "We're not that famous. This thing blew up beyond my wildest dreams. It wasn't supposed to happen like this."

"Yeah, nothing went according to your plan. I met with her." Liam pulled away from the curb and blended into traffic.

"And?" He couldn't hide his excitement. "You made progress with her, right?"

"Not exactly." Liam maneuvered around the different lanes of the freeway and drove away from the airport. "She's a professor. Creative writing and she seems happy. She's also got a kid."

"Kid?" Daryl sagged in his seat. *A child? She wasn't supposed to have a child without me. How'd I miss that detail?*

"And an ex-husband."

"Holy fuck," Daryl blurted. He was supposed to be the father of her children, and her husband. Sure, he'd married Liam and loved him, but she was now supposed to be a part of their equation.

"The boy is in high school. He's a runner and seems cool,

but I haven't talked to him in person." Liam gripped the steering wheel. "I ran the trails where he practiced. He's good. Not super-fast, but good."

"Stalker much?"

"She intrigues me and I wanted to observe the boy. I met with her at the college." Liam pressed the button to put the car into the speed control setting. He stretched his right arm, then settled. "We had lunch and talked. It was idyllic and sweet."

"But?" Daryl gritted his teeth. Liam was stalling. He hated when Liam wouldn't come right out and tell him the problem.

Liam sighed and drummed his fingers on the steering wheel. "She's scared, evasive and I don't know exactly how you two split, but she's still scared. Every time I thought she'd melt a little, she'd turn the tables and put up walls. When I kissed her I told her we wanted her. I was honest. We want to be with her. That didn't seem to matter. She kept pushing me away."

Daryl stared at the fields of corn alongside the road. His head swam. *She* was hurting? What about *him*? She'd dumped him right before he was supposed to go to California. He smoothed his hand over his mouth. She wasn't telling Liam the whole story. He'd better clear the situation up a bit. "She left me," Daryl murmured. "She walked away from me right when I needed her the most." *How's that for size?*

"No, the way I understand it, you decided to follow your dream and left her behind. I know how these things work. I had a girlfriend in my former high school that I broke ties with when I came to California because I didn't want her to wait for me for nothing." Liam grasped Daryl's hand. "Be honest."

Christ, he was *trying* to tell the truth. Liam wasn't listening. Daryl let go of Liam's fingers. "She was supposed to meet me at the airport. At the last minute, she said she had to do something and our friend Lyndy rode with me on the bus.

I assumed Sarah was having her mother take care of her car or something. Anyway, I wasn't thinking about anything beyond getting on that plane. Lyndy kept telling me Sarah wasn't coming. Something about she'd chicken out. Then Sarah showed up." He shook his head and laughed without mirth. "She said things were better this way, or something along those lines, and that I'd catch my dream if I didn't have her holding me back. She said she'd do the dumping so I didn't look like the asshole. She can hurt all fucking day long, but she left me when I needed her. I want her, but I haven't forgiven her for walking away."

Liam pulled onto the ramp to the state route. When he stopped, he glanced over at Daryl. "I met you the month you came to San Francisco. You'd been in California for three years by then and you sure as shit didn't look like you were sad. You were living it up with every woman you could find."

"Call it fucked up therapy. If I sowed enough wild oats, I'd get her out of my system." His heart ached every time he thought about that day eighteen years ago. He should've fought harder for her and told Lyndy to stuff it. But he hadn't. He'd wanted his dream, just like Sarah had said.

"Didn't work, did it?" Liam drove down the two-lane highway toward the sunshine. "It doesn't look like it anyway."

"Because nothing has helped me forget her. I miss Sarah. The way she smiles, laughs, smells, the noises she makes when we have sex...then there you were and I thought my life was perfect." He'd fucked over Liam. Christ. He'd thought with his dick and messed with the love of the one man who hadn't given up on him.

"Well, it's a good thing I'm smitten with her, too. Otherwise, I'd think I'm losing my husband to another woman." Liam grinned, then sobered. "I've done a lot of thinking while I've been here. You have to realize she's scared because she has a kid, she's got an ex-husband who, from my investigating, is an ass who beat the hell out of her and we're celebrities. For all I know, she doesn't think she can handle us."

"I can't change my past." But he sure wanted to change hers.

"Neither can she."

"She doesn't want me, does she? Just you?" Motherfucker. Why did he have to sound so emo all of the sudden? He usually kept his feelings under wraps and his head level. Put Liam and Sarah together in his brain and he lost all control.

"Try neither." Liam turned onto the main route leading into Kenton. "First, we got her onto television and the Internet. She's been keeping a low profile. She's being talked about on those silly tabloid shows like she's a non-person. They've discussed her weight, her hair, her looks and made her seem unappealing." He put his hand up. "She's got curves, yes, but you'd think she's less than human if you only saw those shows. She's so much more than they've made her out to be, but because she's not one of our past conquests or a rail-thin chick from Hollywood, she's been deemed inadequate. Think of how that has to make her feel."

Daryl drank in the sights of Kenton, but his thoughts remained on Sarah. "They fat-shamed her? For real? She's curvy."

"Well, according to the different tabloid rags, anything over a size zero is huge," Liam said. "Then there's you and me. We're famous. She feels like we're doing her for publicity."

"No." Now he knew he had to talk to her.

"I know that and you know that, but she doesn't believe us. She's been through a lot and she doesn't seem to like me because I came on too strong at the college and you're supposed to be in a relationship."

"Liam…" He was partly right. He and Liam were married — so yeah, definitely in a relationship. But according to the studio, he was seeing Elisa Mornay. Not quite. "The studio set that up so I'd appear more bankable. I'm only with you."

"I know the truth, but if you're looking at us from the outside…it sure appears you're seeing Elisa," Liam snapped. "I don't know about Sarah, but I'm tired of sneaking around. We're married, Daryl. You're my husband. I'm tired of people thinking I'm that fifth wheel tagalong because I'm just not as hot as you."

Liam had a point. He deserved more than to be a footnote in Daryl's life. Daryl draped his arm around the back of Liam's seat and toyed with the hairs at the base of Liam's head. "You're right. I'm tired of hiding, too. From now on, we're honest with each other and the world." He kissed Liam on the cheek. "You're my husband and the rest of the world can suck it."

"Cute." This time Liam smiled and the sparkle shone in his eyes. "But what about Sarah?"

"We persuade her." Not that he had the whole plan sorted out, but finding her, explaining the situation and hoping for the best had always worked before.

"If we show up at her house and demand attention, it won't be successful."

"Well, then let me think." Daryl continued to stroke Liam's hair. Touching his lover tended to calm him down and helped him think rationally. "If we show up and gang up on her, she'll feel double-teamed or that we've tried to pull a publicity stunt."

"Right."

"What if we met her on her terms? Like visiting the college? I've wanted to set up a scholarship fund since I made my first movie. I bet if we did that, we'd look more like we belong on the campus." Daryl grinned. He liked the idea he'd harbored for the last ten years.

"Um…that still smacks of a publicity stunt. You'd have to do it on the sly first and second, it'd bring the papers no matter what." Liam parked in the lot of the hotel. "We're here. Home sweet home for now. Let's take your shit upstairs and get you settled, then worry about our half-assed plan."

"I knew I loved you for a reason." He climbed out of the car and hauled his bag from the backseat. Daryl followed Liam into the lobby of the hotel. No one seemed to notice them and he thanked God for the anonymity. Once in the quiet of the elevator, he abandoned his bag and threw his arms around Liam. "Love you."

"You've always been a sucker for elevator sex." Liam kissed him and brushed his nose along Daryl's. "But this isn't a long ride." As Liam said the words, the bell dinged and the doors opened. "See?"

"You timed it, didn't you?" He let go of this lover and grasped his suitcase.

"Of course." Liam led him down the short hallway to their room.

Daryl waited for Liam open the door, then he held it for him. "You first, babe."

"Romantic." Liam yanked Daryl's suitcase into the room. "It's pretty standard. They've got room service until one in the morning, which is nice. Wi-Fi is strong." Liam shrugged. "It's livable."

"Uh-huh." He collapsed on the bed and closed his eyes. His jeans pulled tight against his cock. He grunted. He wanted a blowjob and a couple of hours' sleep.

"Are you sure you want to do this?"

The bed dipped as Liam settled beside Daryl. Daryl stretched his arm out over Liam's chest and belly. "Define this."

"Sleep with her again," Liam said.

Daryl opened his eyes. "Yes. I've never been more drawn to anyone besides you in my life. I can't stop thinking about her. Hell, the entire time we reshot that love scene, all I focused on was being with the both of you. The director actually thought I was getting hard because of my co-star."

"You never stopped loving her, did you?" Liam rolled onto his side and pressed his jean-covered erection into

Daryl's hip.

"No."

"Not even after you married your wife?"

"Not a chance." He met Liam's gaze. Desire swept over him and he hated himself for neglecting Liam for so long. "I haven't had the chance or sense in my head to tell you I'm happy to see you." He shifted to face Liam and kissed him. "I missed you so much."

"I know." Liam shrugged. "I missed you, too." He knew how to play off his hurt more than Daryl had ever mastered and Daryl hated him for it.

"I'm sorry I've been a dick. I've got no excuses." He cupped Liam's cheek. The day-old whiskers abraded his palm. He brushed his cock against Liam's and wished they were already naked.

"It's okay." Liam shrugged again. "Things happen."

"No. You're more than my best friend. You're my husband. You're the piece I've been missing and I love you. I need to show you how I feel more often." He wound his arm around Liam and stuffed his hand into Liam's back pocket.

"What about Sarah?"

He nuzzled Liam's cheek, then kissed along his jawline. "She's the glue. We're better as a team. You fell for her, too. You understand." Besides, he couldn't imagine being with Sarah without Liam.

"I did fall for her." Liam's eyes flashed. "The way I did for you."

"Show me." He nipped Liam's bottom lip. "Strip. I've waited too long to be naked with you."

Liam left the bed and whipped his shirt off. He tossed the garment onto the floor. His nipples beaded. He closed his eyes and pinched the tight bundles of nerves. A smile curled on his lips and he drew in a sharp breath. He rocked his torso, flexing his abs.

Daryl's mouth watered. He loved watching Liam perform. He swept his gaze over Liam's body and paused.

His husband had shaved the thin patch of hair from his chest. His upper body shimmered. Was he wearing glitter or something to make his muscles shimmer? Didn't matter. Daryl appreciated what he saw. He scooted to the edge of the bed and caressed Liam's pecs. A growl started low in his throat. Damn, he needed this man now.

Liam rolled his hips and eased closer to Daryl. "Like that?" he whispered.

"The shine? Yeah, I do. You've always been sexy, but now? I'm hooked." He dragged his lips across Liam's soft skin, imprinting Liam's taste on his memory.

Liam threaded his fingers into Daryl's hair and tugged. Daryl gasped at the burn. He yearned for the power shift. Liam knew when to push him and when to submit—when to give and take. God, this was why he loved his husband. Daryl kissed his way along Liam's sternum to his navel and swirled his tongue around the divot in Liam's belly.

"Feels great." Liam tipped his head back and tightened his grasp on Daryl's hair.

Daryl mashed his face into his husband's abdomen and smothered his smile. He liked pleasing Liam and loved being inside him even more. He popped the button on Liam's jeans. The denim slid down Liam's hips. Daryl groaned. The low-slung, open look always appealed to Daryl, but especially on Liam. He shoved his lover's pants and boxer briefs down around his ankles. The clothing landed in a heap.

Power surged through Daryl. Love, desire and need filled his brain. He couldn't live without this man. He needed Liam more than his next breath. When the rest of the world went to shit, he could trust Liam to be on his side. He nibbled along Liam's abs. The man kept him balanced and grounded.

"Do you remember the first time we fucked?" Liam asked.

"Made love," Daryl corrected. He dragged his teeth across Liam's stomach. "You kept calling it fucking, but it was more. We made love." He curled his fingers around

Liam's shaft. "But yeah, I remember." How could he forget one of the few nights that had changed his life in an instant?

"Me, too." Liam eased forward, rubbing his cock in Daryl's fingers. "Seems like yesterday."

"Uh-huh." His time with Liam had flown by. They'd shared so many good days and plenty more hot nights. Some of their moments weren't that great, but the positives far outweighed the negatives. He brushed his face over Liam's belly again, then dragged the blunt end of Liam's erection across his lips.

Liam shivered. "Damn."

"Of course. I want you right there. Right on the edge." Daryl pressed his thumb over the top of Liam's cock. Liam managed to blow his mind every time they were together. He bottomed most of the time and never complained. Now he deserved preferential treatment. Daryl scooted off the bed and onto his knees. He settled between Liam's legs. He glanced up at Liam and grinned.

"Daryl?" Liam's eyes widened. "What?"

Daryl traced the seam of his lips with the tip of Liam's cock. Salty pre-cum slid over his tongue. *So good.* He cupped Liam's balls. "Such a hot dick. I want it."

"Me, too, but yours." Liam palmed the back of Daryl's head. "Let me pleasure you."

"Not yet." *Oh God.* The desire to allow Liam to suck his shaft overwhelmed him. But this was what Liam did to him. He had Daryl on the edge of control and drowning in raw desire. He plunged his mouth down on Liam's dick. He buried his nose in Liam's pubic hair then swallowed.

"Shit. Fuck." Liam jerked. He released his grasp on Daryl's hair. He rocked his hips and shoved his cock deep into Daryl's mouth before pulling out again.

Daryl moaned around Liam's erection. He enjoyed being used. He kept stroking Liam's balls while he bobbed his head. When Liam whimpered, Daryl touched the soft patch of skin behind his lover's sac.

Liam jerked and groaned. His knees wobbled. "Daryl."

He loved having Liam close to coming apart. He kept his rhythm up, pulling most of the way out before taking Liam to the back of his throat again. He palmed Liam's thigh for stability.

"Oh Jesus." More strangled cries came from Liam as he curled forward. He moved his hips until his thrusts turned frantic and jerky.

Daryl tapped Liam's asshole. The move, although tiny, always managed to push Liam the rest of the way toward climax.

Liam opened his eyes and sucked in a ragged breath. He rammed his dick into Daryl's mouth. "Can't hold back." Liam tensed. "Please?"

"Come," Daryl said around Liam's cock. He craved the taste of his lover on his tongue.

"Oh fucking hell." Liam palmed the back of Daryl's head. He tried to pull out, but Daryl held fast.

No way Daryl would miss this.

Liam grunted and shot his load into Daryl's mouth. Daryl swallowed everything Liam gave him and hummed. He bobbed his head a few more times until Liam stopped trembling. The man tasted delicious. He lapped at Liam's shaft, cleaning up every last bit.

"Oh shit." Liam pulled out and eased around Daryl, then sagged onto the bed. "I love how you wring me out. You know what to do." He wriggled his ass. "Take me?"

"I do want you." Like every minute and in every way.

Liam managed to prop himself up on his hands and knees. He glanced back at Daryl. A lazy smile curled on his lips. "I'm yours." He wriggled his butt again. "I need a big dick in me."

"You do." First, he needed lube. *Fuck.* "Babe, where's the stuff?"

"My bag." Liam sighed. "Plenty in there."

Daryl left Liam alone long enough to rummage through his duffle. He spotted the tube and grinned. He should've known Liam would be a few steps ahead of him. He noticed the glass dildo nestled among Liam's boxer briefs. "Should I use this, too?" He held up the toy. "I didn't know you had this."

"I pretended it was you." Liam spread his knees apart and swatted his own ass. "I'd rather have you fuck me."

He'd rather be the one giving Liam pleasure, too. Daryl grabbed the lube then knelt behind Liam. He rubbed his face on Liam's ass cheek. He loved this man so much and couldn't see life without him. He caressed Liam's hole. *So pretty and pink.* He tapped the puckered skin.

"Yeah," Liam whispered. "Fuck."

Daryl dragged his nose along Liam's' rump then massaged lube onto his asshole. He dribbled more of the clear fluid onto his fingers. Liam moaned and backed into Daryl.

Daryl chuckled. "I love how responsive you are to me. Need me?"

"You know I do." Liam flexed his hips. His cock bobbed between his legs. He stroked himself a couple of times then braced his hands again. He grunted. "Jesus. I came already and could come a second time."

"Then keep doing that." He wanted Liam to orgasm a second and maybe four times. He needed Liam to crave him as much as he craved Liam. "I love watching you." He drew circles around Liam's hole with the tip of his index finger.

"Nice." Liam backed into Daryl and pushed onto Daryl's digit.

"Yeah." That was what he desired—Liam hot and bothered, just for him. He smeared lube over the second knuckle then continued pushing. He flicked his tongue over the tight pink skin of Liam's ass.

"Shit." Liam sucked in a tight breath. "I love that."

"I know you do." He tongued Liam's hole. At the same time, he used his free hand to tug on his lover's balls and caress the soft skin behind his sac.

Liam wriggled his hips and backed into Daryl's face.

"Naughty." Daryl swatted Liam, leaving a red print on

his skin. He couldn't argue with Liam, though. He'd made his lover wait long enough. He needed to be inside Liam. First, he had to prep him. Daryl lubed his middle finger then eased both digits into Liam's ass.

Liam reached between his legs and tugged on his dick. "Need more."

Daryl worked his fingers in and out of Liam's hole, curling and twisting to stretch his lover out. He caressed Liam's prostate and when Liam whimpered, then jerked, Daryl grinned. "So nice." He continued to tease the puckered skin and swatted Liam twice more.

"Put your dick in me." Liam shivered. "Stop the foreplay. I want it. I want *you*." He moaned and pressed his face into the bedding. "Daryl."

I love to hear my name on Liam's lips. Sweet music. He pumped his fingers a few more times, then withdrew. He kissed Liam's asshole.

Liam dug his toes into the blankets and another groan ripped from his throat.

"Just a second." Not that he could blame Liam. Sexy, needy and right on the edge was exactly where he wanted his lover because he felt the same way. Now it wouldn't take long for him to come, too.

Daryl stood and drenched his dick in lube, then lined himself up with his lover's hole. As much as he wanted to barrel forward, he eased slowly into Liam. He pushed past the tight ring of muscle and buried himself deep in Liam's ass.

"Uh…oh God." Liam tensed.

"Breathe out and bear down on me." He palmed Liam's waist. "Come on, babe. Breathe."

Liam whimpered and relaxed a little. Daryl slid to the hilt into Liam and paused. *So tight and hot.* He could stay right there forever.

"Oh, sweet Jesus, yes," Liam said. "Fucking balls."

"Yeah." Daryl worked his hips, pulling most of the way out before shoving all the way in again. He loved the delicious pressure. Blood coursed through his veins. The rest of the world and all of his troubles melted away. Nothing mattered except for Liam and the moment.

Liam shuddered and met Daryl thrust for thrust.

His restraint snapped. *Holy shit.* Daryl tipped his head back and gasped. He squeezed Liam's hips. No matter how fast he pushed into his lover, it wasn't enough. This had to be what giving in to abandon felt like. He wanted Liam to experience the feral need with him. "Stroke yourself. Come with me."

"Thank you." Liam grunted. He arched his back and flexed his asshole.

Daryl couldn't see the action, but he felt Liam's trembles as he writhed beneath him. The noises coming from his lover turned Daryl on. The orgasm started low in his belly and spiraled through his veins. He stopped fighting the climax and allowed the overwhelming desire to fill his body. He curled forward and continued pumping his hips. Skin slapped skin and the noise echoed. "Come with me. Oh. Fuck." He slammed into Liam. A bead of perspiration slipped down Liam's back and sparkled on his skin. He sank his dick to the hilt into Liam and filled his lover's ass with cum.

"Fuck me." A ragged cry erupted from Liam. He shuddered again and arched his back, then collapsed on the bed.

Daryl settled on top of his husband. He wasn't ready to be two separate souls just yet. He craved the togetherness. A moment of sadness washed over him. He hadn't spent nearly enough time with Liam. The tenderness coming from Liam helped Daryl to make up his mind. He had to make this moment last. He held Liam and didn't remove his dick from his lover's ass. Neither he nor Liam spoke. The simple act of existing was enough.

Liam groaned first and split the silence. "Damn."

"Yeah." He kissed Liam's shoulder. "Hot, too." Forming a complete sentence beyond a couple of words was beyond him.

"Uh-huh." Liam sighed. "I want you to hold me forever. No leaving. Time standing still. Just us. Right here."

Daryl raked his teeth between Liam's shoulder blades, then kissed the reddened skin. "Deal."

"But I should clean up the wet spot first." Liam wriggled. "It's gooey."

Daryl snorted. "Fine." He eased out of Liam and flopped onto his back. "At least it's at the foot of the bed. Then we don't have to sleep in it."

"True." Liam left the bedroom long enough to retrieve a towel. He wiped up the cum on the sheets then dried his belly. With care, he dried Daryl. Instead of speaking, he grinned then returned to the bathroom. When he came back, he snuggled in the sheets with Daryl.

"What are you thinking about?" Daryl asked. He draped his arm around Liam. "You're unusually quiet."

"Nothing." Liam didn't look at him. "Really."

"Right. Want to try for a real answer or are you going to stall?" He held Liam tighter. "Fess up. What's wrong?"

Liam groaned. "I'm worried. Part of me believes you when you tell me you love me and we're tight, but I'm scared you're going to be here on your old stomping grounds and when you see Sarah, you'll realize you want her more than me. I'm not jealous of her. I'm worried you'll go to the one you love more and that's not me. You said you were coming out to everyone and letting them know we're married. What if you change your mind? Sarah's beautiful and she'll fit your image better than I can. It's probably silly, but that's what I'm thinking."

"Not silly at all." He should've seen this coming. Should've considered Liam's feelings more, reassured Liam that he wanted him no matter what. "I'm not leaving you or lying about who I am." Daryl kissed Liam's shoulder. "You're mine."

"And you're willing to tell anyone who asks if that's the case?" Liam glanced back at him. "Or was that a lapse in judgment?"

"Fuck 'em. I have a husband." He'd shout it from the roof, but he doubted he'd be allowed up there. "You're mine and those vows we wrote weren't for nothing."

"What if Sarah doesn't want both of us?"

"She will. Without her, I'd never have figured out I was bisexual. She…" He wanted to explain, but the words wouldn't come. "I tried pegging with her. She's the only woman I've let fuck me." He held Liam tightly. "Go to sleep. We'll worry about her in the morning."

"I'll try." Liam ground his ass against Daryl's soft dick. His breath warmed Daryl's skin and within moments, he fell asleep.

Daryl tried to nod off, but no matter how hard he tried, he couldn't shake the excitement and annoyance in his brain. Part of him couldn't be mad that she'd moved on and had a kid. Who could blame her? She deserved a life, but still. She had a chemistry with him and with the triad. They were perfect as a threesome.

But the annoyance crept back in. She couldn't be with someone else. Not while she slept with them.

Still, he could've come back long before now. The what-ifs and what-could've-beens ate at him. If he'd stayed, they'd be together. If he'd have argued for her to come along and put his foot down, they might not have forged a future together. His career was nice, but Liam and Sarah made it perfect. He'd convinced Liam the triad would work. Now he had to get Sarah on board. *Talk about the near impossible.*

Chapter Six

The next morning, Daryl woke but the anger hadn't dissipated. His stomach ached and the thoughts clouding his mind hadn't gone away. He sat up and rubbed his face with both hands. The scent of pancakes wafted through the air. He sniffed, then opened his eyes. Liam sat at the table and grinned.

"I had room service bring up breakfast." Liam pointed to the other plate. "Have some."

"Thanks." Daryl left the bed but didn't bother to dress. *Fuck it.* He strode naked over to the table and sat opposite Liam. He had a thousand questions on his mind. He stuffed a forkful of pancakes into his mouth and chewed. The pillow-soft breakfast melted with the butter in a delicious mess. He groaned.

"I know, right? This place makes the best pancakes. We'll gain ten pounds just from breakfast, but it'll be worth it." Liam finished his food. "You tossed and turned all night. Want to talk?"

"I do." He held up his fork. God help him, but he needed his hands when he talked. "Where'd you find her? What building? She teaches creative writing? In the lecture hall or a dinky classroom?"

"Okay." Liam smiled. "She's teaching creative writing, yes, and the college. The Leonard building, I believe, and it's a lecture hall. We can come in shortly after class starts and hide in the back. She didn't see me until I walked down the main aisle."

"Great." He sat back in his seat and stared at his breakfast. "I'm excited and nervous. I bet she's dynamic."

"She is." Liam tipped his head. "What are you thinking? We just show up? She'll freak out or they'll throw us out."

"Nah." He'd find a way to meet with the dean of the arts college and set up a scholarship like he'd planned. One for a student with aptitude in the dramatic arts and acting but with little to no financial aid available. Then he'd do the same thing but for a needy journalism student. Part of him debated putting his name on a building, but he decided against that. He'd contribute to the alumni fund, too. He'd graduated from Kenton and they didn't owe him a thing, but damn it, he wanted to be on campus and not get thrown off.

"Just cool it. We'll get this sorted out." Liam left the table and wandered into the bathroom. "If we go slow, we might get more than we expected."

"Deal." He'd have to believe Liam. He finished his pancakes and wiped his mouth before he joined Liam in the shower. "You're hot as hell, you know that, right?" He massaged soap onto the washcloth and cleaned Liam. "Might make me forget why I'm here."

"I doubt it." Liam kissed him, then ducked under the water. "You're obsessed with Sarah, but it's a good thing because I'm drawn to her, too."

"You're smart and sexy. The best combination." He washed his hair once Liam left the shower. "You take the world's quickest shower, too. Geez."

"I hurried." Liam left him alone in the bathroom.

Daryl rinsed the lather out of his hair and slathered soap over his body. When he stepped under the spray again, the tension in him flowed into the drain. Today, he'd get the woman he loved back into his arms and he'd have the man he loved right there with him. He turned the water off and dried himself, then dressed.

Ten minutes later, he climbed into the car with Liam and rode across town to the campus. The moment he stepped out of the vehicle, a wave of nostalgia hit him. He hadn't been back to Kenton State University in so long. The place smelled the same—like dried leaves and hope. Did hope have a scent? He'd always thought so. The students seemed younger, too. Or was he just old? Even though he'd been gone a long time, he knew where to find the Leonard building.

"Know where we're going?" Liam chuckled. "Lead the way."

"Of course." Daryl grasped Liam's hand. He'd declared he wasn't afraid to admit they were a couple or married. Time to put that into action. He kissed Liam. "Let's go."

"You...in public...kissed me." Liam stood rooted to the spot. "Are you sure?"

"I am." He wound his arms around Liam. "I don't care who sees us or asks questions. I'm not ashamed and I'm tired of hiding. I said we're going public, so we are." He loved Liam and wanted the world to know.

Liam's lips parted. He sagged into Daryl. "I like that."

"Me, too." He kissed Liam again and rested his forehead against his.

"Get a room," a girl shouted. "Jesus."

Daryl laughed. He might not have Sarah back, but he and Liam were in a good place. For the first time since his last movie had started, he had few worries and felt lighter. "We should go."

Liam nodded and allowed Daryl to clasp his hand once again. Daryl walked beside Liam. Of all the things he'd been through, he wanted to share his past at KSU with Liam. "The music and theater building is on the north end of campus. We'll see that later, but this building is the arts one. Sarah and I took a history class there and she dared me to model nude for a semester. I did it and made sure it was for her drawing class. She wanted to kill me." He could still see the way her eyes had widened when he'd lost the robe the first time.

"I bet she loved that. You probably got the phone numbers of the women in the class." Liam bumped shoulders with Daryl. "Did you ever want to cheat on her?"

"I did get numbers and I shared them with Sarah. Back then, we were on the same wavelength. She wasn't worried about me cheating and I had no desire to do it." He kissed Liam's temple. "Just like with you." He stopped at the main drag and nodded to the south. "That huge structure down there is the student center and basketball arena. I never went to the games, but I saw a couple of local bands play. Over there is the pottery building. Gotta have a place for ceramics classes and glass blowing."

Liam laughed and snorted. "Oh my God. I thought you were going to say dick blowing."

"You're juvenile." But he'd said the same thing so many times. He crossed the road and tugged Liam's hand. The moment he spotted the Leonard building, the breath lodged in his throat. "There it is."

"I know." Liam grinned. "I've been here. Remember?"

"I do." He opened the door for Liam. No one seemed to notice them. Then again, there weren't many people in the halls. He'd expected the corridors to be jammed. Liam pointed to the doors to the lecture hall. Daryl dipped his head and grasped the handle. He blew out a long breath and followed Liam into the large room.

The lights in the back of the space had been turned down, but were brighter on the stage and podium. He eased into the last row and sat beside Liam. No wonder Liam had been able to sneak in. When he spotted Sarah, Daryl held Liam's hand tighter. Her jeans clung to her curvy frame like a second skin and the sweater seemed more like something to hide in. She'd pulled her hair back in a ponytail. The vibrant blue showed in her hair. He heard her speak but paid no attention to the words. She mesmerized him. He longed to snag her in his arms and hold her between him and Liam.

"Told you," Liam whispered. He palmed Daryl's thigh. "I could listen to her forever."

"Uh-huh." He'd fantasized about making love to her in a classroom when they were back in college. He'd also wanted to fuck Liam on more than one of the movie sets. He shivered. *Hell.* He should make a movie about a teacher and her student or the parents of her student. Maybe make Liam the teacher...he didn't care. He added the concept to his mental list of film ideas.

"Remember to bring those outlines and the first three chapters on Monday." Sarah closed her book and moved to the edge of the stage. She sat on the steps and a few students approached her.

Daryl gripped the arms of the chair but Liam squeezed Daryl's leg and stilled him. "Give her about five minutes. They clear out quick. We'll get down there. Be cool."

"Yeah, I will." *Tell my brain to be cool. Christ.* He wanted to run down the steps to her. He waited as long as he could — probably not five minutes — then left his seat. One of the female students turned around just as he hit the bottom step. Her eyes widened.

"Are...you?" A wide smile curled on her lips. "Dare Evans? Oh my God."

He could lie, but when he met Sarah's gaze, his desire to be fake evaporated. "I am. I graduated from Kenton years ago."

"That is so not in the brochure." The girl whipped out her phone. "Selfie with me?"

"Sure." He hadn't planned on being on the Internet, but he'd opened a huge can of trouble. He posed with her then signed her notebook. She shrieked as she hurried up the stairs and he shook his head. Yeah, he'd invited trouble to Kenton.

"You certainly haven't lost your charm." Sarah tucked her papers and a leather journal into her messenger bag. "It's good to see you again, Dare."

She wasn't looking at him and had called him by his stage name. *Shit.* "Sarah."

"It's good to see you, too, Sarah." Liam eased around Daryl and opened his arms. He enfolded Sarah in a hug. Her eyes flashed and she blushed from her hairline to her collar.

"Liam." She stumbled into him. "I thought I'd scared you off."

"Nah. I'm tougher than you think." He stared at her a little longer than Daryl liked. "You're hard to walk away from, too." He kept his arm around her and met Daryl's glare. "I've also awoken the beast."

"Oh yes. He can be possessive at his worst." Sarah shrugged free from Liam. "I've got to go. Unless you're enrolling in my class, and I sincerely hope not, you don't need me."

"I don't know. I might enjoy creative writing." Liam paused. "Looks like we've got company."

Daryl gritted his teeth. Damn it, he didn't want to deal with another fan. He glanced over his shoulder. A young man with dirty blond hair and blue eyes strolled down the steps. *Who in the hell is he?*

"Todd." Sarah smiled. She draped the handle of her bag across her body and rushed up to him. "Well? How'd it go?"

"I'm in." Todd frowned. "Who are these two?" He stepped between Sarah and Liam. "What are they doing here? Students? They look a little old to be students."

"You're a little young to be here." Daryl stood toe-to-toe with Todd. Jealousy hit him hard. He didn't like the shit jumping in on his game. "Who are you?"

"I'm here to see my *mom*," Todd snapped.

"Would you believe he dated your mom?" Liam asked. "I met her in Vegas. She's a wonderful person. I like her a lot."

Daryl wobbled on his feet. He'd been told she had a kid, but he'd pictured a child…not a young adult. *Her son…his mom…holy fuck.*

"You didn't date her. I know. I've been around." Todd glared at Daryl. "So don't try to bullshit me. And you." He turned to Liam. "I don't know where you met her, but just leave her alone. She's been through enough."

What? Like? He had a thousand questions for Sarah, Todd

and Liam. How much did his husband know? What was Sarah not telling him? And why did he have the feeling there was more to Todd's story than he was letting on as well?

"Todd, let's go. I want to know how your interview went." Sarah waved to Liam and Daryl. "Bye, guys. See you around. I'm sure there will be a swarm in the hallway." She started up the stairs with Todd.

Liam hooked his index fingers into his belt loops. "So you fucked that up." He faced Daryl. "We should've given her a chance to sort things out for everyone."

"Yeah. I did." Daryl shook his head. He needed more time. Needed to process what he'd been told and how he'd ask the questions he wanted to learn the answers to without being an asshole. His phone vibrated. *Fine time to get a call or a text.* He slipped the device from his pocket and glanced at the screen. A text from his agent. "I have a meeting with the dean of the arts department and the president of Kenton in ten minutes. Special notice."

"Good. Then it gives me the opportunity to talk to Sarah while you set up your scholarship fund thing." Liam kissed Daryl on the mouth and gripped his shoulders. "Hey. We'll work this out. She didn't exactly push me away. Chances are she won't push you, either, if you be cool." He kissed him again, then darted up the stairs after Sarah.

Daryl massaged his temples. He'd had such big plans when Mischa had called. He'd win Sarah back, have Liam and life would be good. Then he'd found out Sarah was at the college. He'd added the scholarship idea to the mix. Still a perfectly smart idea. What he hadn't planned on was Sarah pushing him and things not going to according to his desires. He'd been so used to people doing what he wanted almost without even his asking. She not only challenged him but expected more from him. Plus, she had a teenage son.

Damn it. He had no idea what to do. He sighed. If nothing else, he had the meeting. He trusted Liam. If his husband said he had the situation in hand, then fine. He'd give Liam the benefit of the doubt. Liam hadn't let him down before. All Daryl knew was that he couldn't live without Liam and Sarah. How he'd get to that point, he wasn't sure.

Liam hurried out of the lecture hall. In the corridor, he surveyed the area. North, south...no Sarah. When he glanced out through the bank of windows, he noticed her on the sidewalk. She stood with Todd. Both were smiling and she hugged him. Liam's heart clenched. He missed that closeness with his family. They'd stuck by him when he'd married Daryl, but they lived in Pennsylvania. Not exactly a hop, skip and a jump from Hollywood. He shored up his gumption and continued after Sarah.

He opened the door. Unlike Daryl, the students didn't seem to notice him. He snorted. For being a movie star and believed to be so famous, he could still move about in relative anonymity. He strode up to Sarah and Todd.

"God. Don't you stop?" Todd snapped.

Sarah put her hand up. "It's okay, kid. He's nice."

"That's what you said about Rick." Todd gripped the straps of his backpack. "I'm not doing this again."

"Good, because I don't know what this is, but I don't want to do it, either." Liam stood tall and didn't crowd into their space. "First, I'm sorry about Daryl. He's on a hair-trigger. He just finished a movie and he's always touchy right afterwards. Second, we weren't trying to embarrass or upset you. Third, I hear you had an interview," he said to Todd. "Was it good?"

Sarah tilted her head and stared at him.

Todd's brow furrowed. "Hold it. You just apologized and now you're asking about my life? Who are you?"

"Liam Turner." He offered his hand. "Actor, voice actor and general pain in the ass to my directors. You must be Sarah's son. It's a pleasure to meet you."

Todd shook hands with Liam, then met his mother's gaze. He groaned and turned his attention back to Liam. "I was accepted into Kenton next semester for post-secondary classes. We have to re-apply each semester. Anyway, I'm on the path to have my associate's degree when I graduate from high school."

"Nice." She'd raised a smart and protective kid. "I'm proud," Liam said. "That's wonderful."

Todd rolled his eyes. "Sure." He shrugged out of Liam's grip. "Mom, I'll see you after practice. Thanks for getting my car out of the shop. Liam…nice to meet you." He waved then started off down the sidewalk.

Sarah folded her arms and bowed her head.

"I'm impressed," Liam said. "You've done well, Momma."

"It's a lot easier when you've got a good kid to begin with." She sighed. "So… Daryl's here and so are you. What's next?"

"Well, I thought we'd talk." He draped his arm around her waist. "I noticed a set of swings down on the grassy area at the foot of the hill. Why don't we find one?"

"What about Daryl?" she asked.

"He's meeting with the dean and the president of the college. He wasn't kidding about the scholarship thing."

"Wow. I didn't think he had it in him." She fell into step beside him. "What did you want to talk about?"

"I'm sorry Daryl flew off the handle." He guided her down the hill to the row of two-seater swings. "He doesn't…" *How am I supposed to explain this?* "He thinks and leads with his heart. He moves, then worries about the damage." He stopped at the first empty swing. "Care to sit with me?"

"Sure." She smiled and eased onto the seat. "I know about Daryl. He's a good man — well, he was."

"He still is." He draped his arm across the back of the swing and pushed to start the motion. "He loves you very much."

"I doubt that." She didn't lean in to him, but she also didn't pull away. "He loves any and all women."

"What if I told you that's not the case?"

"I'd tell you to stop lying. I've seen the shows and read

the articles on the Internet. He's a dog." Sarah chuckled. "He's got the looks and the attitude for it, so I won't knock him."

He stared at the students walking across the field. He'd been young and innocent like them, what seemed like a lifetime ago. Then his career and the Hollywood lifestyle had gotten hold of him. He'd changed just like Daryl. He'd grown harder around the edges and less trusting. He had to get through to her and make her see that Daryl wasn't as bad as she'd thought. But how?

"He's still gorgeous." Sarah patted Liam's thigh. "So are you. If I had to have a lapse in judgment, then I'm glad I had it with the both of you."

Shit. He'd hoped she wouldn't call their burgeoning relationship a lapse in judgment. "Sweetheart, Daryl and I aren't fooling around. We're more than a little in love with you. He never fell out of love with you." Liam trailed his fingers over her shoulder. "He doesn't fall easily and not at all with every woman he meets. The tabloids and the studios make stories out of nothing. You have to believe me. Daryl wouldn't carry your photo in his wallet if he didn't still have feelings for you. The fact that you're a mom endears you to him almost as much as it does to me. I can't think of anyone else I'd rather be right here with." Except for maybe with Daryl on her other side. Soon.

Sarah stared at him. She hadn't expected Liam to say a thing about Todd other than he was proud. He liked that she was a mom? Most guys wanted to date her once Todd was out of the house. Part of her wanted to believe Liam, but the rest reserved say.

"How old is Todd, then? Eighteen? Seventeen?" Liam asked.

"He turned seventeen in January." She rubbed her arms. Despite the sweater, the chill seeped through to her bones.

"Huh." Liam nodded. He didn't speak for a long time. Instead, he continued to move the swing. "You and Daryl split eighteen years ago, didn't you?"

She tensed. Was he putting two and two together? He seemed like a smart enough man. He had to know the deal. "Yeah, we did."

He shifted in his seat to face her. "What exactly happened when you split? Tell me the truth."

She'd wanted to get the story out for so long. He deserved answers. Daryl even more so, but he wasn't there. "I left Daryl at the airport. I knew I'd be a noose around his neck. You've seen what all he's done. He'd never have been in those movies or won those awards if..." She sucked in a ragged breath. Saying the words out loud made them seem so final.

"If you'd stuck around?" Liam tipped his head to meet her gaze.

"Yeah." In her heart she knew Daryl deserved to know the truth and to be able to decide on his own path, but she'd done what she'd thought was best.

"Well, we've got the right now and I'm not going anywhere. No matter what you tell me, I have no plans to leave." He rubbed her shoulder. "I like you, Sarah. I want to see where this goes."

His words were comforting. She rested her head on his shoulder. "You're crazy, but if that's what you want...I won't argue." She didn't have the strength to — not now.

"Good." He kicked at the ground, moving the swing again.

Just like with Daryl, she couldn't deny the attraction or the safety she felt in Liam's arms. He knew how to touch her and make her crave him. She wasn't worried about how he'd treat Todd or even if Todd would like him in return. A few dates or a possible relationship could happen.

"There you are." Daryl strode up to the swing. He'd stuffed his hands into his pockets. "The meeting went well. I just donated a hundred grand to Kenton in order for students like us to get through school with as few tuition bills as possible."

"Good job," Liam said.

A hundred grand? She couldn't fathom having that much money, let alone being able to give it away without a second thought.

Daryl leaned against the frame of the swing structure. "I also ran into Todd."

Her heart dropped and bile rose in her throat. Todd didn't take to strangers well and she doubted he'd get along with Daryl. He'd become too protective of her in the last few years.

"And?" Liam asked.

"He's a good kid. He doesn't believe I dated his mom, but it happens." He crossed his ankles. "Is there anywhere we can go that's a little more private? Once word got out that I'd donated money and was on campus…let's just say we won't be able to talk for much longer without someone interrupting. Besides, I want to apologize for earlier."

She sighed. She should've known being with a movie star and having his best friend around would bring unwanted attention.

"He's being serious." Liam tipped her chin to meet his gaze. "He never apologizes."

"I know." She'd seen Daryl at his worst back in college. Even if she had him dead to rights, he wouldn't back down on his position. To have him admitting he was wrong now blew her mind. She patted Liam's thigh. If they wanted privacy, she'd do the best she could short of going to the house. "I have a place. I doubt we'll all fit, but it's a place." She stood and pulled away from Liam. She'd never move forward if she didn't start now. Without looking back at either Daryl or Liam, she headed across the field to the staff office building.

Liam grasped her hand and neither man spoke until she reached the doors. Liam stopped short. "Wait," he said. "You told me you didn't have an office."

"I lied." She headed up to the third floor. When she rounded the corner, she sent up a small prayer that her office would be empty. The lack of light under the door served as a good omen.

"Brat." Liam slipped his arm around her waist. "I should spank you."

"I might like it." She stuffed her key into the lock and turned the knob.

"Wait," Daryl said. "You never talked to me that way."

"I grew up." She opened the door and thanked God her office mate wasn't there. She scooted to the side and waved her hand. "There's not much room and nowhere to sit besides on my desk, but it's private." Truth be told, she didn't want to chat. Being so close to both men brought out her inner desire to do naughty things with them. Another round of sex like in Vegas sounded perfect. She shook her head. Now wasn't the time to think about making love.

Daryl leaned against the empty wall and Liam leaned against her desk. She closed the door and blew out a long breath. She had to be crazy inviting them to her office.

"Huh." Liam laughed. "This looks like such an office."

"It's nothing exciting." She kept her back to the door. "I rarely use it."

Daryl met her gaze. "I can tell, but you've always been a minimalist." He hooked his thumbs on his jeans pockets. "I'm sorry about the Todd thing."

"He's a kid. They get testy and protective. It's been him and me against the world for a long time." Longer than needed. Because of her past, Todd had been forced to grow up quickly. He'd been the man of the house for far too long. "He's no more of a threat than Matt is."

"Who?" Daryl's eyes flickered with passion. Or was that anger?

"My gay best friend. Remember Addie's brother? I'm sure you met him." She pressed herself into the door. As much as she liked the conversation, she wanted to escape. The overwhelming desire to tell them she wanted them was too much. She needed to stop thinking about fucking.

"I do." Daryl nodded. "How is he?"

"Fine." She gasped for air. How in the hell had things become so uncomfortable? Had the temperature kicked on?

Liam eased up to her. Instead of acting jealous, he seemed to take everything she'd said in stride. He bumped shoulders with her. "We won't push you."

"We? That's good to know. But how exactly are you not going to push me? There isn't a *we*. There's you two and me." She switched her gaze between Daryl and Liam. They'd spent a lot of time together, but the only way there would be a *we* was if she allowed it. She still wasn't convinced being with Liam was a good idea.

Daryl smiled and his eyes flashed again. "Yeah. *We* want you."

"Right. For another one-night stand? Or is it an affair between movies?" She held up her hands. "Now no one will see us or anything. I get it." They wanted her as a plaything for the moment. *Yeah, not going to happen.* She might want to have sex with them and have a good time, but not at the risk of being used.

"I don't think you understand." Liam brushed her hair from her neck. "We want you."

She sucked in a ragged breath. Liam Turner, heartthrob of the big screen, sure as hell didn't sound like he was kidding.

"Sweetheart, there is only one woman for us." Liam kissed along her throat to just behind her ear. "You."

"For now." She bit back a moan. She'd always loved when a man kissed her right there. If he continued, she'd forget her arguments for keeping him and Daryl at bay. She sagged into Liam and whimpered. "Don't do what you don't mean," she managed.

"Never." Liam palmed her breast through the cotton of her sweater. "Can't."

Can't? Can't what? Before she could argue, Daryl eased up to her other side. He cupped her other breast. When she turned her head to meet his gaze, he kissed her hard on the lips. "We need you."

Her thoughts blurred. Two movie stars wanted her. As

much as her common sense screamed for her to run out of the office, her desire for Daryl and Liam outweighed the doubt.

Liam eased his fingers under her sweater and grazed her belly. She sucked in her stomach. *Fuck.* They'd notice she needed to visit the gym...like a hundred times over. Liam caressed her breast beneath the lace of her bra. "You're perfect the way you are," he murmured and resumed kissing her neck.

She shivered. Holy shit. This was real. She leaned into Liam's touch as Daryl curled his fingers under her chin. He feasted on her mouth and tongue. He stole her breath. She ground her ass into the door. She'd never been so...she wasn't even sure how to explain the way she felt. Exposed and vulnerable, but protected.

Liam tucked her to his chest and kneaded her breast. He pinched her nipple through her bra. The bit of pain added to her pleasure. She whimpered into Daryl's mouth. Daryl unbuttoned her jeans and worked his hand beneath the elastic of her panties. She widened her stance as much as she could between their hard bodies.

"Holy shit, I want you." Daryl nipped her earlobe. He worked his fingers down to her pussy. "Christ, you're wet. Can we fuck in here?"

"I..." She'd never thought about it before. Her office was utilitarian — not for sex.

"Haven't been this hard in a while." Liam chuckled. "Nor this suave."

The words *yes, fuck me* resonated in her mind, but when she opened her mouth, no sound came out. She massaged the bulge in Liam's pants and the one in Daryl's, too. Two dicks, hard and ready for her.

Daryl managed to turn her and situated his thigh between her legs. He continued toying with her clit. Liam fell in behind her and cupped both of her breasts. At the same time, he rubbed his denim-covered cock against the seam of her ass.

"I've dreamed about you since Vegas. That kiss." Liam raked his teeth along the side of her neck. "Can't get enough."

She closed her eyes. Even if they became an item, she'd never get over Daryl or Liam. Something rattled. She shrugged and continued to kiss Daryl. He'd probably bumped the door and made the handle rattle. The sound came back. The lock mechanism only made that sound when someone turned the knob.

Turned the knob… Sarah pushed Daryl away and opened her eyes. Someone was trying to enter the office. *Fuck, fuck, fuck.* She focused on the lock, then turned the tab. The gesture would buy a few more seconds for her to think. Although he pulled his hand out of her pants, Daryl didn't appear pleased. Thank goodness he hadn't said anything. She placed her finger over her lips. *Please, God, let them understand.*

Daryl covered his mouth with his hand and Liam did likewise.

Sarah bit back a groan. She'd gotten them into this jam by allowing Daryl and Liam to romance her. Now she had to find a way back out.

Chapter Seven

The knob rattled again and Sarah adjusted her clothing, then steadied herself. "Sorry, the lock's jammed." She pressed her full weight against the door. She couldn't see the person on the other side, but the scent of perfume wafted around her. The only person she knew who wore perfume that thick was Mischa—her office-mate.

"For the love of fuck," Mischa snapped. "This thing is always messed up. I'll get the fucking janitor."

Sarah pressed her ear to the door and listened for Mischa leaving. The sound of Mischa's high heels on the tile floor dissipated. She dragged a deep breath into her lungs then let it out slowly. "Okay." She shoved her hair out of her eyes. "Go out the back way. Remember? The way we'd sneak in here when we wanted to make out?"

Daryl nodded.

"Make out?" Liam grinned. "I love it."

"Well, you'll love it a lot less if she comes back." Sarah opened the door and checked the hall. No one. She waved to Daryl and Liam. "Go. I'll catch up with you in the C lot. The last thing I need is for Mischa to catch us. I'm not in the mood to deal with the hell she'd give me."

"Forget her. You've got us," Daryl murmured. He darted out of the room.

Liam kissed her on the cheek. "We'll make it up to you." He winked, then followed Daryl around the corner and out of sight.

Sarah sagged against the wall just outside of the office. She'd have to do a lot of explaining to so many people tonight. The click of stiletto on tile grated on her nerves.

It also signaled Mischa's return. The woman certainly had timing — good or bad, Sarah wasn't sure.

"That doesn't look stuck to me." Mischa waved her soy latte at Sarah. Her oversized purse jangled on her other arm.

Sarah half-expected to see a teacup dog pop its head out of the purse. "I got the lock to work. Someone must've jammed a pencil or something in the mechanism. A few turns and the shavings fell out." God, she was a horrible liar.

"Good, I couldn't find a janitor." Mischa barreled past Sarah into the office. She crinkled her nose. "Smells like cologne in here. Men's cologne."

"I just talked to a student, then Todd came by." She really needed to stop fibbing. Sarah gathered up her messenger bag. Some professors loved their office and crammed every last book and paper into the space. Others barely visited and kept nothing of importance there. She fell into the second category, but not by choice. Mischa's fashion posters, books, papers and patterns took up almost every available inch.

Mischa plunked her bag on her desk and flipped her lamp on. "Have you heard from your Vegas boys?"

"No." 'Heard' wasn't the right way to put things. Kissed, touched and argued with sounded correct.

"Sad. They really seemed to jive on you. I hooked up with Dom." Mischa waved her hand. "The best forty-eight hours of my life."

"Oh, good." She gripped the strap of her bag. "I'm glad."

"He wanted to go public, but I didn't want that glare in my life." Mischa sat on the edge of her desk. "He needed someone with him all of the time and I'm not ready to give up my career here at the college. I saw you got press for your hook-up. Did the dean speak to you?"

"No." She hadn't heard a thing, but wondered if she should've. Fear crept into her brain. There weren't rules against going to Vegas or having a relationship out there.

The last she knew, the professors were just supposed to act with dignity. Being in a tabloid magazine wasn't the best for her image, but it wasn't awful.

"Well, watch your back. Those morality clauses are a bitch." Mischa filed her fingernails then checked her work beneath the light of the lamp.

"I wasn't immoral." Out of her element, maybe, but she hadn't done anything wrong.

"No, but you did bring unwanted attention to the college." Mischa frowned. "I understand, hon. You were letting your guard down and the wrong people saw. Anyone would've done the same thing." She patted Sarah's arm. "I'm sure it'll blow over."

"Yeah." Her stomach soured. What in the hell had she done to her life? There wasn't any guarantee the thing with Liam and Daryl would last and her teaching job brought in the cash to feed her son. If she lost her position at the college, they'd be in a world of hurt.

"I forgot to tell you. I called Daryl." Mischa clasped her hands together. "He was so good, too."

"What?" This was news to her. Daryl had his problems, but cheating wasn't his style — even if all they were having was a fling.

"Hon, you dumped Daryl and the poor man was crushed. That's why they haven't called. Liam moved on to a Tracy? Terry? I can't remember." Mischa's eyes gleamed. "And poor Daryl needed someone to lean on. I was that shoulder. You know how that works."

"I do." She didn't believe Mischa, but now she'd seen her true colors.

"We didn't get the press you two did, but that's because I value my position here at Kenton. You understand." Mischa stood, then opened her bag. "And because I'm going to start seeing him, I can't do your promotions any longer. You understand. I mean, I'm here for fashion and I can't waste time on something that's a conflict of interest. I've got students and Daryl to think about. He wants me to quit, but I don't know. I love my students. I love Kenton."

Sarah pasted a smile onto her lips. Despite Mischa's best efforts, her attempts to lie were transparent. Sarah knew Daryl and Liam enough to see through the stories. Was this how the whole relationship with Mischa had been? One lie after another in order to get what she wanted? Sarah gritted her teeth. She'd been a fool to trust Mischa with anything, least of all her hobby. No wonder she never managed to have any book signings and her online numbers stunk. She wasn't going to get press if her publicity department worked against her.

"I've got to get to work. Thanks for fixing the door. Are you going to be hanging around?" Mischa asked. She sipped her drink. "I've got so much to do."

"I was just on my way out." Sarah swept her gaze across the room. She hadn't left anything behind. As of now, she wasn't coming back to the office, either. Seeing Mischa was just too painful. "Have a good one. Hope you get lots done."

Sarah darted out of the room and down the corridor. Bringing Liam and Daryl to the office wasn't bad. Hell, she appreciated finding out the truth about her business associate. But the mention of the dean bothered her. For all she knew, Mischa could've made that up, too. She didn't remember a morality clause in her contract. She sighed and started toward the staff parking lot. She'd made a mess of her life and now she had to hope the damage wasn't permanent.

When she reached her car, Daryl and Liam weren't anywhere around. She sighed and pressed the unlock button on her fob. Part of her wished they'd show up so she wouldn't be alone. She hated parking lots at dusk. But the rest of her couldn't help but be relieved. She'd had one hell of a day.

Headlights shone against the side of her car and when she turned to argue with the driver of the car, her irritation deflated.

Liam rolled down the window and grinned. "We

would've waited and walked you out, but I wasn't sure which car was yours."

"It's okay." She gripped the handle of her door. "What are your plans for this evening?"

"Ours?" Daryl leaned forward in the passenger seat. "You ask us that after what went down in your office? Um, we'd like to continue. Preferably in your bed and all night long. It is Friday and you shouldn't have class in the morning."

She sagged against the side of her car. "I don't, but my son has a cross-country meet. He runs at nine-thirty and the meet's over in Akron." She massaged her temple. "Look, I usually make a huge pot of spaghetti. Addie — you remember her — and her husband, Hammond, and Alyssa, their daughter, also known as Todd's sometime girlfriend and fulltime best friend, have dinner with us. Matt should be coming over, too. Why don't you join us?"

"Matt?" Liam asked. Daryl frowned but said nothing.

Fucking hell. "My best friend and Addie's brother. Did you forget?"

"Yeah, for a minute I did." Liam pointed straight ahead. "We'll follow you. Tell us where and we'll go."

"I'm going with her." Daryl hopped out of Liam's vehicle and darted over to Sarah's. "I've spent plenty of time with him. It's your turn."

Liam rolled his eyes. "Okay, I'll follow."

"He's childish." She shook her head, then opened her car door. By the time she settled on the seat, Daryl was already beside her. She sighed. "You're childish."

"I'm working on my maturity." He clicked his seatbelt into place. "I thought we could talk while you drove."

"Wonderful." She backed out of the parking spot and started down the main aisle of the lot. Like he promised, Liam stayed behind her. She gripped the steering wheel. "What did you want to talk about?"

"I've missed this campus. Is that nuts?" Daryl placed his hand on her thigh. "It has to be crazy. I forgot just how big and small this place was. When we were here, it seemed like a huge campus. Like the world revolved around Kenton. Then I left and I realize now how quaint it was."

"You're a shark in the ocean. We're guppies in Lake Erie compared to you." She pointed to the strip of cafes and the bookstore. "They put that in five years after we graduated. Then the alumni group decided to rehab downtown. It's brought in so many more students. I can't complain. I'd rather learn on a clean campus."

"I agree." He massaged her leg. "So Addie's still around? Anyone else?"

"No. The group you ran with all went west. A few took a little longer than you, but they're all gone. I'm the only one from my circle of friends who bothered to get a job here. Kenton has its charm, but it's not for everyone." She flexed her fingers. Thinking about the kids she'd gone to school with pricked her conscience. So many friends had faded from her life. No calls or forwarding addresses, just gone.

"Briar Lane is so much bigger than I remember. Was it always a divided road?" Daryl sat up. "Wow."

She turned onto the street leading to her development. "They improved it about ten years ago. They do a mile at a time. Bricks and flowers, then the little maple trees. I guess the city planning department felt that if the town had some homier areas, families would want to stay here. It worked. I bought half of a duplex on Ridge Road." She made the left hand turn onto Ridge. "See?"

"The houses all look the same." Daryl leaned forward. "Like they came out of a retro magazine. How do you know which one is yours?"

"The massive truck." She pulled into her driveway. "That's Todd's baby." She parked in the garage and waited for Liam to stop, then she exited her car. "He loves that godawful truck. Rebuilt the engine with Matt's help." Speaking of the devil, only Matt could be out at twilight trimming the hedges in front of the duplex and wearing just his jeans and sneakers. *Who am I trying to impress?*

"You always have the gardener working at near dark?"

Daryl rounded the trunk of the car. "Or was this for our benefit?"

She shrugged then turned her attention to Matt. "Show off."

"You know it, babe." Matt strode up to her and kissed her full on the mouth. "Company?"

"Kind of." She stared at him. "Why are you doing this?"

"Hi." Liam bounced up to her and Matt. "You must be Addie's brother."

"I am." Matt's eyes flashed and he let go of Sarah. "And you are...? Liam Turner? And Dare Evans? Addie wasn't kidding. Sarah? Did you know about this?"

"Since one rode with me and the other followed, I'd say I knew." She folded her arms. She'd never known Matt to be starstruck over anyone—not even flashy ex-boyfriends. "Have you seen Todd?"

"Ah, yeah. He's in with Alyssa. They had math or something." Matt shook hands with Liam. "It's a pleasure to meet you."

She rolled her eyes again. "I'll start supper." She waved to Daryl. "You're free to stay out here and shoot the shit or you can help me. I don't care." She tended to make the spaghetti on her own while she waited for Addie to get off work. Hammond was no help in the kitchen and she'd never asked. Sarah ducked into the house and left Daryl and Liam with Matt.

She dropped her bag on the bench just inside the door. Todd thundered down the back steps and stopped in the kitchen.

"Hey, Mom." Todd leaned on the counter. "What's with the fakers on the front lawn?"

"They're my friends." She dug the soup pot out of the cupboard. "They wanted to visit and I invited them over for dinner."

"Right." Todd took the pot from her and filled it with water. "Mom, they're lying. That's not Liam Turner or Dare Evans. They wouldn't be caught dead in Kenton. They're

111

taking you for a ride. You're a mom and they could…"

"Have anyone but me?" she finished. "Because being a mom makes me so gross?"

"No." He turned off the water and placed the pot on the stove. "If they are truly who they say they are, then they're doing this for a reason. I mean, why have fast food when you can have gourmet?"

She plucked the box of spaghetti from the pantry. "So you're saying I'm fast food?" She'd wondered why Liam and Daryl would stoop to being with her when they could be with a slew of prettier women, but she wouldn't tell her son that.

"I'm saying…they're actors and you're my mom." He drizzled olive oil into the water then turned on the heat. "Are you sure they're who they say they are? I saw the performance at the college. If that's how they are on set, then they stink."

"They aren't lying." She popped open the end of the box. "I knew Dare back when he was still Daryl. I should. I dated him in college."

"Mom." Todd frowned and the crinkles in his forehead deepened.

When she glanced at her son, she understood why he'd stopped talking. Liam stood in the doorway.

Todd notched his chin in the air. "Be honest with my mom." He stepped between Sarah and Liam. "Tell her this is a con. I know you're bullshitting her. You're not even the real guy."

"I'm real. William Turner Walsh, but my screen name is Liam Turner." He offered his hand to Todd. "Remember? We met on campus." When Todd didn't shake hands, Liam tugged his wallet from his pocket. "See?"

Todd glared at him. "I don't believe you."

"I didn't think you would, but I'm not lying. I'm him. The same guy from *Kaleidoscope* and twenty other movies." Liam shrugged. "Sorry to burst your bubble."

"So you know his filmography. It doesn't mean anything,"

Todd snapped.

"I like your mom and I have no reason to lie. Neither does Daryl." Liam inched over to Sarah.

"Right," Todd snarled. "Next thing I know you're going to tell me you're going to date my mom. Please. She's my mom and she's not dating anyone—famous or not."

"She's a sweet woman."

"Translation—she's good for now. Yeah, I don't think so." Todd insinuated himself between her and Liam again. "Get out of Kenton before you screw her over, because I know that's what you're going to do."

"I don't plan on it." Liam tipped his head. "I applaud your protectiveness, though."

The arguing had to stop. "Enough," she shouted. "Just stop. I'm an adult, but I'm feeling like my life is being decided for me. Jesus. Todd, they're real. I dated Daryl in college. Yes, he was my first..." She couldn't say 'lover'. *Hell.* Her kid didn't need to know that. Besides, once one secret came out, the rest would follow.

"What?" Todd glared at her. "He wasn't your husband, so don't tell me that. No, you married Richard, the asshole."

She wobbled against the countertop. *Well, shit.* She blew out a long breath. If the whole story had to come out, then she preferred to be the one disclosing the details. "Where's Daryl?"

"He stopped to talk to Matt. He'll be in." Liam met her gaze. "We all have things in our past we're not proud of, but that's what makes us who we are."

His calm demeanor and soothing tone helped, but not much. She wanted to crawl into a hole. Everything she'd kept on an even keel for so long had gone ass end up. As much as she wanted to shut the whole situation down, she pressed on. Todd had the right to the truth.

"What? Like mistakes?" Todd snorted. "Richard lied and cheated. He was a joke."

"Hon?" Liam side-stepped Todd. He held his hand out to her. "It's okay."

Nothing was okay. She stared at the floor. Talking about her ex-husband sucked, but she didn't have much choice. "When Daryl and I split, I didn't date for three years. I focused on raising Todd. Then I met Richard. He seemed nice and was handsome. I thought he could be the one." She hadn't trusted her heart. Only her common sense and even that hadn't been reliable.

"Could be?" Liam curled his index finger under her chin and tipped her gaze. "What do you mean?"

"I was a single mom and he seemed to like Todd. I figured I couldn't be too choosy and when he asked me to marry him, I agreed." Her stomach ached. Everything having to do with Richard was a mistake. Christ, she was foolish, but she'd wanted to be loved and at the time she hadn't thought anyone would love her.

"The guy was a jerk. He screamed at Mom," Todd said. His voice cracked. "He wouldn't let her write and he got her fired from her job at the college."

"It was bad," she murmured. "I didn't think I was worthy of anyone except him. I was a mess. I missed Daryl so much, but I couldn't call him. I wasn't even sure where he was or what he was doing." She willed her stomach to settle. "But I got us out of the situation and it's been Todd and me since." Half of her secrets were public.

"I'm not letting some asshole actor and his sidepiece screw my mom over." Todd folded his arms. "She deserves the best and I don't think that's you or Dare Evans."

She gripped the edge of the counter for stability. She couldn't hold the secret any longer. "You're going to have to get used to them, Todd. They're sticking around."

"Why?" Todd asked.

"I like them." The answer was too easy. She switched her gaze between her son and Liam. More than like, she'd never been out of love with Daryl and she'd fallen fast for Liam—not that she'd tell them so just yet.

"Oh my God. Mom… You dated him? So what? You've always said you don't owe them anything. Whatever you did in Vegas was just a date. Don't do this." Todd shook his head. "Don't. We've had enough upheaval."

She should've trusted her son to be level headed and to speak his mind. "It's stickier than that." She grabbed the box of spaghetti. She needed something to do with her hands and to take her mind off the tension in the room. "Jesus." She dumped the pasta into the water then set the timer. Sarah faced her son. "Daryl is your father." She held her breath. There. She'd said it. Liam and Todd now knew the truth.

"No." Todd backed away from her. "You said it was a guy named Dean or Dave." He forked his fingers into his hair. "Mom. Don't do this. Don't lie."

"It's true." She scrubbed her palm across her mouth. She needed to sit down. Her life was so messy and now even more of a disaster. She'd just started over with Daryl and given Liam a shot—kind of—but now? The stability she'd craved for her son and the positive environment were all shot to hell and all because she'd kept a secret for far too long.

"I'm going to Alyssa's." Todd shook his head again. "Fuck this shit. Just...fuck it." He darted out of the room, leaving Sarah alone with Liam.

She sank onto the closest chair. "Well, I told him." She leaned forward and rested her head on her hands. "I told him."

"I know." Liam eased onto the other chair and rubbed her back. "I bet it's a weight off your mind."

"This wasn't how it was supposed to go. I had a plan." She had half of an idea of what to do, but blurting wasn't part of it. She picked up her phone and dialed Addie's number. As the call rang, she turned her attention to Liam. "Give me a minute."

He didn't pull away or seem repulsed by her. *Score one for him.*

Addie answered the phone. "Hi. So, you told him."

"I did." She wiped her face. Tears she hadn't realized

were streaming down her face, wetted her palm. Liam kept his hand on her back and rubbed. His bit of calm helped. She wanted to curl up on his lap and shut her eyes. Maybe the world would melt away and she could have a do-over.

"He's here and I'll keep an eye on him. I'll feed him, too. Give him some time and he'll settle down. I promise," Addie said. "It'll sort itself out."

"I made a mess," she blurted. "How can you be sure? I don't see a good end in this."

"He had to find out eventually, Sarah. Stuff happens. You opened up. That's huge. Now don't kill yourself over this." Addie paused. "Is he with you? Either he?"

"Liam's here. I'm not sure about Daryl. He was outside," Sarah said. Liam cleared his throat and when she looked up, she noticed Daryl in the doorway. "Never mind," she said. "He's here."

"Tell him. It'll hurt worse the longer you keep it inside," Addie said. "I've got Todd. You take care of them."

"Thanks." She appreciated her friend being honest and forthright, but Addie hadn't said anything she wanted to hear. Sarah dried her face. She had no choice but to tell Daryl everything. She sighed and stood, then tucked her phone into her back pocket. *Time to stir the pasta.*

"Do you have sauce?" Liam asked. "I'll heat it up." He took the wooden spoon from her hands, then murmured, "Talk to him. I've got this."

"It's in the pantry. Over there. The small saucepan is in the cupboard on the left." Sarah hesitated by the counter. "Thank you."

"You're crying. Liam? What'd you do?" Daryl stood rooted to the spot. "Does this have anything to do with why Todd ran out of here glaring at me like I stole his birthday? Did he just run away? Should I go after him?" He stuffed his hands into his jeans pockets. "Tell me what's wrong. If Liam and I can't fix it, we'll do whatever we have to in order to get it fixed."

Sarah fortified her courage and laced her fingers together.

If she didn't talk now, she'd never tell Daryl the truth. "He ran away to Alyssa's. Addie will watch him." She paused. *Now or never.* "We need to talk."

Daryl rocked on his heels. Those words were never good. 'We need to talk.' Bad things came out of that sentence. He nodded to the table. "Mind if I sit?" Seeing her in tears jarred him. She wasn't a crier. If something upset her, she kept her emotions bottled up. If she was emotional enough to sob, then there was a problem.

"I'd appreciate it." Sarah's hands shook as she moved the other chair.

"It's best to get it talked out." Liam half-smiled, then returned his attention to the sauce. "Just trust me. Both of you."

"You already know?" He bit back his anger. Of course Liam would be in on the scam. He'd been in the room with her. He focused on Sarah. "Is Todd okay?"

"He's mad as hell, but he'll be okay." She flattened her palms on the table top. "Promise."

He tried to suppress his emotions but he didn't understand what the hell was going on. His heart hammered and he left hot spots on the table from his sweaty palms. "Then what? My ex-girlfriend, who I'd like to be my current girlfriend, is planning on running away with my husband?" He'd jumped to a huge conclusion, but his thoughts blurred and he couldn't think straight.

Her eyes widened and the color drained from her face. Her lips parted. "What?"

The muscle in Liam's jaw tensed. He glanced over his shoulder and narrowed his eyes. "Great job." He growled. "Sarah, where's a colander?"

"Same cupboard with the pan." She rose from her chair. "I'll help."

"You'll talk to Daryl," Liam said, his voice firm. "I've got this."

Daryl covered her hand with his. "What are you going to

do?"

"I don't know. I didn't realize you were married." She hopped up from her seat and backed up against the counter. "Oh my God. I've fucked everything up."

"How? Unless you're really running off with Liam? Are you?" He didn't like the way she paled or shrank away from him. "Sarah?"

"When did you get married?" She hugged her body. "Why didn't you tell me? I would've sent a wedding present or something." She closed her eyes, then bowed her head. "Oh my God. I have feelings for you. This isn't right. I told my son about you. About us."

"I figured that much. He hates my guts." Daryl remained in his seat. "I'm not a bad guy."

Liam snicked the dials on the stove to turn off the burners, then pulled the smaller pan off the heat. He didn't turn around. "You're not exactly Mr. Wonderful when you're angry and you didn't endear yourself to him this afternoon."

Daryl bit back a growl. He couldn't argue. Liam was right and knew him too well. Instead of lashing out at his husband, he snarled at Sarah. "So what did you tell him? Huh? I'm a horrible person? What?"

"You're his father." Her shoulders sank and defeat clouded her voice. "Jesus, Daryl," she whispered. "He's yours." She leaned against the counter then collapsed onto the floor.

Liam sprang into action and knelt beside her. "When she told Todd the truth, he flipped out." He held her against his chest and petted her hair. "It's a lot to take in."

"No shit." Daryl sagged in his seat. *My kid?* He wasn't father material. He was more like an overgrown child in a man's body. Liam was the adult one in the relationship. He pinched the bridge of his nose. He needed facts and time to process them. "Okay. Wait."

"I've now messed up four lives. I didn't know you were married. I'm…" She shook her head. "I thought I was doing the right thing. Giving you your space and dreams while I gave Todd stability. But I fucked it all up. I'm embarrassed." She sobbed against Liam's shoulder.

His heart ached for her. She'd done a few things differently than he might have, but she wasn't a bad person. He left his chair and settled on the floor with her and Liam.

Liam stroked her hair. He held her like a parent. Daryl couldn't help but be jealous. He ran around like a bull in a china shop but Liam was the sweet one.

"No, sweetheart, it's...complicated," Liam said. "Daryl and I are married, yes, but we kept it quiet because of our career. He's supposed to be the hottest man in Hollywood and the hottest bachelor. I'm the sidekick, the guy who tags along and is cute enough to be fun. Some in the business might be fine with us being together and married, but a lot aren't. They see us as a commodity. The studio threatened to fire us if we came out."

"That's why they kept setting me up on dates." Daryl grasped her hand and squeezed. "They wanted to keep up my image. Hanging out only with Liam made people ask questions."

Her mascara smeared down her cheeks and the skin under her eyes had puffed from crying. Daryl didn't care. She still looked sexy as hell.

"What about me?" she asked. "Why are you messing around with me?"

Daryl grasped Liam's hand. "There's always been a missing piece. At first, we were enough for each other and had an awesome time. Then things changed." He'd lost his words. He wasn't sure how to explain the disconnect.

"He'd tell me about you and how he loved you. He's got the photos, like I said. I don't know. I guess I fell under your spell or the perfect vision he had of you and I tumbled head over heels. Then Mischa called. I don't know how she knew to find Daryl or what, but Daryl and I talked. We knew. Then once we were together...you fit our puzzle." Liam grinned. "I call it fate."

"I love Liam completely, but I never stopped loving you." He clasped her hand and Liam's together and kissed their knuckles. "Promise." He still hadn't wrapped his head around having a kid or that kid being nearly an adult, but as long as he had Liam and Sarah he'd figure things out.

Chapter Eight

Daryl scrubbed the back of his hand across his mouth. This wasn't how he'd wanted the evening to go, but he also didn't regret what had happened. They were together and he had more family than he'd ever dreamed of.

"But you don't love me now." She shook her head. "You can't."

"The only thing that would make me hate you would be if you told me I couldn't see Todd now that I know or if you couldn't handle Liam and I having sex." He half-shrugged. "Even then, we'd find a way to make this work."

A tear slipped down her cheek. "Sounds kind of hot to me. You together."

He'd gotten through to her. *Good.* When Liam met his smile and grinned in return, Daryl nodded. "You're the reason I like pegging. That's not horrible." He treasured the time they'd learned and grown together. "You were and are the only woman who understood and wasn't put off."

"Besides, you're sexy as hell," Liam said. "Dumbass here has a movie to prep for in a month, but I'm free for the next six months. We want you and Todd in our life. No settling or lowering our standards. We want to make things right and be there for you. Todd deserves to know his dad."

Once again, Liam had a point. Daryl tried to remember the wording in his contract. The picture would start principal shooting in December and he had a clause written in giving him the second half of the month off as well as every other weekend. If he worked with Liam and Sarah as a team, they could make this turn out well.

She shook her head and sighed. "I don't know how it'll

work." She paused. "But…if Todd approves, we can try."

"Easier said than done," Liam said. "But we're up to the challenge."

"No kidding." Sarah rested her head on Liam's shoulder. "How do you feel about it? I don't know how you don't hate me."

"Well…" Daryl rubbed the top of Liam's hand. "Part of me is still pissed. You kept a pretty big secret from me. Not only that, but you stole time and experiences I could've had with Todd. Birthdays, holidays, first steps, first words. I would've liked to have been here for those."

"I have movies," she whispered. "And lots of pictures."

He took note of what she'd said. Later, he wanted to find said photos and movies. Until then, he had to reassure her. "But as much as I'm angry, I also understand. I never forgot what you told me at the airport. You were letting me go so I could do big things. You saw my potential when even I didn't. I'm not saying I wouldn't change the course of my life, but I'm also not saying I'm holding a grudge."

"You never would've left Kenton." Sarah met his gaze. "Your dreams would've been put on hold. I couldn't do that to you."

"We chose to fool around without rubbers. That was just as much my decision as yours." He leaned in and kissed her. "Why didn't you tell me later on? Or even in the last few years?"

"Remember the Lane scandal?" she snorted. "Yeah, that's why."

How could he forget? He'd nearly lost his career because a woman he'd never slept with claimed he'd fathered her child. He'd forgiven her and offered her money to get her back on her feet, but the image of her clutching the baby and crying had never quite left his mind. The studio had backed him, but also reminded him another scandal would be the end of his working with them. But Sarah wasn't Melody Lane. "This situation is different. I never slept with her, but we did so many times. Other than Liam, you're the only person I've ever loved. I would've loved to have been here when Todd was born, was little and to watch him become the man he is, but I'm here now. *We're* here now."

"You deserved to have your dreams." She half-smiled. "And you did."

"But you should've had them, too." Daryl shook his head. "We both created life."

"I had mine." She scooted off Liam's lap and stood. Sarah seemed to regain some of her confidence. "I did. I wrote in the evenings — still do — and teach at the college during the day. Todd is a good young man. He's already ahead of the curve. He'll graduate a year early and with his associate's degree from Kenton. I'm good and so is he."

"But are you happy?" Daryl asked. He had a pretty decent idea as to how she'd answer.

She shrugged. "Yeah."

Daryl left the floor and crossed to where she stood. "I believe and I think Liam agrees that you deserve more. We want to be the men in your life. The ones who erase your ex-husband from your memories and who build you up while making you the woman you want to be."

"What about Todd?" She balled her hands, but didn't push him away.

"He's almost a man. That doesn't mean we won't try to convince him to come around. We want to be there for him, too. I'm proud of the man he's become. I can't wait to start this chapter of our lives." Daryl brushed a lock of her hair from her face. "Todd will come around. If I can wrap my head around this, then he can, too. If Liam can make room for me and you in his heart then you can do the same for us."

"I can and already have." Liam slipped his hand into Daryl's back pocket and draped his other arm around Sarah's waist. He kissed her temple. "You both make me happy."

"This is so messed up," she said. The corner of her mouth kinked.

"If Todd says no, then we give him time." Daryl enfolded her and Liam into his embrace. "We've got plenty of time." He hugged them for what seemed like an eternity — a perfect, blissful eternity.

"Sarah? Your butt is vibrating." Liam let go of her. "Your phone?"

She stared at him for a moment. "Huh?"

Daryl patted her ass. Sure enough, the phone was vibrating in her pocket. "Yep. It's you, not me."

She disengaged from Daryl and Liam. "Shit." She whipped the device from her jeans pocket and answered. "Todd. Hi." She paused. "Yes, they're here." Another pause. "He's still your dad. It won't change. Okay, sperm donor, but it wasn't like that." She groaned and ran her fingers through her hair. "Will you at least come home for supper? We can discuss this and I'll tell you everything you want to know." She paused, then pulled the phone from her ear. "Well, I'll get some pasta in him tonight. He'll be mad and may not sleep well and there's a good chance he'll hose himself over at the race, but he's coming back to the house."

"Fine." Daryl nodded. *Time to properly meet my son.*

* * * *

An hour later, Daryl sat on the couch in Sarah's living room and laced his fingers together. He stared at Todd, who glared at him. The more he looked at the young man — *my son* — the more he saw himself in Todd. The same dirty blond hair, the smirk, the way he tipped his head to make a point and his defensiveness. Unlike Daryl, Todd had good reasons to keep people at bay. Even though Todd hadn't grown up around him, they acted a lot alike.

"Mom's upstairs. With Liam?" Todd snorted. "Bet that burns your ass."

"Liam ran to the hotel to get phone chargers and a few other things." Ah, he should've known his offspring would have his tendency for snappy comebacks.

"So you're really him? Really Dare Evans?" Todd asked. "And you dated my mom? But back then you were Daryl and not famous."

"I did." He liked the way Todd didn't trust him and the way he seemed to be continually considering the situation. *Smart kid and on point, too. She's done a good job raising him.* "I've always been Daryl. Dare was the name the studio said I needed to sound more...dangerous." He thought the stage name a tad overblown and not at all representative of his true self, but in Hollywood, no one cared about anyone's true self.

"You love her?" Todd narrowed his eyes. "For real?" He gripped the arm of the overstuffed chair.

"I do." He didn't have to think about his answer. He loved her down to his soul and in ways he couldn't understand.

"Why'd you wait?"

Was Todd testing him? He'd challenge right back. "To?"

"Return to Kenton." Todd clipped his words. "You know, to her?"

He sighed. He had to face a whole lot of truth he'd buried for a long time. If he wanted to get to know his son, then he owed Todd the unabridged story. "I was scared. We left on good terms—kind of. She told me to do good things and be famous. Said I was meant for more than Kenton could provide and that she'd be my biggest fan. She practically pushed me onto the plane. I wanted to argue, but I did what she wanted. Once I made it and honed my skills, I thought about finding her, but I freaked. What if she didn't like me? What if the whole *I wish you well* stuff was just bullshit? What if she'd moved on? I didn't want to be rejected." He wouldn't have been able to handle it if she pushed him away again. Back then, he'd seen everything like a dream. He'd grown in the years since he'd left Kenton and saw life through a high-definition focus.

"You could've asked. Aunt Addie would've told you. I heard you talked to her over the years." Todd's face remained expressionless save for the smirk.

"True and I did, but I made her promise to keep my secret." He wished he could take back that decision. If he'd known the truth about Richard and whatever Sarah had been through, he'd have come back to Kenton in a heartbeat.

"Are you going to ditch her now?" Todd asked. He folded his hands on his lap.

"I don't plan to." If all went according to his wishes, they'd be a happy family—all four of them.

"You married Liam Turner. If you're so in love with him that you married him, why are you moving in on Mom?"

Good question. Thankfully he had a solid answer. "Because I love them both."

Todd shook his head once and snorted. "Um, so you're famous and decided you need a husband and a wife? That's messed up."

He shrugged. Life wasn't exactly clean and pressed at all times. "Yes and no. It's more complicated than it sounds, but with the three of us, the relationship just works." Besides, he didn't want to go into the intricacies of his love life with his son. But he'd try to explain a bit. "It's like when you realize you're straight. You know you're attracted to girls. Or if you're gay. Same thing—but with guys. For me, I've been attracted to both but not at the same time. Your mom and Liam are like the other sides of my equilateral triangle. Without them, I'm not me."

"You're seriously messed up."

"Nah." Maybe a little, but his preference for Sarah and Liam had nothing to do with it.

"And you're my dad? Jesus. Of all the people my mom could've...she had to pick you. Lame." Todd perched on the edge of the chair. "*You're* the lame one, not her."

"Maybe I am lame. I've been called worse, but you shouldn't swear. I'm not saying it to be a dad. I've told Liam so many times I'm not the best father material." He probably should've kept that tidbit to himself. At least he had some practical advice to pass down. "I'm saying it because I've been in your shoes. It doesn't make you sound any older or cooler."

"I saw *Turbo I* and *II*. You swore like a sailor."

"For the character." Not that the explanation made much of a difference.

"Right, and the swagger in all of those interviews was just…a show? Come on. Alyssa likes to watch the red carpet shows. We've seen you unfiltered."

He'd made a mess of everything—which was probably why he and Sarah fit together so well. Liam was the anchor and the cool head. Now it was Daryl's turn to be the level one. "I've made mistakes. Lots of them. I'm not the best person to go unfiltered, as you put it, in public. I speak my mind and don't always think before I talk. That said, I've learned from those mistakes. I was you. I wanted to impress people and make them think I was cool. If they saw me as dangerous or gritty, then I'd be offered gritty roles. It only worked to an extent. When I acted mature and showed my acting chops without trying too hard to be someone I'm not, the roles poured in. I used my words and chose them wisely. 'Fuck' doesn't make you come across any better. It could be seen as insulting."

Todd rolled his eyes. "Sure."

Well, he'd tried and he'd keep at it. One day he'd get through to Todd. Until then, he'd go with his best cards and use sarcasm. "Or I'm a guy trying to sound intelligent so my kid likes me."

"I don't like you. You're full of yourself, arrogant and I don't trust that you'll stick around." Todd rubbed his hand over the patch of fuzz on his chin. "But you seem to make Mom happy."

Todd had him on the cocky and arrogant parts. He had every right not to trust Daryl, too. By Hollywood standards, Daryl wasn't much of a player, but to anyone outside of the business, he looked like a dog. But he'd made a breakthrough with Todd. "You're not going to argue with me? Not going to throw a punch or give me hell?"

"I have no reason—not really. Mom was the one who

chose to walk away. She didn't tell you about me. You can't change what you don't know about." Todd rested his elbows on his knees. "Besides, if my mom likes you, then there's not much I can say. She'll do what she wants just like with Richard. At least this time I'm old enough to leave if I want. Back then, I was stuck with the bastard."

He really needed to find out what Richard had done. "I don't know. She cares very much how you feel. If you're not on board, she won't do this. Sounds like Richard was a mistake she learned from."

"Yeah, but you're my dad. I can't exactly tell you to go to hell. You have the right to see me." He rolled his eyes for the third time, then groaned. "And maybe I want to get to know you."

"Of course the idea of possibly spending a summer or two working on a film set doesn't interest you at all?" He wouldn't make things easy for Todd if the kid wanted to go into the film industry, but he wasn't above giving a few pointers.

"Maybe." Todd shrugged. "I'll be straight with you. Mom got hurt bad with Richard. I don't want to see her hurt again. She never mentioned your name, but I know she's always cared about you. If you fuck her over, it'll devastate her."

"You're colorful and wise for your years." Much more than he had been at that age.

"I protect her. If you can't, too, then Dad or not, don't bother. I'm serious. If you and Liam can't be a hundred percent all in, then go."

The edge to Todd's words permeated Daryl's brain. *Message received and understood.* "I waited too long to see her again. You've got my word."

"Fine." Todd sagged on the armchair and groaned.

The conversation might be over for Todd, but not for him. He had to ask a few more questions. "Todd?"

"Yeah?"

Daryl rested his ankle on his knee and stared at his son.

He had to word his question just right. "What did Richard do? I understand he was a jerk, but what happened? I need to know what I'm up against, but I want to hear it in your words." Even if he managed to get Sarah to talk about her ex-husband, he couldn't be sure she'd tell him everything.

Todd raked his fingers through his hair, then sat up and leaned forward. He glanced over at the doorway to the kitchen, then dropped his voice to a murmur. "She hates to talk about him. I do, too. I hated him. Still do." He tensed and cracked his knuckles. "Look, he beat her up. He called her names — everything bad. One time she didn't do what he wanted and she argued with him so he rearranged her face. She used a lot of makeup and stayed home until the bruises faded. He wouldn't let her go to the hospital to make sure nothing was broken."

"Wow." The wind rushed from Daryl's lungs. Guilt washed over him. He should've been there. Should've protected her from Richard and been there for his son.

Todd hesitated. "The guy was jealous of everyone and anything. He hated me because I took her time and focus away from him." Todd shook his head. "He had her quit at the school. Locked her up in the house pretty much all the time. She went out for stuff for me for school because he didn't have permission or he would've kept her from that, too. When I was almost eight years old, she told me we were going away. That night she took me to a shelter and started divorce proceedings. He found her and beat her up again, but the women there called the cops. With the amount of witnesses, not only did she get the divorce, but he landed in jail for assault and battery."

"My God." Daryl balled his hand and pounded his thigh. "I had no idea."

"Matt, Addie, Ham and Alyssa live in the other half of our house because Mom was afraid to live alone. Uncle Matt put in the alarm system and Uncle Ham bought a dog. Lyss and I ride to school together so we've got someone to watch our back." Todd slapped the arms of the chair. "That's why

I'm not thrilled she went to Vegas or that you're here. I'm worried this will end badly."

"If I can help it, your mom will have the life she deserves." Daryl still couldn't believe what he'd been told.

"Cool, I guess." Todd stood. "You're okay to talk to and all, but I have to hit the sack. We're supposed to be at the metro park by seven for the meet. You're welcome to come. I run at ten. I should've done my homework, too. I'll do it tomorrow."

"For your college class?" Daryl asked. He hopped to his feet. Should he hug Todd? Shake hands? Let him go? He wasn't sure.

"Yeah. You remembered me talking about that?" Todd narrowed his eyes again. "If I want to graduate early, I could double up on some classes. Next semester will be easier, but right now, I'm up to my eyeballs in work for the history course."

"I'm proud of you. You've got a goal and you're achieving it. Great job."

Todd flicked his hand. "Thanks...I think." He wandered out of the room, leaving Daryl in silence.

Daryl collapsed onto the couch again. Parenting was harder than he'd thought. At least he'd made progress with Todd—more than he'd expected. He debated what to do next. Find Sarah? Wait for Liam? He noticed the sound of voices in the kitchen. After what he'd learned about Richard, he followed his instinct to protect her.

Liam stood in the kitchen and nodded to someone Daryl couldn't see.

"We shouldn't just walk into her house." Daryl clicked the lock on the door. "Knock or something."

"I did. Todd let me in." Liam tilted his head to the side. "How'd it go with Todd?"

"Better than I predicted."

"Good." Liam wrapped his arms around Daryl and kissed him. "Have I ever told you you're sexy when you're flustered? Your cheeks turn red and your eyes flash. It's hot as hell."

"You've mentioned it a few times, but not lately." Desire rose within him. *Forget Sarah's past and making progress with Todd.* The only thing on Daryl's mind was being with Liam and Sarah. He rubbed his burgeoning erection against the bulge in Liam's pants. If he was at home, he and Liam would be naked by now.

"Wow…"

Liam's face lit up and he grinned. Daryl turned his attention to the top of the stairs. Sarah stood with her hands on her hips. She'd covered her hair in a towel and wore a thick robe.

"Hiya, babe." Daryl half-waved. "We were showing off for you."

"Um, I like it, but why don't you come upstairs?" She nodded once. "That way you don't gross out your son."

The more she said those words, *your son*, the more he liked hearing them. He grasped Liam's hand and headed for the second floor.

"Todd's in his room on that end of the house. Mine's over here." She eased the towel off her head and dried her hair. "The bathroom's in the middle. It's an oddly laid out house."

"I think our realtor would call it character." Liam shrugged. "I brought our chargers, wallets and the rest of our valuables. The clothes I left at the hotel. We can get those in the morning or whenever."

"True. Todd said he locked the doors." She clicked the tab on the door handle. "I have no idea what he told you or what you've learned, but I'm glad you're not weirded out. I hoped you'd want to stay."

"Of course we want to stick around. The layout of your house doesn't mean anything." Liam dropped the duffle bag onto the armchair. "I didn't step into this situation lightly. You've got me and Daryl for the duration."

"Yes." Daryl stood in her bedroom. He still couldn't believe he was there. Sarah was back in his life and she'd allowed him into her private space. *Remarkable. Dreams can come true.*

Liam grinned at Daryl, then moved to Sarah's left. "Want you." He kissed her neck and nudged open her robe. Sarah didn't stop him. Instead, she tilted her head and parted her lips. She closed her eyes. Liam groaned as she opened her palm over the bulge in his jeans.

Daryl blew out a low whistle. Seeing Liam with Sarah pleased him. The jealousy that could've been there wasn't. His partners were both needy and excited and that spurred him on. He inched over to her right side and tipped her chin to kiss her. Sarah's eyes lit with fire and she smiled before she met him for the kiss. Liam continued to massage her breast through the cloth of her robe.

Sarah moaned into the kiss. She leaned against Daryl and placed his hand on her other boob. "Whoa," she murmured. She swiped her tongue across Daryl's bottom lip then turned her attention to kissing Liam.

Daryl drank in the view of her feasting on Liam's mouth. He bit back a groan. She needed to be naked. Now. He unknotted the tie and nudged her robe down her shoulder. He kissed along her bare skin and continued to remove the garment until it landed on the floor.

"Jesus." Liam palmed her bare breast. "Beautiful."

"Liam." She arched into him.

Daryl kissed along her neck and flattened his tongue across her pulse. He eased around behind her and tilted her head onto his shoulder. The change in position gave him better access to her mouth. He moaned as he kissed her. He'd never tasted anything so sweet and decadent.

"Damn," Liam said. "Hot."

He had his husband down to one-word sentences. Nice. Daryl walked Sarah backward to the bed and wrenched his mouth free. "Open yourself up to us, sweetheart."

She wobbled, but Sarah managed to sprawl out on the bed. She opened her legs and the blush stretched from her hairline to her breasts. Her nipples beaded. A wild fire lit in her eyes and she panted.

"Gorgeous." Liam dropped to his knees between her legs and trailed his fingers along her inner thigh. "I can't wait to nibble."

Daryl wanted a taste, but he'd wait. Right now he wanted to suck her breasts. He licked and nipped her skin, leaving small red spots in his wake.

Sarah whimpered and moaned. "Liam." His name came out soft but needy. She arched her back. "It's been so long."

Daryl would have to change her perception. Either she hadn't loved what they'd done in Vegas or she meant the craving and desire she needed. He'd bet she meant feeling desired. She deserved to be loved every night until she collapsed and to be pleasured...worshipped. He feasted on her nipples and loved the sounds she made as he flicked his tongue across the tight bundles of nerves. Each moan and sharp intake of breath spurred him on. Electricity zinged through his veins. *Dear God.* He slid his hand over his dick. His balls tingled and he wanted her mouth wrapped around his shaft.

She slid her fingers into Daryl's hair. Each time she tensed, she pulled and added to his pleasure. He'd take whatever she had to throw at him and not complain. He had years to make up for and he vowed he'd give her the love she needed. He continued to rub his cock through the fabric of his jeans. *Shit.* One or two pulls and he'd come apart. His throat ached as he groaned again.

Sarah yanked on his hair and met his gaze. "I want your dick." A lazy smile curled on her lips and she looked up at him from under heavy-lidded eyes. "Now."

He couldn't tell her no. Daryl scrambled to his feet. He fumbled with the sleeves of his shirt. The longer he wrestled with the garment, the more tangled he became. *Slow down. Don't get ahead of yourself.* Once he listened to his own advice, he managed to free himself from the shirt. He tossed the garment onto the floor and unzipped. Eagerness filled his veins. He focused on her and shoved his pants and boxer briefs to his ankles. Sarah palmed her chest and tweaked her nipples. She shivered and licked her lips and drew her knees up around Liam's head.

"Um…" Sarah closed her eyes. She ground against Liam's face. "More."

"I will." Liam nipped her inner thigh and speared two fingers into her pussy. She writhed and moaned. Liam licked her cunt and hummed. "I love it."

Daryl agreed. "So fucking sexy." He stroked himself. Being with Sarah was just as hot as being with Liam. He liked how Liam pleased her. But now Daryl needed more. He patted Sarah's thigh. "Roll over."

Sarah opened her eyes. Her cheeks were infused with a blush. Liam paused, then withdrew his fingers. When Daryl nodded, Liam dipped his head once. Liam helped her roll onto her belly. He folded her legs up and spread her ass and pussy for his use.

Daryl growled. Damn, he loved attentive partners. He climbed onto the bed. He had Sarah where he wanted her and Liam between her legs pleasing her. *Life is so good.*

"Yes." Sarah flattened her hands on the mattress and opened her mouth.

Daryl slid his dick between her lips and bit back a groan. Heaven. His eyes rolled back and he threaded his fingers into her hair. Although she set the pace, he felt compelled to guide her. He moved his hips, pushing his cock in and out of her sweet mouth. She curled her tongue around his shaft and the move added to his joy.

"Fuck," Daryl bit out. "Just…fuck." He wanted to sound more intelligent and sweet, but he couldn't form the words.

"Damn." Liam glanced up at Daryl, then returned to Sarah's pussy. He and Daryl worked in delicious rhythm.

Daryl pushed his dick in deep then withdrew again. Warmth spread through his body and the beginnings of the orgasm hit. He dragged air into his lungs. He couldn't think straight. Instead, he simply rode the wave of excitement. Sarah managed to caress his balls, adding another sensation to the mix. Combined with the way she bobbed her head, she turned his senses inside out. He whimpered. He had two of the most attentive lovers in Sarah and Liam. He couldn't believe he'd stayed away from her for so long and waited what seemed like a lifetime to introduce her to Liam.

His balls tingled and the lush headiness spread through his limbs. He shuddered and increased the speed of his thrusts. *Shit.* She had him right there.

"Ready?" Liam asked. He dug his fingers into her ass cheeks.

Daryl didn't know if Liam meant him or her. He didn't care. He needed to come.

Sarah tensed and hummed, then gasped. She clawed at the bedding. Her strangled cries filtered up to Daryl. He slowed his rhythm enough to let her breathe. She withdrew and curled forward.

"Yes, sweetheart. Come for us." Daryl petted her hair and stroked himself with his free hand. "I'm right there, too."

She drew her arms and legs in tight. More whimpers erupted from her and she shivered.

Daryl yanked on his dick as the climax hit. "Oh fuck." His restraint blew all to hell as he gave in to the orgasm. "Sarah." He shot cum across her back. Shit. *That* wasn't what he'd meant to do. Then again, he wasn't sure where he'd planned to spill his seed.

Sarah didn't jerk or move. She allowed him to ride out the aftershocks. He stroked until the trembling subsided.

"Messy." Liam licked his lips, then dragged his tongue along her spine. He cleaned the cum from her skin and massaged her ass cheek.

She giggled. "That tickles."

"It's hot as fuck," Daryl blurted. "I love it."

"Tastes good, too." Liam flattened his tongue on her shoulder blade and finished lapping up the jizz. "It's hot watching you come and feeling you do it right along with him." He kissed her rump. "I want a turn."

Daryl flopped onto the bed. He wanted to fuck Liam

hard—but after a break. He gathered Sarah to his chest and spooned against her. She laced her fingers with his. "What do you think?" she asked. "Should we?"

"We give him what he deserves," Daryl said. "Strip, babe. We want to see our prize and the man who worked hard to get us off."

Liam wiggled his eyebrows, then whipped his shirt over his head. He stood and flexed his upper body. His muscles flexed and his abs rippled. The man was a specimen and so handsome.

"You've been working out more." Daryl winked. "Keep going. I like it." He loved what he saw and needed more. He draped his arm across Sarah's hip. He couldn't imagine anything better. He had a good life, enough money, two wonderful people in his arms and bed as well as a son. Yeah, he had the best existence a man could ask for and it'd only get better.

Chapter Nine

Liam removed his pants and shivered in the chilly air. The October day had been warm and beautiful, but the temps dropped after dark and chilled him to the core. Still, losing his clothes and baring his body to his partners freed him. He hoped he matched their expectations. His nerves frayed. He craved Daryl and Sarah so much and wanted the pleasure to last for years.

Sarah grinned and curled her finger. "Come here."

He inched forward. Sarah wrapped her hand around his shaft then flicked her tongue across the knobby head of his dick. Sizzles shot through his body. He rested his hands on his hips. His thoughts muddled and he didn't move. If Sarah wanted to suck him off then he'd allow her to do it to her heart's content.

She raked her teeth along the underside and continued to stroke him, drawing a groan from deep in his throat. Sarah managed to bend him to her will. He'd do anything for her as long as she kept licking him. Her mouth was perfection — so hot, wet and addictive.

Daryl crawled around her. While she flicked her tongue over the blunt head of Liam's erection, Daryl nibbled on the shaft. He switched to Liam's balls and caressed the soft patch of skin behind Liam's sac.

"Jesus." Liam groaned. The power in his veins nearly knocked him over the edge. He had two people pleasuring him. He tipped his head back and drew a long breath into his lungs. He shivered. He'd never been so turned on in his life.

Daryl scraped his nails down Liam's thigh. "Happy?"

He nodded. More than just happy, he felt complete. He seemed to glow or maybe it was just the warmth inside of him. He focused on Daryl. "More." He sounded like a caveman, but he couldn't vocalize anything else.

"How about my dick in your ass?" Daryl's eyes gleamed. He stroked himself until he'd regained his erection.

Liam snorted. The damn bastard was hard already. "Yeah, I want it," Liam managed. His knees buckled. Shit, he needed release.

Daryl left the bed and eased up behind Liam. He kissed his husband's shoulder and wrapped his arms around him. "Love you."

Liam angled to kiss Daryl on the lips. "Love you, too." He ground his ass into Daryl's erection. Fucking hell, he wanted that cock in his ass.

"Don't forget about me." Sarah rolled onto her back and spread her legs. She scooted down to where Liam stood and reached for him. "While he fucks you, I want you to fuck me."

"Uh-huh." He focused on her and pleasing her, but damn, holding his attention was hard with Daryl behind him. He wanted Sarah and Daryl so much.

Daryl moved away from Liam, leaving him chilled once more. Liam peeked over his shoulder. Daryl offered up a foil packet.

"You'll want this," Daryl said. He winked again.

"I do." He turned his attention to Sarah. She took the condom from his hands and tore the packet. Before he could stop her, she sheathed him. She reclined on the bed and lined his erection up with her cunt.

Knocked out of his lust-induced stupor, Liam grasped her hips. He situated himself in her pussy. A shiver ran through him. Being inside her was so good. He moved his torso, plunging deep into her then pulling most of the way out. He loved the delicious pressure and despite the condom, he felt every ripple and nuance of her.

"Love it." Daryl kissed the side of Liam's neck. "Want

you."

"Take me." He wouldn't argue. He relaxed as much as possible and grunted as Daryl dribbled cold lube over his hole. A breath rushed out of him when Daryl pushed two fingers into his ass. Liam widened his stance. "Fuck me." He couldn't wait much longer.

"I will." Daryl bit Liam's shoulder. "Dreamed of this. Us. Together." He removed his digits from Liam's rump then lined his cock up with his hole. Inch by inch, he filled Liam.

Liam grunted. The added pressure frayed his restraint. *Oh shit.* So full and so perfect. He leaned forward and kissed Sarah. He moved his hips. When he buried himself balls deep in Sarah, Daryl plowed into him. Within seconds, Daryl and Liam managed to build a smooth rhythm. Sarah draped her arms around Liam's neck and her breath fanned over his skin.

Liam gritted his teeth. He didn't need much to come apart. Being sandwiched between Sarah and Daryl blurred his thoughts. He couldn't breathe and pistoned his hips. The faster he moved, the more Daryl increased his thrusts.

Sarah clutched Liam's shoulders. Her knees trembled and she arched her back. "Fuck," she whispered. "Oh…"

Yeah. He wasn't sure what to say either. Euphoria filled his brain and his pushes turned frantic. The orgasm was just within reach. He plunged into her and his resistance snapped. Why fight the climax he wanted so much? He curled forward and moaned as he came. He filled the condom and shuddered.

"Yes." Sarah dug her nails into his. Her pussy clenched. "Jesus, yes. I needed this." She trembled beneath him.

Daryl clawed at Liam's waist. "Don't forget me." The sound of skin slapping skin echoed in the room as he stretched Liam's ass.

Liam remained within Sarah as Daryl pounded into him. He fixed his gaze on hers. He opened his mouth but no sound came out.

"Fucking balls and hell." Daryl thrust fully within Liam

and his cock throbbed as he came. "Yes," Daryl bit out. "Mine."

He belonged to Daryl, heart and soul. He collapsed on Sarah and cradled her to his body. He couldn't imagine being anywhere else.

She giggled and held him. "I haven't felt this good in forever."

"Yeah." He hadn't felt this complete in a long time.

"Damn. You two." Daryl swatted Liam's ass and eased out of him. He then stretched out beside Sarah on the bed. "Gets better every time."

"It does." She squeezed Liam's shoulders.

Liam dragged a breath into his lungs and paused. He needed a moment to collect himself. He also needed to ditch the condom. Although he wanted to stay buried in Sarah, he pulled out and stood. His knees wobbled as he removed the rubber and tossed it into the waste bin. He should shower, but needed a nap first. He crawled into bed on Sarah's left side and snuggled her.

"You'll wear us out," Daryl said. "In a good way. You're our missing piece."

Liam nodded. She'd been the spark their relationship required to sustain it. "Think you'd give us a try?" he asked. "Like long-term?" He had no idea what Sarah and Daryl had discussed or what had gone down with Todd. Maybe he'd jumped the gun, but he wanted to know if there was the possibility he'd have the two most important people stick around in his life.

Sarah chuckled and toyed with Liam's nipple. "I'm pretty sure I'm past the point of getting rid of you — either of you." She turned her attention to Daryl. "I'm sorry I didn't tell you about Todd."

"I know now and that's what matters." Daryl tightened his grasp on Liam and Sarah, pulling them in close. "You're our missing piece and we're together. We can't do this without you."

Sarah leaned in and kissed Liam, then Daryl. "I agree."

Liam settled against Daryl's shoulder. While Daryl and Sarah eased off to sleep, he couldn't shut down his brain. He splayed his hand on Daryl's belly. Things were going well—save for the whole child thing. Not that he cared about Sarah and Daryl having a kid. Hell, he liked knowing they'd have someone to carry on Daryl's name. If he and Daryl had to pick someone to give them a child, Sarah was the only choice.

But he didn't trust the good times or the way things were happening so easily. Daryl ready to tell everyone they were married. Sarah accepting them. Todd not pushing them totally away. Something had to hit the fan. It always did.

He groaned. He shouldn't be thinking about the negative, but he'd learned to keep his guard up. After his marriage to Angeline had crumbled, he'd had a hard time letting anyone into his life. Sure, Daryl had been there, but when he'd said he wanted to take things to the next level, Liam had freaked out. What if Daryl left? Now Sarah was part of the equation. What if things between the three of them disintegrated?

His anxieties got the best of him. He couldn't breathe and needed to move. Liam eased out of bed and grabbed his jeans from the floor. He donned the pants then crept out of the bedroom. *Jesus. What am I going to do?* Just being all-in on a relationship wasn't enough. He headed downstairs and stood in the darkness of the living room, staring out at the street.

Back home, he'd have to keep the curtains closed and stayed away from the windows. He never knew when the paparazzi would show up and expect to photograph Daryl. They didn't bother him all that much. He only factored in when he went out with Daryl. Sad, really. He'd made just as many movies as Daryl but hadn't received the same recognition. Daryl was the action star, the handsome rogue who could say anything at any time and charm the pants off pretty much anyone.

Maybe it was his dip in confidence or his worries that

something bad would happen, but he couldn't embrace the goodness in his situation.

He settled on the couch and stared at the ceiling until he couldn't keep his eyes open any longer. Hopefully, sleep would come soon. If for no other reason than he'd forget his troubles.

"What are you doing down here?"

Liam jerked awake and palmed the air. *Down here? Huh?* He blinked as he regained his bearings. Sarah sat on the edge of the cushion and brushed his hair from his face.

"Hi." She smiled. "Why'd you sleep in my living room? Did we crowd you out of bed?"

She'd pulled her hair back into a ponytail and scrubbed her cheeks clean of the makeup. He'd never seen a more beautiful woman in his life. Liam managed to sit up and scratched his belly—more for something to do with his hands than a true itch. "I couldn't sleep. Too much on my mind."

"You, too?" She twined her fingers with his. "This is a huge change for all of us. Two weeks ago, I had no idea what Daryl was doing other than making movies and being famous. I lusted after you with each film but never guessed you'd be in my home. It's like a dream come true."

"It is." He yawned, then tugged her onto his lap.

"But?" She met his gaze and grinned. "What are you worried about?"

He had to be straight with her. "Lots of things, but mostly that something will come along to implode what we're starting." He stared into her eyes. *A man could get lost in those eyes.* "Being with us isn't easy. When we're not gone for long stretches of time working on various film projects, we're asked to walk the red carpet and show up at parties. We've had to stick together because we're the only one the other can trust. My ex-wife cheated on me. His had the marriage annulled after three weeks. Other girlfriends— real and set up—can't handle the stress of being with a star. We're like everyone else, but we have crazy schedules. I'm scared you're going to see it's not perfect and want out."

She draped her arms around his neck and shrugged. "I understand. You'd think I wouldn't, but I do. After Richard and even before, I didn't think I was good enough. I had a kid. I was…one guy told me I was used goods and he couldn't be with someone like me. I let it affect my self-worth. Richard was hell. That's why I didn't date. Ask my son. He thought I'd become a hermit, save for working at the college. Trust isn't easy, but it is earned. If this is meant to work, then it will. I know my gut. I might have been wrong in my choices, but when I follow my instincts, I'm usually dead-on."

He cupped her jaw and drew her close. "What does your gut tell you about us? About me?" Dear God, he hadn't been this nervous in a long time. She'd said she liked them, but things could change in the cold light of day.

She sighed and brushed her nose along his. "It tells me that Daryl will be a handful. His heart is in the right place, but life likes to throw him curveballs. It's up to you and me to stick by him. As for you, it tells me you're the rock I've been looking for. When you love, it's unconditional and Daryl and I are the luckiest people in the world."

He kissed her hard on the lips and cradled her to his body. He'd never get enough of her. Daryl had been right all along. She was their perfect third.

"Mom. Seriously?" Todd groaned. "Gross. I'm leaving to catch the bus. See you at Cloverleaf."

"Be careful, don't speed and I'll see you in an hour or so." She pulled away from Liam and laughed as the door clunked shut in the kitchen. "Welcome to having a teenager in the house. He hears most of what I say and does three quarters of what I ask. The rest is angst and hormones in a six-foot tall body." She winked then scooted off Liam's lap. "Would you like to come to the cross-country meet with me? Todd can use all of the cheering section he can get." She offered her hand. "Plus it's nice to have someone to talk to."

"I'd be honored." He left the couch and walked with her into the kitchen. "I've never gone to such a thing, so pointers are welcome."

"Dress warm. It's chilly out today. Have fun." She paused at the bottom of the stairs. "Oh and be prepared to run from point A to point B, C and D. It's not a stationary sport for parents."

"Nice." He palmed her ass. "I'll have to stop at the hotel. My clothes are there."

"We can make a pit stop. We have to wake up Daryl anyhow. He could sleep through a bombing."

"He could." He stopped her about three steps up. "Don't try to kiss him awake. If we're in any kind of hurry, it won't help. He'll want to fuck and we'll be all kinds of late."

"He's still like that?" She laughed and threw her arms around his neck. "I'll keep it in mind."

"I'm the crazy morning person. Give me coffee and I'm set." He scooped her into his arms and carried her the rest of the way up the stairs. Maybe he could embrace the new experiences in his life without thinking about the what-ifs. As he set her on her feet in the bedroom, ideas popped into his head. A place of their own. Ground to stretch out on and the family situation he'd always dreamed of having. With Sarah, Todd and Daryl, he could have what he wanted. *I wonder where I can find a local realtor…*

* * * *

Sarah pulled into the parking lot of Cloverleaf High School. Thank goodness Daryl hadn't taken a full hour to get dressed and ready. He'd always been a slow poke in the bathroom, but Liam kept him on his toes.

"We need to get a truck," Daryl said. "Something with a bench seat so when we go out as a threesome, we can sit together. I hate being in the back. It's lonely."

Liam snorted. "You didn't mind being in my rear last night."

"That's different."

Sarah searched the lot. "I swear this one is full. We'll have to go to the one back by the football field." She hated having to hike up to the race, only to hike around the course, but she'd make it work.

"There's one." Liam pointed to a spot along the sidewalk. "I think someone just vacated it."

"Perfect." She pulled in, parked and turned off the car, but didn't leave the vehicle. "Okay, so ground rules."

"I knew this was coming," Daryl said. He squeezed her shoulder. "We'll behave."

"You'll have to." She turned in her seat to stare at Daryl and Liam. "First, don't act like celebrities. Just be yourselves. Half of these people don't care if you're here. Second, please cheer for Todd. He's not the fastest, but it helps his confidence when he knows someone is rooting for him. Third, Addie will be here. I'm guessing she'll give you hell, Daryl. She'll probably want to jump you, Liam, because she's got a huge crush on you. Fourth, there are other parents here who probably won't understand you both being with me. Just be cool." She hoped she'd touched on the important points. "I'm not trying to treat you like children, but I've got enough problems."

"Noted and you've got my word." Liam winked.

"Show off." Daryl squeezed her shoulder again. "I'll behave. I'm excited to see my kid. This is a whole new world for me."

"Him, too." She left the car. "Let's go." Sarah walked across the lot to the school building.

"Looks like we can go in this way." Daryl pointed to the double doors. "The sign says so."

Sarah followed Liam and Daryl inside. Without missing a beat, Daryl paid the entrance fee. It almost seemed like he'd done this before. She shook her head. Did he have a kid back in Hollywood? Part of her wondered. Instead of asking, she headed through the lobby to the rear of the building. The green space behind the structure was littered with tents for each of the cross-country teams. She spotted the Kenton one but didn't see Todd.

Addie, Hammond and Matt stood with Alyssa. Ham had his hands in his pockets and Matt was twiddling with his phone. Addie noticed her first and grinned, then frowned. "Hey," Addie said. "Todd's out warming up."

Alyssa hugged Sarah, then shucked her jacket. "I need to stretch and warm up, then I'm heading to the line for our race. See ya!" She waved and jogged off.

Hammond elbowed Matt then nodded. Both men left her alone with Addie, Liam and Daryl.

Addie narrowed her eyes. "So. You're him?" The corner of her mouth kinked, then she threw her arms around Liam. "You have no idea. I'm a huge fan…wow. I wish the tats were real, but it's okay."

"I'm pleased to meet you." Liam grinned at Sarah, then Addie. "I get compliments on the art, but I'm not wild about needles, so I'm not going to get any ink anytime soon."

Sarah laughed. At least he'd made Addie's day.

"Interesting," Addie said. "You're honest. I like it." Her grin faded. "You, on the other hand…" She wrapped her hands around Daryl's biceps. "A word?"

"Of course." Daryl glanced back at Sarah, then walked away with Addie.

"She seems nice," Liam said. "Protective, but nice."

Sarah snorted. Addie had plenty of reason to be cautious, but she had the feeling her friend was reading Daryl the riot act. "She's seen a lot." She pointed to the hill. "At this course, I like to watch from up here, then go to the finish line. We'll see the runners three times this way."

"Works for me." He held her hand and stayed beside her.

She marveled at his sweetness. Some men would've been pushy and played the celebrity card, but not him. Sarah bit back a smile. She'd forgotten the pleasantness of being at the race with someone who wasn't a friend. She found a spot on the hill and stopped. "We're set for now. Once we hear the gun go off, that's the time to pay attention."

"Sure." He stood beside her. "I was friends with Daryl long before I met my ex-wife. She was so jealous of him and how much time he and I spent together. Back then, we were hitting the clubs at the same time and we made *Nautilus* together. The whole getting together romantically wasn't on the radar. She'd say I was up Daryl's ass and she hated him. According to her, we were having an affair. It's funny. She ended up being the one to stray from the marriage. Once the ink was dry, then Daryl and I explored our feelings for each other. He was the only person to stick with me and not accuse me of being a dick. I cherished those early years. Still cherish him, but things have evolved for us."

She nodded. She'd seen some of the drama play out on the tabloid shows. Back then, she'd thought Liam was a cad for straying, but if he hadn't then the joke was on her. "I'm sorry. Cheating is never good."

"No, but it made me value the people I already had in my life and the ones who stuck by me—which was mostly Daryl. He's one of the few actors I trust. Men, women—they all want ahead and will do whatever it takes to get there. I got tired of the crap. That's why I took a break. I'm tired of the shit, the backstabbing and the lies. When I come home, it's just him and me...and now you and Todd. That's what I want. The hard, easy, messy, confusing and complicated... the family and the love."

"Yeah." Sarah hugged Liam and breathed in the scent of his cologne. "Me, too." She smiled and allowed herself to relax. She'd found something good with Liam and Daryl. She met his gaze but the gun went off, making her jump. "Oh! They're off." She stayed in his arms but turned to watch the runners. "He'll be near the back of the pack. They've got yellow jerseys."

Liam groaned. "I'm glad you've got Addie, but I wish she'd let up on Daryl. He'll miss the race." He kept his arms around her, keeping her warm. "I bet Addie helped a lot when you left your ex-husband."

"Uh huh." She'd guessed he'd ask that. Instead of

answering, she spotted Todd and switched subjects. "Here he comes. Mid-pack." She sprang free from Liam, then jumped up and down. "Go, Todd. Use your arms. Good strides." She clapped for her son. "Good job. Keep it up!"

Todd shook his head and smiled. He might not have liked her embarrassing him, but he'd heard her. He raced past her and Sarah clapped until he disappeared behind the school building.

"Now we go over here." She stepped across the gravel path out of the way of the runners. "And we wait."

"I'm choked up. He's good." Liam applauded the racers. "Think he'd let me train with him?"

"You'd have to ask." But she appreciated Liam thinking of Todd. Her son tended to run alone on non-practice days. Having a partner would be perfect.

"I will." He draped his arm around her again and squeezed her. "Think Addie is almost done with Daryl?"

"Who knows? Once she gets a burr up her ass, she doesn't let go easily." She cheered and clapped as Todd passed again. "Great job, kid. Keep it up. You've got this." She waited until Todd rounded the far turn, then spoke. "He'll come back once more, then we all sprint to the finish line. The way he's going, we're going to have to hustle or we'll miss him."

"He's doing very well. I'm proud," Liam said.

He hadn't pushed on the topic of Addie, but she still owed him an explanation while they had a little time. "The thing with Addie...we've known each other almost as long as I've known Daryl. We were officially roommates before I moved in with Daryl. When I found out I was pregnant, I told her. I discussed with her what I should do and my decision to leave him. She stuck by me, much like he did with you — well, she did until I married Richard. She knew he was trouble in the same way she saw through Mischa. She's given me the green light with you and Daryl, but I'll bet she's giving him an earful so he doesn't screw up. Something along the lines of if you leave, she'll break your legs."

Liam kissed her temple. "Richard was a bastard. She'd got the right to be protective. I would be if I were her." He slid his hand into her back pocket. "Hell, if Daryl screws you over, he'll have to deal with me. There's more at stake here than just an affair. I'm not taking this lightly."

"You're silly." But she loved his devotion. She needed someone so attentive to her needs and hoped Daryl could be the same. They'd had something strong once and it could happen again.

"I'm in love with two people. What can I say?" He squeezed her ass. "I won't take that back."

"Good," she murmured and buried her face against his neck. She liked feeling protected.

"Speaking of good, here comes the pack. Todd should be around soon." He patted her rump.

She glanced around at the people milling about. For the first time since Vegas, she felt free. Being with someone, even a celebrity, wasn't scary. Being at the race with him wasn't awful or embarrassing. She could do this. She spotted Todd, still mid-pack and going strong. "Proud of you," she shouted. "Keep it up. Come on, Todd. Not much more."

"Great job." Liam let go of her long enough to applaud the runners. He tapped her arm. "We'd better go. He's quick."

"Yeah." She hurried toward the finish line with Liam beside her. The simple act of being together wasn't lost on her. She loved having him there. She caught up to Addie, Ham, Matt and Daryl. She kept clapping and tried to see the clock. "What's his time? I'm too short. I can't..." She groaned. The timer needed to be placed higher.

Liam surged forward. "Come on, Todd. Twenty-one. You've got this."

"Twenty-one," she blurted. "Are you serious?" His best run time was around twenty-four minutes. She jumped up and down in time to see Todd cross the finish line.

"Holy shit," Liam shouted. He threw his arms around

her and turned a circle. "He did it in twenty-one minutes and forty-six seconds. I'm going to have to bust my nuts in order to keep up with him."

She clung to Liam and marveled over her son's time. Twenty-one minutes and forty-six seconds. Todd had outdone himself. Pride swelled in her heart, then she regained herself. "We need to catch him in the corral."

Liam placed her on her feet and kissed her. "We'll grab Daryl, too. I saw him, but we stopped ahead of where they are."

She nodded as Daryl strode up to her. He grinned but didn't say anything. He stayed on her left side and Liam stood on her right. *So possessive all of a sudden.* She brushed off her concern. She found Todd in the corral and hugged him. Tears streaked down her cheeks. "Great job. I'm so proud of you. Personal record!"

"Yeah." He brushed the sweat from his brow. Redness infused his cheeks and his brow furrowed. "I had to run from him."

"Huh? Who?" She hugged Todd again. "Daryl and Liam aren't that bad." She didn't understand.

"No, but Richard is." Todd shook his head and ducked away from her.

"What?" She met Liam's gaze. "What just happened?"

Addie elbowed Sarah and faced her. "Richard is here and he seems to have followed Todd."

She let go of Liam and sucked in a ragged breath. *Richard at the meet? Isn't he supposed to be in jail?* Even if he'd been released, part of the judgment instructed him to stay at least a mile away from her and Todd at all times. She surveyed the crowd. Maybe someone had seen the wrong man. Maybe he wasn't really there. The moment she spotted her ex-husband, her blood chilled. The breath wrenched from her chest and her knees wobbled. "He's here."

Liam swooped his arm around her, holding her up. "Fucker," he whispered.

Richard stood on the other side of the chute where the

runners funneled through after the race. He'd folded his arms and was glaring at her. His brown eyes blazed. He had facial hair now and a ponytail. Tattoos covered his forearms and neck. He'd been strong before, but he'd bulked up in prison.

She shivered. She'd never thought she'd face him again. He hated her and Todd. Why would he come to the meet other than to threaten her?

"We won't let him get to you," Liam murmured. "Promise."

Daryl stepped between her and the tape lining the chute. "Addie said she thought she saw him. We followed Todd and consequently Richard." He turned his back to her ex-husband. "Li, stay with Sarah. I'll contact Al and keep an eye on my son." He strode away, leaving her with Liam.

Sarah shuddered and leaned into Liam. Richard would always be a sore spot and a bad decision.

"Don't dwell on what happened. Focus on now and moving forward." Liam kept his arm around her. "We aren't kidding. We've got Todd, too."

"Jesus," she said. "I'm thirty-eight years old. I shouldn't be this afraid." She rubbed her arms. How could such a nice morning go so wrong? Yes, Daryl and Liam were there. Addie and her family were there as well and Richard hadn't done anything yet, but he was present. His staring unnerved her.

"I'll have our lawyer get the restraining order situation worked out." Liam eased between her and Richard. "He works fast and he's good."

She shook her head. "According to the agreement when he pleaded guilty, he's not allowed within a mile of me or Todd." She didn't know exactly what a mile radius looked like, but she knew Richard was too close.

"It'll be fine. Let's talk to the coach." Liam guided her around the corral. "We'll get this worked out."

She'd never mentioned Richard or his presence to the coach because her ex hadn't been a problem before. She gulped air to hold back her fear, but nothing helped much. Something was very wrong. If Richard was around then the situation was fucked up. She held on to the hope that Daryl and Liam could keep her safe.

"I see you," Richard shouted. "A celebrity boyfriend and his lackey won't do anything. I know where you're weak." He laughed. "It makes you more vulnerable."

She tucked tighter to Liam. Nothing short of Richard landing back in jail would give her peace of mind.

"Don't worry about him." Liam guided her to the team tent. Daryl stood with Todd and the coach. A sheriff's deputy approached and joined the conversation.

The deputy nodded and said something Sarah couldn't hear. Daryl pointed and the sheriff strode away. Daryl whipped his phone from his pocket.

She tensed and whimpered. Daryl angry was never a good thing.

"He's probably calling our security specialist friend, Al." Liam's jaw tightened. "We should've brought Al along from the beginning."

"But you didn't know what you were getting into." Yeah, her life was a little more complicated than they'd expected and she knew it.

She rubbed her arms again. The chill seeped through to her bones despite the warm temperature. A hundred questions filled her mind. Why was Richard there? Why would he come to the meet? Why didn't she know about his release, if he'd even been released? Wasn't there a protection order in place? Would he target them or was he just trying to scare everyone? Was he after Addie and her family too?

"We'll wait until Alyssa finishes her race, then we'll grab her and Todd and go." Liam held her. "It'll be okay."

"How can you be sure?" She'd been there when Richard unleashed his brand of hell on her life. "He's dangerous."

Daryl strode back up to her and Liam. "Al is on his way here." Daryl flexed his fingers on his phone. "Knowing someone with a private jet and lots of access at the ready helped." He grabbed Liam and Sarah in a hug. "We'll protect you and Todd. I can't lose you now that I've got you in my life."

Sarah sagged against Liam and Daryl. She didn't know what to think. Danger was back and she wasn't alone. But for how long? Liam might be honest about sticking around. Daryl had a reason to do so as well, but could she put too much trust in him? She didn't have much choice. She'd have to give Daryl and Liam the benefit of the doubt and put her faith in two actors to keep her safe.

Chapter Ten

Once back at the house after the race and a quick trip to the hotel to check out, Liam went around to every window and door to ensure the locks were secure. Daryl had gone upstairs with Sarah to calm her down. Liam sat at the table with his laptop. He wasn't sure what else to do. Until Al arrived and their lawyer got the paperwork done, Liam and Daryl were helpless to stop Richard.

"No tablet?" Todd sat opposite him at the table. "I figured you'd have the best tech."

"Nah. I like the old girl." He closed the lid on his computer. "She's pretty and reliable. Besides, I don't want another one." He'd searched for properties around Kenton with the proper security or land enough for privacy.

"What are you looking for?" Todd shrugged. "I peeked over your shoulder."

"Houses." He'd been found out. He couldn't lie.

"Why?" Todd asked. "What's wrong with this one? Too small? Not fancy enough?"

Ah, to be a teenager again… "There's nothing wrong with this one, but I want to protect you and your mom. I feel helpless."

Todd snorted. "Richard gets off on that. He wants us to be afraid." He drummed his fingers on the table and twiddled with his phone. "I get it. You want Mom to trust you. She does. She's cautious, but she likes you and Daryl around."

He sighed. He understood why Todd hadn't called Daryl his father, but still. "But?"

"But the more you flip out and act crazy, the more it feeds into Richard's fucked-up-ness." Todd folded his arms.

"He told me one time that there's nothing hotter than the screams of a woman. I didn't understand it at the time, but he meant when she's afraid. If he can't dominate her, then he's not happy."

Although what Todd said made sense, he refused to accept the explanation. "I can't do nothing." He hated being helpless.

"I know. Trust me. I want to run the hell away from here and never see the jerk again, but he'll find us." Todd shoved a piece of paper across the table. "This came today in the mail. It's the notice of his release. They didn't ask her or give her the chance to question it. That's bullshit."

Todd was right. *Shit.* Liam massaged his temples. "I need to talk to your mom and show her this."

"Just…" Todd sighed. "I don't know. You have security guards. Maybe you can station one with her when you can't be there. Get the restraining order sorted out. He'll beat her up. He needs to not be in town. Jail would be best, but out of town is better."

"We can't get rid of him. I'm not part of the mafia." Although he kind of wished he was the character he'd played in *Nautilus*. At least then he'd know what to do.

"I know."

Liam left the laptop on the table. "My friend Al is coming to provide security. Daryl says he's got a couple of his best men working with him, so at least you'll be protected."

"What about when I do my run tomorrow?" Todd stood. "Mom said you were cool about coming along. Want to?"

"I do." At least then he could keep an eye on Todd. Daryl would have Sarah with him.

"Cool. I'm going to work on my homework. I've got a paper to finish. French Revolution. Thrilling." Todd shrugged, then headed out of the room.

He rested his hands on his hips. Al and company couldn't get there fast enough. Liam made his way up to the second floor. Sarah and Daryl's voices filtered out into the hallway. He stopped. He knew he shouldn't be listening in, but he couldn't help himself. His phone vibrated in his pocket. He slipped the device from his pants and checked the message, then blew out a long breath. The text was from Al.

Pulling into Kenton. Will be at the house in ten. Black car. Can't miss us.

"Thank you," he murmured.

Will look for you.

Now he had to talk to Daryl. They needed to have a plan. First, he had to wait for Sarah and Daryl to finish their conversation.

"Are you sure you're not going to leave me? I lied to you for years," Sarah said.

"By omission," Daryl said. "I'm not happy, if that's what you want to know, but I'm getting over it. Believe me, finding out I had a kid was a shock."

Liam leaned against the wall and waited for the right time to enter. Daryl had a point, but he felt for Sarah. She'd put herself in a tough situation and now that she had a way to fix the problem, the solution would take time. Add in Richard and things were all fucked up.

"Babe, I have no plans on leaving. I said I wanted you back and now that I've got you and Liam, I want this triad to work." Daryl chuckled. "We vowed to be there for you. We are."

"I want to say I know," Sarah replied.

Liam forced himself forward. He entered the room and waited in the doorway. He wanted to throw himself into her arms and beg forgiveness for listening in, but he kept quiet.

"Hey." She wiped her face. "I'm sorry you had to see Richard, but now you know what he looks like."

His heart bled for her. She'd been through so much. Despite the hard times, she'd been strong. She'd come out on the other side and not only had her work at the school to show for it, but a few novellas for sale on the Internet and a well-adjusted son. She deserved the world and with Daryl's help he'd give it to her.

"What's up?" Daryl asked. "Everything okay?"

"Things are fine." Considering the upheaval that morning, things had levelled off enough to be manageable. But Liam needed to speak to Daryl. He clasped his hands together. "Al's going to be here at any second."

* * * *

Ten minutes later, Daryl escorted Al into the house. Daryl massaged his forehead. *Okay, we can move forward.* "Why don't we all get acquainted?" He headed to the kitchen. Al stood in the middle of the room. Daryl met Liam's gaze, then nodded once. Al Cramer could be imposing. The man stood over six feet tall, bore tattoos all over his arms and neck and his booming voice could quiet a stadium. Daryl trusted him above anyone else in the areas of security, intelligence and crowd control. If Al couldn't part the Red Sea of paparazzi and get him and Liam to a private jet, then no one could. Daryl placed his arm around Sarah.

"Todd should be here. If this is for protection, then yeah, I want him around." Sarah shrugged out of Daryl's grasp and disappeared up the stairs.

Al stared at Daryl. "Guys."

"Hey." Daryl dipped his head. "The objective is to keep her and the kid safe. The ex never said he was going to hurt her, but he also said we couldn't protect her. Could be a BS move or it's a veiled threat. I can't do nothing and I can't let him do something."

Al's expression didn't change. "We ran a background check on him. The guy's been arrested six times for assault in the last ten years, once for rape, and once she left him, he was sentenced to five years in jail. He's dangerous and gets off on pain. The thing is, he got out on early release for good behavior."

"Are you serious?" Liam blurted.

Daryl gritted his teeth. A pain freak — and not in a good way — plus great at fooling the law. *Shit.* They were all in deep trouble if Richard decided on revenge.

"I'm shocked he got out, but not totally surprised. Some judges believe in rehabilitation. If your boy here acted right and played the part, he could've pulled a judge who bought the whole story. I don't know how, but he must've." Al widened his stance and folded his arms. "He's accused of killing his ex-girlfriend, Carys, but there's no proof. No body and no forensics. Just hearsay."

Daryl's heart dropped. Sarah deserved to know, but damn it. She had no business hearing this. His blood chilled. *An accused murderer...* Thank God Richard wasn't biologically connected to her son. He focused on Al. "So his MO is what?"

"Stalking, threatening then attacking. I've got my buddy Bix installing the security system. It's totally silent and internal. The best tech I can get my hands on," Al said. "Theo and Ken are on surveillance and I'm sticking to Sarah like glue. Where she goes, I do. Denny will do the same with your...Todd."

"Son?" He clapped Al on the shoulder. "It's okay. I'm still wrapping my head around it too, but finding out the truth is the best thing to happen to me." He bowed his head once. "I'm thankful you were able to help and so fast. Liam and I can't thank you enough." He didn't feel the change. Hell, he was still on-edge, but with Al around, he had a little peace of mind.

"Speaking of peace, I've got people keeping an eye out on the neighbors, too. You mentioned he might try to attack them. If something happens over there or with anyone, the police will be notified first, but we'll be there, too." Al gave him a sharp nod. "I'm off. We're turning the area above the garage into the headquarters. Everything is on the down-low and we're good. I'm always watching." He waved, then strode out of the house.

Daryl closed the back door and leaned against it. *Shit.* She'd missed the entire conversation — but that was Al. He kept things short, sweet and informational. "Christ. Life has changed so much."

"You've got more to fight for. We both do." Liam wrapped his arms around Daryl. "No one said this would be easy. We couldn't just drop into her life and make it perfect."

"Maybe, but that doesn't mean I can't try." He tilted Liam's head and kissed him. "None of this would be possible without you. You're my rock."

"And I've got a great ass." Liam laughed. "So do you."

Sarah rounded the corner. Todd collided with her. Neither said anything and instead they stared at him and Liam.

Daryl opened his mouth then closed it. What the hell could he do now? She'd never mentioned not showing he was with Liam to Todd. The kid deserved to know the truth.

"Get a room." Todd rolled his eyes. "At least go upstairs. I don't want to see that stuff."

"Sorry." Liam disengaged from Daryl and scratched his forehead. "Wasn't thinking."

"Stop." Sarah glanced at Daryl, then poked Liam in the chest with her finger. "First, you need to quit apologizing. He's seventeen and I know what I've caught him not only watching but doing. A married couple kissing isn't awful."

"Mom." Todd's eyes widened. "You're embarrassing me."

"Won't be the first time," she said, then turned her attention to Daryl. "Our boy isn't as innocent as I'd like. He's all boy." She placed her palm on Liam's chest. "Now you…you need to stick up for yourself more. There's a tiger in here and it's dying to come out. He wants to protect his family. Let him."

Pride swelled in Daryl's heart. Not just for Sarah finding her backbone, but for Liam and Todd, too. She was right. Liam had guts but he'd been quick to keep them in check. Daryl hadn't encouraged Liam as much as he should've. He tended to put Liam in his place. Not good. Todd might be a little rowdier than Sarah wanted, but Daryl had no room to talk. He'd done his share of getting around during his youth, too. He bit back a chuckle. Sarah had become more than the glue holding them together. She handled all three of them with ease and was much stronger than she seemed to believe.

Sarah rested her hands on her hips and stared at Daryl. "Okay. Give me the rundown. Are we under lock and key? Or what?"

Daryl sighed and explained the gist of what Al had planned. He'd introduce her and Todd to the major players and he'd talk to Addie about their protection.

"So you're putting us all under surveillance?" Todd groaned. "Big brother."

"Kind of." Daryl shrugged. "It's either that or risk something worse. I'm rather fond of you and your mother. I don't want you to get hurt."

"Is all of this going to be for nothing?" Sarah asked, her voice low.

Daryl should've seen this coming. "What if it's not?" He had too much on his mind and the weight of it all nearly crushed him. "I'm expecting to hear from my agent in the next few days. He's going to tell me to report to Massachusetts for a movie I signed on two years ago to do. How in the hell can I be sure my family will be safe if I'm not here?"

Sarah said nothing. Liam cracked his knuckles, but kept quiet too. Todd leaned on the wall and snorted. "Two years ago? You plan that far ahead? I'm not even sure what I want to do after college."

"Yeah, well, I liked the script." Back then, he'd loved it—a small-town coffee shop owner falling for a brilliant billionaire pretending not to be rich so she could experience some normalcy. Now he wished he could pull out of the part. He should be in Ohio with them. Not only did he want to be with them, but he had so much catching up to do.

Sarah smiled and her expression reminded him of the one

she'd worn the day she'd left him at the airport years ago. "You have a job to do and should do it. Liam said he was taking time off...yes? He'll be here, so we won't be alone."

"Exactly," Liam said. "I'm here for the long haul."

"Or until your agent busts your balls," Todd interjected. "Isn't that what agents are for?"

"No." Liam shook his head. "I'm in the clear until June. I negotiated a break when I signed on to do Nash."

Daryl slipped his hand into Liam's back pocket. He relaxed a little but not enough. "It's eight weeks of shooting. Really, it should be less since it's a television film."

"Hon, we'll be here." Sarah toyed with the wrinkles in Daryl's shirt. "I've got tenure with the college and Tod has to finish his senior year. If you have people lined up to provide security, then great. We'll make it work."

"Sarah." Daryl's heart sank. She'd become too agreeable.

"I'm not arguing," she replied.

Then why in the hell does it feel like she's pushing me away? "Talk to me." He hated the uneasy feeling in his brain.

"I'm being practical. Would I like you here all the time? Sure. I've dreamed of that happening for years. But it's not possible. You have to act. It's who you are." Sarah looked him straight in the eye. "Am I wrong?"

"I could work around here." He hated the pleading tone of his voice but he had no shame left. He could do local theater and direct something in Ohio. Truth be told, plans not involving his agent weren't his forte. He needed the structure of his agent, but damn. He wanted to be with his family.

"Daryl, you don't want to do that." Liam eased his arm around Daryl. "You wouldn't be happy. She's right. Acting is in your DNA."

"I can't run off while I'm needed here." God help him, if she said she didn't need him, too, he'd lose his shit.

"I understand," Sarah said. "But you've put plans in action to keep us safe. Liam is here. The security specialists are, too. Richard would be crazy to do something now. There are too many witnesses and obstacles for him to succeed. We'll be okay. Besides, you can't live on your smile."

Liam shrugged. "If anyone could, it'd be him."

Daryl forced himself to laugh. Liam was right.

"True." Sarah grasped Daryl's hand. "You need funds to pay the bills and I can't support all four of us."

"Oh, I'm chipping in," Liam said. "You're not doing this alone."

Daryl scrubbed both hands over his face. She had a point and Liam was already stepping up. It almost seemed like they didn't need him. *But come on. This has to be my mind running away with me, right? Paranoia? Christ.* He could channel the emotions into his work when the camera clicked on, but in real life, he faltered. Still, he had to do his job. "It'll kill me to be away from you. All of you."

"Then after this film, leave extra time between it and the next project." Sarah hugged Daryl and rested her head on his chest. "I'm so grateful you're taking care of us. I'm thrilled you aren't turning away from Todd and that Liam is on board with what's happening." She met Daryl's gaze. "Besides, having two sexy boyfriends is pretty amazing. I'm a lucky girl."

"We're lucky, too." He gathered Liam and Sarah in an embrace. "Todd? Join us?"

Todd stood against the wall and crooked his eyebrow. "I think you're crazy." After a moment, he joined the group hug. "I've got a crazy, messed up family...but I'm glad."

Daryl grasped them tighter. He still wasn't thrilled about leaving for the New England project but he didn't have much choice. Liam, Sarah and Todd needed him to do his job then come back to them. He could do it. Walking away would be hard as hell, but he'd return and everything would be right. As long has he had faith and the ones he loved in his corner, yeah, he'd be fine.

Sarah closed her eyes. *Crisis averted.* She cared so much for Liam and Daryl, but Daryl could overreact if given the chance. He claimed to love her and she understood his devotion. Still, he couldn't ignore his prior commitments just because she had a problem.

Todd groaned. "Mom. I promised Alyssa we'd watch a movie tonight in the basement. Is that still okay?"

She'd forgotten about allowing him to do so. *Crap.* Sarah flipped her hair over her shoulder. "Yeah." She couldn't keep her son secluded forever. "See if Addie and Ham want to come over, too."

"Mom." Todd groaned again, this time with dramatic flair. "It was supposed to be a date."

"Under the circumstances, I think it's best if you just stay where I can see you and have her parents over, too." She needed the extra time to wrap her head around what was going on.

"We can order pizza and make it fun," Liam said. "Right?"

Todd threw his hands up and sighed. "Sure. Whatever. I'll text Alyssa." He left the room in a huff.

Sarah sagged against Liam. "I could blame the attitude on him being a teenager, but he has a point. They're dating and should be able to go out rather than be cooped up here with us."

"Hon." Daryl massaged her shoulders. "Give it a few days to calm down. I know I just flew off the handle a little bit ago, but I've gained some clarity. You're right. If you're protected, you should all go about your business. That said, I'd be willing to bet Addie would appreciate coming over."

"She would." Sarah slipped her phone from her back pocket and handed the device to Daryl. "Call Carlucci's Pizza. Get whatever, but no pineapple or anchovies. The number is still the same...the question is, do you remember it?"

Daryl accepted the phone. "Oddly enough, I do remember." He twiddled with the phone then placed it against his ear. "My boy isn't wild about pineapple and anchovies? Or is that your aversion?"

"He's a lot like you." She hadn't thought about Daryl's

pizza preferences in years, but yeah, he and Todd had the same dislikes. The two of them shared so many qualities and actions, including their flair for the dramatic.

A man Sarah didn't know ushered Addie and Alyssa into the kitchen. Alyssa shrugged away from him and darted from the room. The man nodded once then left.

Addie sighed. "Ham's at work. He didn't want to go, but he has a few more payments to make on Alyssa's braces, so...yeah. Matt went clubbing. He said something about needing a break from the drama." She rolled her eyes. "I don't understand any of this, but I can't say I blame him."

"Join the club." Sarah hugged her friend. "It's all moving at warp speed. These two are back, I told Todd the truth... then Richard shows up. It's nuts."

Daryl handed Sarah her phone back. "The pizza will be here in half an hour and Al will answer the door." He pinched the bridge of his nose. "Sorry. Addie, Sarah, that gentleman who was just in here is Al. He's a damn good security specialist and I trust him with my life as well as Liam's."

"I see." Addie pursed her lips. "And the goons outside of my house are...?"

"Al's team—some of them. I didn't want to risk your family." Daryl smiled but the joyful expression didn't reach his eyes. He tapped Liam's arm and said nothing before he left the kitchen and disappeared up the stairs. The non-verbal communication annoyed Sarah.

"What's the deal?" Sarah asked.

"I believe his agent texted him." Liam shrugged. "He's probably going to call him to hammer out the details for his trip to New England. I don't ask questions. I just let him have his space."

"Oh." *Well, shit.* She'd pushed in on something that didn't involve her.

"It's fine. He won't talk to our agent while I'm in the room. I don't understand why. But he's done that since I've known him." Liam shook his head. "Why don't we start the movie? I'll bring the pizza down when it arrives."

"Deal." Addie left Sarah alone with Liam.

Sarah narrowed her eyes. "I have no right to say this, especially with my past actions, but I don't like secrets. If we're going to keep doing this…relationship, then we talk things out and don't hide." Truth be told, she didn't care about his negotiations with his agent. But if he kept his mouth shut about what he was going to do, then what else would he hide? She'd vowed to be honest with them and wanted open lines of communication with them, too.

"I agree." Liam cupped her jaw. "But I can't make him talk."

"I know." She knew all too well. Daryl seemed to want to save the world and be a superhero, but he'd run himself ragged first trying to keep everything in line. "He's a control freak when he wants to be and stubborn on occasion, too. He'll kill himself trying to keep order."

"Yeah, but that's why you left him at the airport—so he didn't burn himself out." Liam chuckled. "You're the only one who brings him to his knees and makes him so crazy. None of his exes or the women who've co-starred with him and claimed to have slept with him have made the same impact as you. I'm not enough."

"You are." She hooked her fingers into Liam's front pockets. "He wouldn't be here without you, I'm sure."

"You have too much faith."

"I've been told that quite a few times." More than she could count, actually. "But I also have three great men in my life. I can't complain." She kissed him. "You're greater than you know."

Liam rested his forehead on hers. "We'll make this work and make it right, sweetheart. No more fear. I want this to work more than you realize. I don't know if you love us, but I know my heart. I love you and Daryl. I'm so fond of Todd…like he's my own child. I don't want this to fall apart."

She couldn't say the word love even though she did love

them. The words were there but not ready to be said out loud. The fear of losing Daryl and Todd and being alone overshadowed so much. She couldn't help guarding her heart in case they left and she ended up by herself. Todd would be out of the house within a year or so. She refused to hang on to a man or men who couldn't stick around. *Christ.* She didn't trust them as much as she'd thought. They could have her body and bring her pleasure, but she wasn't ready to fork over her heart…again.

* * * *

Three hours later, Sarah sat in the basement. The movie had finished more than half an hour ago. Addie and Alyssa had gone home and Todd had disappeared upstairs to his room. Although he'd brought the pizza downstairs and joined them for a few minutes, Daryl had quickly headed back to the ground floor or maybe the bedroom. She wasn't sure. She hugged her legs and stared at the scuffs on the coffee table. She'd been in a room full of friends and family but had felt so alone.

Liam returned to the basement and plopped next to her on the sofa. "Hey." He slipped her hand into his. "Tired?"

"Yeah." *Try exhausted.* She wanted to curl up in her bed and sleep for a week. Maybe then the nightmare of her ex-husband would be gone. Right now, she didn't want to talk about him. "Would you believe I've met Logan Malone?"

"The hunk in our movie?" Liam crooked his eyebrows. "I don't doubt it. You know some awesome people."

She laughed and palmed his thigh. "He's married to my second cousin, Cass. We email back and forth, but I haven't been to Crawford since their little boy was christened."

"I worked with Logan back when we were both doing soap operas," Liam said. "For a three-week run on the show, we were supposed to be chasing the same woman. He won. I ended up being written off before the end of the season. My character went to college and was never heard from again." He shrugged. "I met my now ex-wife that season. Daryl came along shortly thereafter. Funny how that works."

"Life is quirky." She massaged her forehead. Thinking about her cousin and the charmed life she now lived made Sarah a little jealous. She wasn't sure why. Cass had worked hard to not fall for Logan, but like Daryl, he'd managed to melt Cass' defenses. Sarah stole a glance at Liam. *Who am I to call anyone charmed?* She had two lovers...and a misguided ex-husband.

"Okay, you've stalled enough." Liam dragged her onto his lap and cuddled her to his chest. "Talk to me."

"There's nothing to say. It's been one hell of a crazy twelve or so hours and I'm worn out." She snuggled into his embrace. *Holy shit.* Being held and cherished blew her mind. She hadn't felt so tight with anyone in such a long time. Not just intimate, but part of a two...threesome.

Liam kissed the top of her head and rubbed her forearm. He didn't push or demand. He understood how to be a rock for her and she appreciated him. Despite the craziness, she felt safe. Her mind worked overtime. She knew in her heart that she loved Liam and she'd never stopped loving Daryl, but saying those things wasn't going to happen.

"What are you thinking about, sweets?" He tickled her skin with his light touches. "I can feel your mind working. There's smoke coming out of your ears."

She didn't doubt the smoke. She couldn't shut her brain down and needed to get a few things out of her mind. "I'm overwhelmed." She laughed without emotion. "You have no idea how it feels to be lonely. I didn't feel cherished when I was with Richard and he claimed to love me. I'm not sure how to have a relationship anymore. I'm scared this is all a farce." The words flowed out faster than she could keep them straight. "What if I wake up tomorrow and he's back to hurt me? You might decide you only want Daryl and he'll leave." *Oh my God.* She sounded so whiny. *Shit.* "What if I never tell you how I really feel because I'm

167

scared?"

He didn't stop stroking her hair, but remained calm. "How do you feel?"

She opened her mouth but no sound came out. *No, no, no.* She needed to speak her mind.

"I'm not going to try to persuade you of anything," Liam said, his voice soft. "I know how I feel and the same for Daryl. We also understand more than it seems. We've been lonely. I've been in a room full of screaming fans who want nothing more than to say they slept with me and to use my celebrity to boost their own status. I know because they've told me. They want the fame but they'd never be able to handle the real me. Daryl understands me and so do you. I fell for you long before I met you. I know you love me, but the words won't come. That's okay. I'm a patient man."

She looked up at him. Her jaw slackened. He might not be trying to persuade her, but he'd done a good job. The walls around her heart melted and her confidence boosted. She'd fallen for him all over again and harder this time.

"Am I wrong?" Liam whispered.

"No." Sarah flattened her palm over his heart and his pulse thrummed against her skin. She wrapped her free arm around his shoulders. Warmth flowed through her body. She pressed her knees together. She wanted him so much. "I like how you hold me. I miss it."

"I'll hold you as long as you'd like. So will Daryl." He brushed his nose against hers and his lips grazed her mouth. His breath feathered over her cheeks. He smoothed his palm over her ass. "I like keeping you so close."

She believed him all the way down to her soul. Her heart thudded and desire overwhelmed her. "Make love to me?"

"You never have to ask." He threaded his fingers into her hair and kissed her. The connection, passionate and demanding, but exciting, spurred her on. She craved him. Sarah worked her arms free of her sleeves then eased away from him long enough to whip her shirt over her head. Her breasts strained against her bra and she longed for him to tweak her nipples.

Liam palmed her waist but didn't grab her. Instead, he tugged her closer and resumed kissing her. He sucked on her bottom lip, then her tongue. She shoved her hands under his shirt and massaged his taut skin. She groaned into the kiss. Damn, he was so handsome and muscled.

"Oh yeah." Liam moved his hand to her breast. "So soft and perfect." He kneaded her tit. "Love."

She loved how he touched her, too. The strap of her bra slipped down her shoulder and revealed more of the upper swell of her boob. She glanced over at the staircase. If Daryl or anyone else came looking for her, she'd hear them and could duck behind the couch out of sight. *Oh, what the hell.* She unhooked her brassiere and the lingerie landed on her lap.

Hunger shone in his eyes. He licked his lips then buried his face in her cleavage. She gasped and leaned into him. His teeth raked against her skin and fire burned in her veins. She threaded her fingers into his hair. Each time he bit her, a whimper ripped from her throat. She closed her eyes and tilted her head back.

"Yeah, babe. Tell me you like this." Liam patted her ass. "Love when you make noise."

"Fuck." She curled forward as he sucked on her breast. "Liam." She grasped the hem of his shirt and nudged him away long enough to divest him of the garment. She'd waited for too long and allowed her emotions to get the best of her more than she should've. Now she needed him to take care of her.

"Wow…" Daryl said. "Can I join in?"

She looked up and grinned. "Of course."

Chapter Eleven

Daryl hesitated in the doorway for a moment and drank in the image of Liam and Sarah together. Part of him wanted to be a tiny bit jealous. She and Liam made a sexy pair. But he couldn't muster the emotion. He liked what he saw and wanted to jump into the middle. He rubbed his crotch and blood rushed to his dick.

"You're not joining us." Sarah curled into Liam. Her nipples puckered and she shivered. "Daryl?" she asked.

"I'm enjoying the view." Daryl closed the basement door and clicked the lock. He didn't want any interruptions. "Touch him."

Sarah tilted her head to the side, then focused on Liam again. She offered up her breasts. Liam groaned then mashed his face into the pillow of her chest.

Damn. Daryl popped the button on his jeans and unzipped. The denim remained on his hips as he worked his hand into his pants. He curled his fingers around his shaft. Seeing her with Liam and Liam so happy filled his heart with joy. She was the missing piece.

But now he wanted to have a taste too. He stopped stroking himself and crossed the room. He settled behind Sarah. "Come here." He placed her on his lap on the floor. While kissing her shoulder, he eased his arms around her and palmed her tits. He rolled her nipples in his fingers, pleased when she whimpered.

"Never thought we'd end up like this." She tipped her head back. Her hair tickled Daryl's face. "Can't imagine being anywhere else."

"Uh-huh." He scraped his teeth across her neck and

pinched her nipple. When he caught sight of Liam, he grinned. Liam licked his lips. Was he feeling ignored? Or horny as hell? "We should indulge Liam."

Sarah twisted to meet his gaze. Her eyes flashed and a smile spread across her face. "I agree." She reminded him of a goddess, glistening with a hint of perspiration over her naked breasts. She scooted onto the carpet beside him and raked her nails along Liam's thigh. With Daryl's help, she freed Liam of his jeans. Liam's cock throbbed and pre-cum shone on the tip.

Daryl kissed Sarah again, then nodded once. "Shall we?"

Sarah must've known what he meant. She sucked Liam's dick into her mouth and bobbed her head. Daryl gathered her hair into his fingers and held the tresses out of the way. She set the pace, though. He winked at Liam then joined Sarah on his husband's shaft.

"Oh my fuck." Liam balled one hand on the couch and palmed the back of her head with the other. He slid down on the cushions and a muscle in his jaw clenched. "Christ, I'm on the edge."

Good. Daryl licked his way down Liam's dick to his balls. When he sucked one of Liam's testicles into his mouth, Liam jerked.

"Oh shit," Liam blurted. "Two mouths. I'm dead and in heaven."

"No, you're here with us," Sarah said between licks. She resumed bobbing her head.

The moment overwhelmed Daryl. He wasn't sure what he wanted to touch—not when he had two people to choose from. He palmed her breast then nipped his way up to Liam's cock. "My turn."

Sarah backed out of the way but leaned into Daryl's touch. "Remember when you and I used the clips...way back when?"

He replied, but his 'uh-huh' was lost around Liam's erection. He pictured Sarah in his mind, wearing the nipple clips. *Fucking balls.* She'd screamed when she'd come that night. He'd have to find another set. Maybe Liam would enjoy them, too.

Power radiated through Daryl. His nerve endings misfired and his thoughts jumbled. How had he stayed away from her and denied Liam for so long?

"Love when you're licking my fucking dick," Liam murmured. "Christ, I'm going to come just from watching you."

He might orgasm from sucking Liam dry. Daryl fought back a shiver.

"Switch." Liam yanked on Daryl's hair. "I want your cock."

Daryl wiped his mouth with the back of his hand. *Holy hell.* He wanted his cock licked, too. Sarah spread Liam's legs wide then returned to sucking Liam's shaft. Her hair covered her face but her whimpers echoed in the room.

A fresh wave of zaps washed over Daryl. He stood long enough to shuck his pants and boxers then climbed onto the couch. Liam took control and grasped Daryl's cock. Within seconds he had Daryl deep in his mouth.

Daryl braced his hand on the back of the couch and his knee in the cushion. The sight before him awed and amazed him. God, she was beautiful with her mouth around Liam's dick and Liam pleasuring Daryl turned his senses inside out. He grunted and increased his speed, fucking Liam's face.

Beneath him, Liam tensed. He rocked his hips as much as he could. The muscles in his calves trembled and the tempo of his licks on Daryl's erection turned feral. He ripped his mouth away long enough to groan, then resumed sucking. Without looking at Sarah, Liam nudged her away. He palmed his shaft. Three quick pulls was all he must've needed. He shot his load onto Sarah's breasts. The sight of Liam coming pushed Daryl over the edge. A shiver ran the length of his spine as he curled forward. Liam held on and swallowed Daryl to the back of his throat.

"Jesus." Daryl tensed as the orgasm hit hard. From his

head to his toes, he wobbled. He gripped the couch and added a few more thrusts until the trembling subsided.

"I sound like a broken record, but that's hot." Sarah sat back on her heels. "Too bad we forgot the lube. I so want to see Liam fuck you."

Daryl puffed, then collapsed on the couch. He held Liam's hand. "I didn't forget."

"He's always prepared." Liam tugged her onto his lap again. Cum smeared between her body and his. "And we're making a mess. Where's my shirt? I'll clean you off."

"No, I want some of that. I've got it." Daryl bent over and licked his husband and Sarah clean. Nothing tasted as good as Liam...except Sarah.

"We did forget rubbers." Liam sighed. "Kind of important."

"True," Daryl said. He prided himself in having the supplies with him at all times and now he'd fallen down on the job. "I'll run upstairs and get some...once I find my jeans."

Sarah picked up her blouse and covered her breasts. "It's okay."

"No, it's not." Daryl smoothed her hair from her face. "We want to protect you." He wasn't a total ass.

"You're clean, right?" she asked, but seemed to tuck into herself. "You haven't been with anyone but each other and me...right?"

"Still. We want to keep you safe," Liam said. "Although giving Todd a baby brother or sister isn't repugnant." A dopey smile stretched across his lips. "I don't know. Increasing the family sounds good."

Daryl nodded. *Another child?* He hadn't thought about that, but liked the idea...until he met her gaze. Sarah scooted off Liam's lap and clutched the shirt to her chest. She didn't speak but her tense, drawn-in manner did. Daryl reached for her and when she backed away, he focused on her. "What aren't you telling us, babe?" They shouldn't be having this conversation in the nude, but fuck it. He wanted answers. "Talk to me. We'll fix it, whatever *it* is."

"There won't be another baby." She backed up. "There can't be." She notched her chin in the air. "Sorry."

"I don't know. If you're worried we'd insist you raise the kid without us, you're wrong. I want to be involved. Nannies are out, too. If we create another child, then we raise him or her together." Daryl left his spot on the couch and hurried into his boxer shorts. "Don't run away. Talk to me. To us. What's going on? We went from hot passionate to ice cold in a second. What'd we say? The baby thing?" He shrugged. "I never got to see you pregnant or be there when you had Todd, but if we could have the chance again... I'd love it."

She shook her head. "No."

"Then talk." Liam stayed on the couch, but covered his nakedness with his wadded-up boxer shorts. "We're here for you."

She kept the shirt in front of her breasts and groaned. "I didn't want to have this conversation now or even later." She blew out a long breath then settled on the arm of the couch. "When Todd was thirteen, I had a hysterectomy. They took everything but my ovaries. There won't be any more babies. Ever. I don't have the works. So...rubbers aren't necessary as long as you're clean."

"Sarah?" Daryl stared at her. She could've knocked him over with her index finger. He couldn't comprehend what she'd been through. "What happened? They don't just take those things out without reason." *Fucking hell.* He'd missed so much and she needed him. "Honey." He gathered her into his arms. "I'm so sorry."

"I wasn't until you mentioned kids." She gazed up at him. Tears slipped down her cheeks. "I can't believe we're discussing this now. I shouldn't be crying. It's not a big deal."

"I can't think of a better time to get this out." Not when he could get answers now. Daryl petted her hair and held her tight. "Tell me everything."

She hesitated, then splayed her hand over his heart. "I was full of fibroids that weren't getting smaller. People thought I was pregnant because I had so many. They weren't cancer or anything—just annoying and now they're gone." She tried to smile. "I kept the playpen but got rid of the crib."

"Sweetheart." Liam dropped the boxers and joined the embrace. "You're a trouper."

"No," she whispered.

Daryl knew nothing about fibroids, but he'd learn…later. She was there in his arms and okay as far as he could tell. He hadn't doubted his feelings and his love for her grew. "After all you've been through, you inspire me."

"Yeah." Liam rested his forehead on hers. "Let us show you respect and how much we love you."

"You don't think I'm broken? After everything?" she asked.

"Nope." Daryl patted her ass. He wanted her even more. "Strip, babe. Show us everything."

She scooted off his lap again, then stood.

Daryl took the shirt from her hands. "Have I told you how beautiful your breasts are?" He hooked his fingers into the waistband of her jeans. Liam stepped up behind her and opened her pants. Sarah shivered as he pushed the denim down her thighs.

"Better," Daryl said. He helped her step out of her wadded up clothes. "Liam? On the couch. Sarah, I want you on top of him again." He loved orchestrating their antics.

Liam stretched out on the couch and stroked his dick. Sarah crawled across his body and settled on his thighs. She wrapped her fingers around his shaft. "Oh, fuck," he murmured. "Like that."

"Thought you might." Daryl kissed along her spine. "Ride him."

She glanced back at him then leaned forward. A moan escaped her lips as she settled on Liam's cock. Her toes curled and she tipped her head back. Liam palmed her waist.

"Jesus." Daryl kneaded her ass. "Beautiful." He understood her so well now. She was an odd twist of strength and fragility. She'd been through so much and kept her head high. He'd give her the controlled pain she needed while doing his best to save her from ever having to fear again.

"Liam." She bounced on his cock. "Oh, my God."

"Like that?" Daryl whispered. He swatted her rump. "His dick in you and my hand on your skin?" He bit her shoulder. "Say it."

"I love when you spank me. Want more." She dug her fingers into Liam's shoulders. "Oh…"

Daryl dug through his jeans for the bottle of lube. Once he located what he needed, he returned to Sarah. Her hair slipped in front of her eyes and a fine sheen of perspiration sparkled on her back. He drenched his fingers in lube. He wanted to possess her and set her free.

"Who does this belong to?" He tapped the pucker of her ass. "Who?" When she didn't answer right away, he spanked her. The swat left a red mark on her skin.

"You." She flipped her hair over her shoulder and rode Liam harder. "I'm on fire."

"Yeah?" He worked his middle finger into her hole, pushing past the tight ring of muscle. "Bear down on me. Breathe."

"I can't." She backed into him. "Fuck."

"We will soon." He worked his digit in and out of her hole, prepping her. Sarah squirmed but didn't argue with him. His heart bubbled with love. She could handle him more than she realized. Power radiated through his veins. He swatted her once more then dragged his fingers through her cream. Shit, she was wet. He needed to be inside her.

A strangled cry escaped Liam's throat. "Daryl."

"Right here." He twisted his wrist and added a second finger to her butt. With each pump into her body, she managed to renew and invigorate him. "I want in." Daryl removed his fingers and dribbled lube over his cock.

Sarah shuddered and rolled her hips. "I need to come."

"Not yet." Daryl lined his dick up with her asshole. "Breathe, babe." He grasped her waist and pushed into her body. The farther he slid into her, the more she spurred him on. *So tight.* "Fuck," he bit out.

"Daryl." She tensed. "I'm so full."

I'll bet. Daryl caressed the reddened skin on her rump and paused deep within her. A groan rumbled in his chest. He'd come not long ago and could again. Like now. When she whimpered, she pulled him out of his stupor. He worked into a smooth rhythm with Liam, pushing in when she rocked forward, then seating himself deep once more. The blood thumped in his ears and he groaned. *This won't take long.*

Daryl planted his left foot on the floor and his right knee in the couch cushion. He moved with abandon. These two people were his. No questions. They belonged to him and he wasn't about to let go. The orgasm started low in his belly. His restraint splintered.

Sarah trembled and moved between him and Liam. Her head lolled on her shoulders. "I can't... Need to come."

"Yes, babe," Liam said. "Come for us."

Good thing Liam could think straight. Daryl's brain misfired. He only noticed her and Liam. The warmth enveloped him. He couldn't hold on much longer.

"Daryl. Liam." Sarah writhed on Liam's cock. "Shit."

"Fuck, I'm coming." Liam braced his feet on the couch and surged into her. Sarah shivered then collapsed against his chest. Her pussy throbbed.

"Yes." Daryl embraced the climax and buried himself to the hilt in her ass. He worked his hips a couple more times as the waves of pleasure hit. The love for Sarah and Liam grew. He'd filled her ass with his seed. Liam owned her pussy. But she...she owned their souls.

He managed to pull out and stagger over to the other half of the sectional couch. "I'm wrung out." He flopped onto the cushion and closed his eyes until the room stopped spinning. Liam and Sarah were still within reach — right where he wanted them.

"I am, too," Sarah said. "I don't think my legs will hold me up."

"Good thing we don't have to leave the room right away." Liam cradled her to his chest, then reached for Daryl. "Right?"

Daryl grasped Liam's fingers. The two people he'd chosen to share his life with were truly incredible. Liam understood in him so many ways and knew how to play the Hollywood game. He loved with his whole heart and Daryl had that heart in his hands. Sarah had gone through her own trials and come out stronger on the other side. She was still the woman he remembered, but better and more sure of herself. The relationship burned brighter than anything he knew and he loved it.

Daryl stared at the ceiling. He had to tell them his news, but man…he didn't want to ruin the mood. "We don't have to leave just yet, but I'll have to soon."

"What did our agent have to say?" Liam asked. He propped himself up on his elbow.

Sarah sat up enough to fold her hands under her chin and rest them on Liam's chest. "Good things?"

He sighed. "Good in that I've got work, but bad because I have to leave tomorrow for Boston." He didn't want to go. Hell, he wanted to stay right there in the basement snuggled up with Sarah and Liam. The rest of the world could disappear — well, for the most part.

Sarah scrambled to her feet and fumbled with her clothing. "So fast?"

"They decided to move it up?" Liam wrestled with his shirt, then stood. "Weather or better scheduling?"

"They got a deal on the buildings we need for the outdoor shots and a tax break." Daryl offered up Sarah's jeans. "Trust me. I'd rather have a few more days here, but it'll be over faster." He scrubbed both hands over his face then sat up and leaned against the couch.

"We'll be fine." Sarah stepped into her jeans then balled her socks, panties and bra in her fist. "We'll be lonely without you, but we'll manage."

"You're taking this well." He wriggled into his pants. Part of him wondered about Sarah's attitude. Was she truly being that cavalier about him leaving or was she just hiding her worry? "Gonna have lots of sex without me?" He'd been mean in his question, but he couldn't help himself.

"Daryl." Liam frowned. "Are you serious?"

He stood and hooked his thumbs into his belt loops. "I'm just worried."

"We can tell." Sarah wrapped her arms around him. "It makes sense. You're going and the idea that I might want him over you isn't unreasonable. What is reasonable, though, is for you to believe us. We're a good triad. He's your husband. I'm the girl in the middle. I like my position. It's warm, cozy and safe. Plus, this time feels like before, but better."

Daryl stared at her. "Sarah?"

"She's right." Liam embraced the three of them. "I like mine, too. I've got the best lovers and I'm not letting go of either one."

"Then I'm not, either." Daryl gathered his clothes and followed Sarah and Liam up to the bedroom. After brushing his teeth and taking a quick shower, he climbed into bed with his partners. Sarah and Liam drifted to sleep within moments but he couldn't. He tucked his arm under his head and thought about his life. He'd chewed her out for no reason and regretted questioning her. The worry had gotten the best of him. He closed his eyes. Downstairs, he'd succumbed to his fears, but now? He reconsidered his position. He had a life many people would kill to have and two lovers who suited him perfectly.

He couldn't complain and the more he thought about his gifts, the more he appreciated everything. The movie would be done in less than two months – unless something went drastically wrong and he doubted that would happen.

He kind of looked forward to doing it because once it wrapped, he'd be back home. He smiled and snuggled into the bedding. If home was where the heart was, then his was nestled right between Sarah and Liam.

* * * *

Sarah finished up her lecture and stepped away from the podium. In the last two weeks, she'd settled into an odd routine of going to the college for her morning classes, sharing lunch with Liam in one of the empty classrooms, then teaching the afternoon courses before Al drove her home. She spent her nights ensuring Todd had his homework completed and finished his cross-country practices without a hitch. Liam kept her informed on any possible Richard sightings. If someone had asked her six weeks ago if she'd thought this would be her life, she would've laughed. Now she thanked God she had Liam and Daryl in her life.

She answered questions for a couple of students, then packed away her notebooks. When she looked up, Mischa stood in the aisle. "Hi," Sarah said. "Would you believe, I haven't had the time to write? I'm so behind." She doubted Mischa cared about her 'hobby', but she wasn't sure what else to say.

"I bet not." Mischa perched on the arm of the closest seat. "So. You've kept 'em around. It's lasted longer than I expected. I had the affair over after Vegas. I bet it wouldn't make it out of Vegas, actually."

"Oh." She shrugged, trying to hide her concern. "I'm full of surprises and not enough time to write."

"Well, if you'd spend a little less time in bed and more on your classes..." Mischa waved her hand. Her blood-red fingernails glimmered. "I saw Dare Evans donated a hundred grand in a special scholarship fund."

"He did." She nodded. "Liam Turner is matching it." Pride swelled in her heart. They'd done something good for those who might not be able to attend college otherwise.

She wished she could've pitched in too.

"Nice." Mischa remained on the chair arm.

Sarah finished packing away her things and draped her bag across her chest. "Well, I'd love to chat longer, but I've got to meet up with..." What the hell could she say? Her driver? Her security specialist? *Shit.* "A friend."

"The burly guy outside?" Mischa asked, her voice low.

"Ah...yes. I messed up my car and the guys got me a driver." *What a shitastic lie.* "They're too nice and it's only until I get mine fixed. Probably another day or so." She smiled and hoped Mischa hadn't caught on.

"Oh. That's thoughtful." Mischa tapped her foot and folded her arms. "Is it cool? Having a driver?"

"It's irritating. I can't just hop in the car and go. I have to ask." She crinkled her nose. She needed to get moving. Al would wait as long as she needed, but lingering unnerved her.

"I'd be grateful if I were you. Not everyone can have a driver." Mischa smiled, but her face reminded Sarah of plastic, as if she'd practiced the expression and the meaning had gone out long before.

"I suppose you're right." She gripped the handle of her bag. "I need to go. See you." She brushed past Mischa and hustled up the stairs. Before she reached the doors at the back of the lecture hall, Mischa caught up to her.

"Did Dare ever tell you the truth?" Mischa asked.

She stopped and turned on her heel. "About?"

"About how he and I got in touch? How I was able to set up the romantic weekend?" Mischa rested her hands on her hips. "Did you ever wonder?"

"No, he never said and no, I never asked." The topic hadn't come up but she'd ask Liam at home.

"I didn't think so." Mischa cocked her hip. "You should know the truth."

"I guess I should." Not that she wanted to. She couldn't be sure what Mischa said was the truth. She'd already caught her former friend in a lie.

Mischa stood in front of the door, blocking Sarah's exit. "We were lovers for two years." She crossed her ankles and seemed at ease. "We kept it low profile and the split was amicable."

"I see." *Hardly.* "At least it was amicable."

"We don't talk about it out of respect for the baby." Mischa's eyes glinted and the corner of her mouth kinked. "You know."

"Baby?" What the hell? She hadn't known anything about a child other than hers.

"Our daughter, Sam."

"Congratulations?" She hoped she sounded sincere, especially since that was not how she felt. Once she got home, she'd have to talk to Liam.

Mischa leaned in close. "Try condolences. Our daughter died at two days old. Her heart."

"I'm so sorry." If he wasn't mistaken, Mischa seemed almost pleased. Was she really happy to disclose this secret? "Wasn't it fully developed?"

"Something like that." Mischa eased away from her. "Sad."

"It is." She wasn't sure what else to say. Mischa's response bothered her. *Something like that.* If she'd lost a child, she'd know for sure what caused the child to perish.

"He wanted to connect with you and I thought it was cute." Mischa's words came out hard. "Now I see you're together and it breaks my heart." A tear slid down her cheek. "We said we'd never love again after Sam."

She pressed her lips together. The whole situation was awkward and confusing. If the baby was real and Daryl knew, he should've told her about it and Mischa. She might have thought twice about hooking up with him.

Mischa blotted her tears with the back of her hand and glared at Sarah. "The next time you see him, all you'll see is my face and you'll think of my broken heart. We could've been... but he destroyed me so he could be with you." She whimpered, then ran out of the lecture hall.

Al rushed into the room and stopped Sarah. "Are you okay?"

"I am." Mischa had shaken her faith in Daryl, but she'd manage. There were two sides to every story. He deserved to have his say. "Let's go home." She stayed beside him on the way to the car and instead of climbing into the backseat, she slid onto the passenger side. No matter how hard she tried, she kept thinking about the conversation with Mischa.

"I saw the woman you spoke with." Al locked the car doors and engaged the engine. "Mischa Delbonne. I'm having the boys run her information." He spoke into his headset but she ignored him.

Sarah didn't want to think about Mischa. The topic of the baby had rattled her. Daryl had seemed so surprised about Todd. A man with multiple children or who had been through something so crushing wouldn't be so shocked... right? Maybe he would. If he thought he'd never have another chance to have a kid... *Could be the deal.* She wasn't sure.

"I have some news." Al gripped the steering wheel. "A little of everything."

"Oh? Lay it on me." She wasn't sure she wanted to deal with anything else tonight, but she didn't have much choice.

"Your ex, Richard Nelson, has left the area. I've got people trailing him, so rest assured he didn't slip under the radar. He's in New York and it looks like he's trying to change his identity."

"So he's not in Ohio." She sighed. *Wonderful.* Not that she felt any better. "Does he know you can see him?"

"Doubtful. We pride ourselves on security."

"Don't underestimate him," she said.

"I haven't. I found out how he managed to get out and that's what has me on high alert. He was granted early release by a female judge in Summit County. I'd question her, but she's dead. She left a suicide note saying she'd been used, lied to and her career ruined by Richard. She fell prey to him—his charms, I'm assuming—and she agreed to release him. She had second thoughts and instead of facing up to her mistake, she committed suicide. Richard, the ass, ignored the no-contact order. He's on the police radar, but he's about six steps ahead of them. We're in contact with the police in New York and Ohio so that's a plus."

Christ. He'd become more dangerous. She shivered. "I'm going to be sick."

"We'll get him. Promise."

She wanted to believe Al, but didn't. She kept quiet until they reached the house. Once in the garage, she hurried inside and dropped her things on the counter. She gulped and fought back tears. Shit. She hated to sob. She couldn't adult any longer, not with so much to deal with. Her brain and body didn't want to comply.

Liam turned around at the sink. "Hey you." He wore an apron she'd forgotten she owned and soap covered his hands. "How...? Are you okay?"

"No." She raked her fingers through her hair. "Why are you soapy? The dishwasher works."

"I made rigatoni and needed to clean the machine." He dried his hands then removed the apron. "Thought you might like it if I made dinner."

"I don't have a rigatoni machine." She leaned against the counter. "I appreciate the gesture. I hate coming home to make supper."

"I bought the machine. The kitchen store in town had a nice one and it's easy to clean. Plus, it gave me something to do." Liam left the towel and apron beside the sink then nodded to the table. "Sit."

She hesitated before complying. *Might as well do what he wants.*

"How about you talk to me? Tell me what's wrong. Did Richard make a move? I've been in contact with Al most of the day." He sat opposite her at the table.

She filled him in on Al's intel and balled her hands. She didn't want him to see her tremble.

Liam sighed. "The asshole. He came, he saw, he terrorized."

"Pretty much."

"That's not the big thing though." He slipped her hand into his and caressed her knuckles. "Well?"

She'd been through so many complications in the last few weeks. She should've seen this coming, but hadn't. "Remember the woman I was with in Vegas?"

"Mischa. Sure. What about her?"

"When did you meet her?" She needed to know.

"Vegas." Liam frowned. "Not in person until then. Why?"

"Are you sure?"

"Positive."

"How'd she know Daryl wanted to find me?"

Liam clasped her hands in his. "It's a stupid story."

"I'm listening."

"We'd already gone to Vegas two weeks before the night we all met up. He had to attend a party and I tagged along for something to do. He had to go with his co-star and I stayed at the hotel. I got bored so I went for a walk. I saw the sign for your book signing and texted him a photo of the ad. I asked him if you were the Sarah he'd been looking for. He left the party right then and met me at the book store. He practically mauled the store owner when she wouldn't give him your information. She referred him to Mischa, saying Mischa was your representative. He took the initiative and called her. It was back and forth for, Christ...four days? He offered to have a friend of ours send a jet to Ohio... she insisted we buy the tickets, hotel room and entrance to the club. He did without question. She set it up, but the night before she wanted to meet up — just her with him. We weren't in Vegas yet, so it didn't work out. We got there within three hours of our meeting."

"That's the only time you saw her?" She wasn't sure what to think.

"Yeah. I was with him the whole time we were in Sin City. I promise."

"Did you know he had a baby with Mischa?" she asked.

He snorted and sobered within seconds. "I'm sorry.

185

What?" He held up his hand. "Wait. What?"

"She said he fathered a child with her. Said the kid died within two days of birth and had a weak heart. They weren't talking about it." Tears threatened at the corners of her eyes again. "She said they were lovers for two years."

"That's not possible." He shook his head. "I can attest to that. He might have acted like a player in Hollywood, but he wasn't. He spent his free time, most of it at home, with me. There wasn't anyone else and when he kissed Salissa Green on set, he told me about it within seconds. If he'd have fathered a kid, first, he wouldn't have come home and second, he would've said something. We thought about adopting."

She pulled away from him and rested her head on her arms. Her brain ached. All the thoughts overwhelmed her.

"Hey. I don't know what she's playing at, but he didn't have an affair on me until you came along and I was involved in that. As for a kid, not a chance." He rubbed her forearm. "When he comes home tomorrow for a break, we'll ask him."

"Fine," she snapped. She shouldn't be upset with Liam. He hadn't done anything wrong. He'd been there, but if Mischa had lied then he was innocent.

"Sarah. Don't do this." He scooted closer to her and curled his fingers under her chin. "Honey, we'll get through this. I know Daryl. Whatever Mischa has said is garbage. You know him. He's the same guy he was before."

Her head ached. Liam made sense, but damn it. Something wasn't right. "I don't have time for this. I have a son I should be worrying about, not this. Instead, I welcomed you both into my home. I didn't think things through and my world is falling apart." Okay, she'd been a tad overdramatic, but still. Her messy life was more complicated now.

"Sarah." The worry lines etched deeper around his eyes and his brow creased. "You don't mean that."

"I'm serious. I should've seen this coming and anticipated..." Her voice cracked. "I just can't do this."

"Hold up." He didn't grab her and there wasn't an edge to his voice. "We jumped into this relationship quick. None of us did a whole lot of thinking. We acted. Compounding the situation is Todd." He held up both hands. "Before you flip out, I don't mean that in a bad way. I mean, him being Daryl's son is a complication. Once you told Daryl the truth, you couldn't go back. He deserved to get to know Todd."

She gritted her teeth. He had a point but she wasn't ready to admit that yet.

"Yes, your ex-husband came back. From the way Al talks, Richard would've shown up either way, but we exacerbated the situation. He wanted a reason to scare you. Any man you chose to be with you would've been a catalyst as much as we are. Richard wanted a fight."

He was on a roll. *Damn it.* She massaged her temples and left her chair. He could stop at any time. She needed out.

Liam stood, but stuffed his hands into his pockets. He fixed his gaze on hers. "I can't speak for Daryl, but I've gone out of my way to keep the media out of your life. Our celebrity status isn't your headache. I've kept my head down and I love it. I could shop without being hassled and attend functions with my partner without the worry of being spotted. I love it."

Her fury melted. There wasn't much point in keeping up the argument about her life being out of control. He'd done his share to help her.

"I've tried to keep Todd as the top priority. We want him to stay safe and out of our spotlight. You said he'd be okay with us and I haven't pushed. I've tried hard to make him like me without coming across as a jerk." Liam widened his stance. "I'll do whatever it takes."

She threw herself against his chest and curled her arms around him. She needed his security and stability. "I'm overwhelmed. You know how to handle this and I don't."

"Not entirely. I can dodge paparazzi and manoeuver around a film set. Walking a red carpet and knowing when to turn and smile is easy. But being myself...it's hard—

except when I'm with you and Daryl. I get overwhelmed, too. That's why it's a good thing we've got each other."

"Yeah." He'd reassured her. She couldn't ask for much more right now.

Liam petted her hair. "We said we've got you. I love you, Sarah, and I won't let you down."

"Thanks." She'd been sure before, but he made the feeling stronger. She loved him. Not just as Daryl and Liam, the package deal, but in his own right. If he said they'd be fine and he'd protect her, then she believed him. Her faith in herself and them had gotten her this far. There wasn't much reason not to hold tight to it now.

Chapter Twelve

"Why don't you grab a shower or better yet, a bath?" Liam asked. "It'll give you time to relax and decompress." He rubbed her back and held her to his chest.

"Are you trying to get rid of me already?" A small smile curled her lips.

"Nope. Once I'm finished cleaning up, I thought I'd join you. We've got forty-five minutes until Todd gets home from practice and making supper won't take more than fifteen since the rigatoni is fresh." He kissed her hard on the lips. He'd never get enough of her. "Does that sound good to you?"

"Okay." She patted his chest. "I'll get the bath started. Don't goof off too long." She brushed her palm over the growing bulge in his jeans. "I want to use this." She winked, then left the room.

He stood still for what seemed like an eternity. *Holy shit.* He had to get a hold of himself. If he didn't finish his tasks, he'd never get anything accomplished. He drained the sink then hung up the towel and apron. Once he checked the staircase, he whipped out his phone and dialed Daryl. He needed answers.

The line rang three times and he expected to hear Daryl's voicemail greeting. Instead, Daryl answered.

"Hey, babe," Daryl said. "I was just thinking about you."

"Hi. I didn't think you'd be available." He listened for the sound of running water on the second floor. *Thank goodness.* He ducked into the living room.

"What's up? You missed me as much as I missed you?" Daryl asked. "I'm coming home in the morning. Isn't that fast enough for you? Trust me, I'd rather be wrapped up in you and Sarah than being here."

"Did you finish filming early?" he asked. Christ, this was awkward. He wasn't sure how to inject the problem into the conversation without the help of a well-written script. "Or are you between shots?"

"We got the love scene done early."

"They have those on sweet, Christmasy movies? I didn't think the studio did those any longer."

"Well, that's what we filmed. It's tasteful and the door closes before anyone loses clothing, so it's a love scene in theory." Daryl paused. "You sound tense. What's wrong?"

"Lots." He wasn't sure what to say.

"Richard?"

"It's a little closer to home." Not the right words, but getting better.

"Todd? He's hurt?"

"No."

"Sarah?"

He'd never get this over with if he didn't just barrel into the conversation they needed to have. "Do you remember Mischa?"

"Blonde, leggy and irritating?"

"Yes." *To a T.*

"What about her?" Daryl asked.

"When was the first time you met her?" He held his breath. *Don't lie.*

"Met? Like in person?"

"Yeah."

"The Saturday night we caught up with Sarah. I'd only talked to her on the phone. You know that. You were with me," Daryl said.

"You're sure?" He hated to keep questioning Daryl, but he understood how Sarah felt. If he were keeping something from them, she'd be gutted. Then again, so would Liam.

"Of course I am. Why?" Anger tinged Daryl's voice. "You're pissing me off. You know when I saw Mischa because you were there and you kept telling me I had tunnel vision concerning Sarah. Remember?"

He did. Liam sighed. He had to be straight with his husband. "Mischa claims you had a two-year relationship that resulted in a kid who is now dead from heart problems. Sarah doesn't know what to think, but she's devastated."

"Whoa. Wait." On Daryl's end of the call, the line quieted, then something slammed. "I had to hide in my trailer. If they want to resume filming, they can wait a few minutes. Now...are you for real? What'd I do that I know nothing about?"

"You heard me. She cornered Sarah at the college. If she's lying, then she seems to believe her story. I need to know the truth. You didn't cheat on me. You'd have told me about that and if you had a kid, right?"

"I never cheated," Daryl said. "Once we got together as lovers, that was it—until Sarah came back into my life. I've never seen Mischa outside of the club that night and I've never spent time alone with her. There's no child other than Todd. I don't know what she's trying to do but I'm not interested in being with anyone but you and Sarah."

"You'd better tell Sarah that. She's rattled." He didn't feel much better, but he believed his husband.

"I'm sure." Daryl sighed. "My flight out is in the morning, but I'm going to call in a favor or two from Webb and see if I can get a ride out tonight. I'll let you know either way."

"Deal." He sat on the arm of the chair and scrubbed the back of his hand across his mouth. Things would improve. Somehow, they would.

"Liam?" Daryl asked, his voice soft.

"Yeah." He left the chair. "I'm here."

"I do love you. I'm all yours and Sarah's."

He shouldn't have worried. Just like Daryl had said, he'd been there. He'd gone to the store and talked to the owner. He'd listened in when Daryl had spoken to Mischa. He never should've doubted Daryl's commitment. "I know. I love you, too."

"I'm sorry this happened, but I'll make it right."

"I know you will." He just needed to hear Daryl say the words out loud.

"I'll call you when I'm in town."

"I'll be waiting."

"Bye, babe," Daryl said.

"Bye." Liam hung up and checked the time on the phone. He still had half an hour until Todd returned home. He clicked the lock on the back door then hurried up the stairs. Maybe the water would still be warm. He tossed his phone onto the bed. Although he tangled his arms in his sleeves for a moment, he soon freed himself, then shoved his pants and boxer briefs down around his ankles. He stopped short in the doorway leading to the bathroom.

Sarah sat in the water and reminded him of a soap-covered goddess. She'd piled her hair on her head and pink infused her cheeks. The tops of her breasts shimmered beneath the suds. When she reached for him, bubbles slid down her arm.

Liam steadied himself and removed the remainder of his clothing. She kept showing him why she was perfect for them. He managed to move forward and eased into the water behind her.

"Gave him hell, didn't you?" She leaned into him and rested her back on his chest. "Called him as soon as I left, right?"

"What makes you think that?" He snatched the washcloth from the rack and wetted the cloth. He rubbed it over her arms. "You're right, though." He situated his dick between her ass cheeks. Blood coursed through his body. His mouth watered. He'd been so lucky not only to realize his feelings for Daryl, but to be able to explore the ones for Sarah too.

"I know you and that's what I would've done. I don't like being lied to." Sarah wriggled on his cock. "Even though that's what I did to him. It wasn't my finest moment and I still regret it. But…now that the secret is out, I'm free."

"He is, too." He washed her shoulders and the back of her

neck, then dragged his tongue along her damp skin.

"I see." She turned to face him, then took the cloth from him. "Do tell."

He groaned as she dragged the cloth across his chest. His nipples beaded. "He claims it's not the same thing—your lie and the others. You didn't try to take him for a million bucks. He and I aren't convinced this story Mischa's telling isn't a money grab in the making. He's coming home as soon as possible to get this worked out."

"Sounds like he's worried." She wound her fingers around his dick and met his gaze. "Yes?"

"More like he's aching for you and me and the crap Mischa's putting you through has him angry. He hates being conned. That's probably why he accepted Todd so easily. He knew you weren't trying to dupe him." He brushed a lock of her hair from her cheek. "Promise."

"If you say so."

"Trust me." He brushed his nose against hers. "I wouldn't lie to you. There's too much at stake."

"I believe you and I do trust you." She dropped the cloth into the water and wound her arms around his neck. "It's just hard."

"So am I." He bit back a chuckle. "But I understand."

She smiled. "Despite your predicament and my misgivings, I'm here. I'm worried, sure. Being with Richard meant not trusting anyone, even him. He clocked me so many times. Because of him, I'd get this feeling—I still do around some people—that warned me off. I'm nervous and a little scared around you and Daryl because I love him so much and never stopped. You're getting there. I worry you'll find someone prettier or skinnier. What happens if you start believing the press and go for someone more your equal?"

"Or believe the hype and stay with my husband only?" he asked.

"Yeah." Her smile wobbled. She toyed with the hair at the base of his skull. "That's silly, huh?"

"Not at all. We've all got the things that make us uneasy. Then there are those that help us shine. For Daryl, that's acting. It's his life, just like you said. For me? I'm happier behind the scenes. I prefer to stay quiet about my relationship with him because the shadows are safer. I'd rather be his secret than risk losing him. *That's* silly. I trust him, but I know the industry we're in. I don't blame you for worrying."

"You're more than a secret."

Her faith in him renewed his own. "I am, but I'd rather be behind the scenes. Directing or producing...I like those better. But no, I'm not a secret and neither are you." He kissed her. "Daryl makes me happy, but he's right. You have been the catalyst we needed to be great—as a threesome."

"You're a goof."

"You love me that way." She might have meant to push him away or minimize what he'd said, but he wasn't giving in.

"I do." Her eyes sparkled. She scooted forward on his lap and arranged his dick between her pussy lips. She eased onto his erection until he filled her. "Oh, Jesus, yes." Her breasts pushed against his chest and her hard nipples tickled his skin. She dug her nails into his shoulders.

She managed to wrench the breath from his throat. She made him happy. He'd rather have Daryl there, too, but this was better than good. He slid his palms under her ass. He loved touching her skin—so soft and pliable.

Sarah rested her forehead against his. She set the pace, moving up and down on his shaft until she eased most of the way back again. She met his gaze and her eyes dilated until only a thin ring of color showed. Pink infused her cheeks down to her chest. "Liam," she puffed.

"Right here." He couldn't be rough with her like Daryl. He didn't understand that sort of play and didn't want to. He preferred softer, gentler touches. He grasped her hips and increased the speed. The slipperiness of the soap helped. The suds shimmered on her skin and the perfume wafted around him. She consumed him and built him up at the same time. Water sloshed with each thrust and a few of the bubbles landed on her cheek. She tilted her head back and groaned.

Warmth filled Liam. His nerve endings tingled. Every sense came alive. Being with her was easy and fantastic… like coming home. He nipped her throat. She tasted like the finest wine. When she leaned forward, a thin hank of her hair slipped free from the clip and tickled his face. He shivered. They hadn't used a condom and without the rubber in the way, he felt every ripple of her cunt. Truly like two people becoming one. She clenched once he filled her to the hilt.

"Oh shit, the way you're holding me." She turned his senses inside out. "Sarah."

She trembled, then buried her face against his neck. She muffled her cries against his skin as she clung to him. "Liam. I'm…oh…"

He moved her up and down on his cock. He'd combust at any second. Holy shit, he needed to come. He rocked her on his lap, faster and deeper. He raked his teeth over her throat. "Fuck," he whispered. "Oh fuck." He wanted to be more eloquent but he couldn't think straight. Hell, he could swear his brain had turned to mush. But the orgasm was right there. "Sarah."

She tensed on his lap. She tightened her arms around his neck and trembled. A whimper ripped from her throat. "Can't hold back." She shivered. "Yes…"

Her coming apart was all he needed. He surged into her and spilled his seed. He gasped. The world around them ceased to exist. Just her, him and their moment in the quiet bathroom.

Sarah didn't move from his lap and kept his dick within her as he worked his hips a few more times. She sagged against his chest and laughter bubbled from her.

He breathed in the scent of her hair and chuckled. Being with her was truly freeing. The water settled and he noticed the puddle on the floor. They'd made a mess but had had fun along the way.

When she sat up, he wiped the bubbles from her cheek. "Did that relax you?" he asked.

"Very much so." She kissed him and smeared more bubbles on his face.

She made sex and love fun—just like Daryl. He'd fallen hard for her. He could stay with her in the tub forever—or until their skin turned wrinkly and the water cooled. He opened his mouth to speak but she placed her finger over his lips.

"Someone's coming," she said. "I hear them on the steps."

Well, shit. They'd been found. He didn't want to lose the perfectness of their hideaway, but he knew life would come crashing in eventually.

"Mom?" Todd knocked on the door. "Probably on the phone," he grumbled. "Are you in there?"

She put both hands over Liam's mouth to keep him quiet, not that he had much to say.

"I'll be out in a moment," Sarah called.

"Are we eating soon? I'm starving," Todd said. "I saw someone made rigatoni."

"Welcome to the never-ending food monster known as a teenaged boy," she whispered. She sat up straighter and spoke louder. "Liam did. We'll eat in a bit." She stifled her giggles against Liam's shoulder. "Let me get dressed."

Liam listened for Todd's footsteps in the hall. "Teens," he whispered. He kissed her again. "I can't remember if I locked the bathroom doors, so it's a good thing he didn't barge in. Why don't you go first? I'll clean up, drain the tub and get dinner around while you relax some more."

She stared at him for a moment. A smile curled on her lips and her eyes sparkled. "I love you. Thank you." She gave him a peck on the cheek then eased out of the tub. She darted from the room before he could say anything.

He chuckled as he left the tub. He drained the water then wrapped a towel around his midsection. She'd said she loved him. He hadn't expected her to utter those words for a while longer. He sopped up the puddles. At least they hadn't made a huge mess and left the floor soaked. He grinned and hung up the wet towels. Life was good. He had a sweet woman and a hot man in his bed. Her son was a smart young man. Coming to Kenton had been better than Liam had imagined. Yeah, he wouldn't change his decisions or trade his life for anything.

* * * *

Daryl packed up his cell phone cord, his mp3 player and a couple of granola bars for the flight. He checked his watch again. According to Webb, he'd have a driver there by eight. He'd better get moving if he wanted to be on time. A text from Webb popped up on the phone screen.

Fueled & ready. Meet me @ the airport

Good. He wanted to get the hell out of New England and home to the ones he loved. He draped his bag over his shoulder and headed out of his trailer. A black car waited in the gravel lot. *Must be my car.* He strode over to the vehicle and reached for the door. A shiver ran the length of his spine. *Damn it.* He hated Richard and the fact that his family was scared of the man. He wished he could get rid of their fears and ensure they were truly safe, but that wouldn't happen until Richard was back in jail.

He climbed into the backseat of the car and closed the door. When he glanced to his left to put his bag down, he noticed he wasn't alone. For a split second he wondered if Webb was bringing someone else from the set to the airport, but once he zeroed in on the other passenger's face, his blood chilled.

"Richard," Daryl said. He hoped he sounded more confident than he felt. He palmed his thigh. He'd left his phone in his pants. Maybe he could get a message out before something bad happened. He pretended to reach for the door and opened it enough to hide the light from his phone as he dialed Al. *Please God, Al, please answer.* He set the phone to the speaker setting.

Just as he'd expected, Richard grabbed him and yanked Daryl back into the car. Daryl dowsed the light on the phone, but kept the line open. He clung to the hope Al would hear the situation and call the cops or get someone to triangulate his location.

Richard aimed something at Daryl. The flash of the muzzle told Daryl exactly what would happen — Richard had a gun and probably wasn't afraid to use it. *Fuck.*

"You weren't supposed to come back to Kenton." Richard jabbed the barrel of the gun against Daryl's side. "You fucked up my plan. She's mine. A few more weeks and she would've begged me to come home, but then you showed up. It should've been me there with her. *You* should've listened to Mischa."

"Why?" He had a pretty good idea, but he had to keep Richard talking.

"She knew the truth about you. You can't keep your dick in your pants." Richard shoved the gun tighter to Daryl's side. "You're an actor."

"What's that got to do with anything?" Daryl asked. "And what about Mischa? You make no sense."

"Fucker. She's in love with you, not Sarah." Richard scowled. "Why are we still talking? You should be with Mischa and my wife should be with me."

The driver fumbled with the handle and managed to open the door.

Richard ripped his attention from Daryl long enough to point the gun at the driver's head. "Don't move or I'll put a bullet in your head."

"We'll get out of this," Daryl said, his voice calm. He had no idea what would happen, but he didn't want to see anyone killed. "Richard. Stop. We can work this out."

"Want to bet?" Richard clicked the safety on the handgun. "You have no idea what I'll do. You're stalling. Won't work." He reached around the headrest.

Daryl couldn't see the muzzle of the gun, but the instant he heard the boom, he knew. The world seemed to move in slow motion as the driver wobbled in his seat. Bits of brain and blood splattered across the windshield. Daryl reached forward but there wasn't much he could do. The driver slumped forward and his head collided with the steering wheel. The horn blasted. Daryl's stomach dropped and he fought the urge to puke. He stared at Richard.

"Want to be next?" Richard asked.

Fucking hell. If he kept still, he'd be dead. If he tried to be a hero...he'd probably meet his maker. The only way he'd get to see Sarah, Liam and Todd again was to do something drastic. Daryl lunged forward and tackled Richard in the back of the car. Power and rage fueled him. The bastard wasn't going to hurt anyone else if he had anything to say about the situation.

"Motherfucker." Daryl yanked the weapon from Richard and with strength he didn't realize he possessed, he kicked the door. "God damn it." He braced his knees and held the gun to Richard's chest. *Let the fucker try something. I'll end it.*

Lights flashed outside of the car and someone shouted. Richard's side of the car opened.

"Freeze," the guard thundered. He clicked his gun and aimed it at Daryl and Richard.

Another guard with a gruff voice opened the front door. "Shit. It's Louis. Call for an ambulance."

Daryl shoved Richard out of the vehicle and into the waiting arms of the guards. "This asshat shot Louis." He held off until the guard wrestled Richard into the back of patrol car, then Daryl heaved up his supper. He'd never get the memory of Louis' final moments out of his head. He collapsed on the ground on his hands and knees. Another wave of nausea hit him. He thanked God he hadn't had to shoot Richard. He'd never fired off real bullets before — only blanks. Fucking hell...he could've lost his life, too.

"Is this your phone?" the gruff voiced guard asked.

He didn't look over his shoulder. "Maybe. I don't know." The stench of vomit lingered in his nose. He sat back on his heels and tipped his face to the sky for fresh air. "What's it say?" *Does the phone really make a difference now?*

"Al's on the line. Still." The guard crouched beside Daryl and rubbed his back. "Good thinking on your part. Your call to him alerted us. I wish we would've gotten here in time for Louis."

"Me, too." He didn't look at the guard. Instead, he closed his eyes. "What happened to Louis?"

"They're taking him in the ambulance, but it's not good," the guard said. "He had kids and a wife. I'm not sure he'll make it."

"Fuck. I'm sorry." He opened his eyes and blinked back tears. "I wish I could've done more. What's going to happen to Richard?" His hands trembled and his stomach ached. "He'll claim I did it."

"For a guy in shock, you're doing a good job of keeping your head on your shoulders." The guard—Norman, if Daryl remembered correctly—toyed with his radio. "According to the cops, there's no way you could've shot Louis. The trajectory is off. Your calling Al helped too. He recorded the whole thing. There's a dozen security cameras around here. They've got to have caught a view of what happened and the cops have it all in their possession." He nodded to the phone. "Al's still on the line. Answer him and we'll take care of this. Just don't go anywhere."

"Yeah." He held the phone to his ear. He wanted to talk to Liam and Sarah…just to hear their voices. Al would have to do for now. "Hi."

"Are you okay?" Al asked. "Daryl?"

"I'm…I'll live. I'm not hurt." He sighed and raked his fingers through his hair. "I'm going to throw up again." He'd seen a man die, wrestled another one down and nearly lost his own life. He had no idea if Liam and Sarah knew what had happened or how they were reacting.

"It's expected after what you've been through," Al said.

"Use your head and cooperate when they ask for your statement."

"Sure." He scrubbed his face with the back of his hand. "What about Sarah? Liam? How are they?"

"Webb sent the plane. They'll be there in a couple of hours...probably about the time you're done talking with the police." Al's end of the line crackled. "The set doctor will probably want to see you. Do what they say. I'm getting your agent there as soon as I can."

A series of flashes went off to his left. *Fucking hell.* The paparazzi must've found him. He turned his back on the streaks of light. If the tabloids wanted to watch him, they'd have to work harder. He wasn't in the mood to play ball. Daryl shook his head. He didn't want to think about the attack. He wanted to go home. The world needed to go away for a while.

* * * *

Four hours later, Daryl sat in the gymnasium of the town school building. He'd given his statement to the police, stripped and turned in his clothes as evidence and offered up DNA samples. He'd spoken with the set psychiatrist as well as allowing the doctor on location to check him over. According to the physician, he was still in shock. *No kidding.*

His friend and co-star, Simeon Webb, strolled over to him. "Daryl? They're here."

"Who now?" he snapped. He didn't want to talk to anyone else.

"Your family." Webb nodded once to the door. "You're welcome."

"Sorry," he muttered. He'd apologize formally later. When Daryl turned around, he spotted Liam, Sarah and Todd. The sight of them relaxed him a little. A cop remained beside Liam. Daryl jumped up from his seat and bounded over to his family. He dragged everyone except for the police officer into his arms.

"Why don't we go to the trailer?" Liam asked.

Daryl allowed them to drag him from the gym. He'd rather be anywhere else. The trailer wasn't all that big, but it was private. As he crossed the set, he noticed the extra cars parked everywhere.

"There are a lot of people here for such a little movie shoot." Liam opened the door to Daryl's trailer. "After you."

Daryl waited until Todd and Sarah were in the building before he kissed Liam. He needed the quick connection.

"Missed you, too," Liam whispered. He patted Daryl's ass. "Get in there before the paparazzi see us."

"I don't give a fuck if they do." He complied, but still. The press could go somewhere else. Once he entered the trailer, he wished they weren't in the tight quarters. "Sorry." He shoved a pile of clothes into the hamper. "I'm a slob on set."

Liam shut the door. "It's nice to see you're still a slob. It's even better to know for certain that you're alive."

Sarah threw herself into Daryl's arms. "He's really gone?" She trembled. "Gone, gone?"

"Yeah. They took him to the hospital, then he'll go to jail. Jenkins, the cop who took my statement and my clothes, says there will be two armed officers with him at all times since he doesn't require surgery." Daryl embraced her tightly. "He can't hurt you any longer." He recounted the incident, but without as many details. Hearing the course of events for the fourth time made them sound disturbing all over again.

Sarah met his gaze and paled. "He killed someone?"

Todd didn't say anything. A muscle in his jaw twitched. He remained beside Sarah.

"Why?" Liam asked. "That's nuts."

"Louis tried to escape." A wave of nausea hit him hard. "He won't get away with it."

"The bastard needs to go away to the highest super max prison," Todd snapped. He paced the length of the small room. "Why would he do that? Kill someone?"

"He's a sick man," Sarah murmured. Tears wetted Daryl's arm. She wiped her face. "He needs help."

"Don't feel sorry for him," Todd growled. "He doesn't deserve it."

"No. I don't." She pulled away from Daryl and sat on the couch with Liam. "I'm numb. I can't imagine a time without him lurking."

Liam held her close. "We're all sort of stunned and overwhelmed."

Guilt washed over Daryl. He'd protected everyone and no one at the same time. If he'd been home, then he'd have been able to keep an eye out for Richard. No one would've had to die. He leaned against the wall.

"What are you thinking?" Liam asked. He offered his hand. "Just work on healing, babe."

"Heal? I fucking beat the hell out of a man and tried unsuccessfully to save another. I should be in jail for assault. How am I going to come back from this? Huh?" Daryl shoved his fingers into his hair. "Just...fuck." He needed to get out of the trailer. Being with his family calmed him, but right now he wasn't any good to anyone. Liam didn't deserve to be screamed at and Sarah needed time to process what had happened. He hadn't been able to help himself when the anger hit his boiling point. He strode over to a grove of trees and leaned against a tall maple. The area offered some privacy, but room to breathe as well.

"Hey." Todd stood beside him. "You really lit into Liam."

"I did and I'm sorry." More guilt hit him. *Damn it.*

"You should apologize to him, not me." Todd widened his stance and folded his arms. "I've wanted to yell at him a hundred times."

"Liam?" Daryl asked. He'd thought Todd and Liam got along just fine.

"Richard."

"Oh." That was what he'd suspected. "Part of me wanted to kill him. Of course, I thought of that after he'd been hauled off in custody. I hate him and what he did to you and your mom."

"He was a bastard." Todd shrugged. "He'll get his."

"I'm glad I'm not the one who gave it to him. I don't want killing someone on my soul," Daryl said.

"Smart."

He stared at Todd. "How are you so level-headed?" God knew he wasn't. He could lose his shit again at any moment. Then again, he'd just been through hell and Todd had some separation. Still, Todd exuded a sense of calm that Daryl wished he had too.

"I'm angry, trust me." Todd notched his chin in the air. "There isn't a level of hell bad enough for Richard. I want him to rot for what he did, but…me getting mad isn't going to do anything to make him suffer. He doesn't care. He got the high he wanted. Mom was walking scared. You and Liam installed all those guards. Yeah, he got off on it."

Todd had a point. Daryl stuffed his hands into his pockets. "You're wise beyond your years. Are you sure you're seventeen?" He admired his son and wished he'd been able to get to know him much sooner. Still, he had time now.

"I'm sure," Todd said. "I've spent a lot of time in therapy and watching Mom. Therapy taught me to sweat what I can control and to not believe the Richard thing was my fault. As for Mom, she's kept her head held high after a lot of crap. She showed me how to be strong. Richard, the guys who refuse to date a woman with a kid or be with a chick with a brain…the guys who saw her having a career and not wanting to be a stay-at-home parent as a liability… it was tough. She met some real winners, but managed to stay Mom."

"I'm sorry." He'd said that a lot lately. But this time he was truly sorry he hadn't been there. He would've kept her from having her heart broken if he'd known.

"I am, too, but I'm not. I've learned to pick my battles. Mom says that a lot, but she's right. Richard is the cops' problem now, not hers. You and Liam are hers."

"You don't like us?"

"I do, actually, but even if I didn't, I wouldn't tell her that. You make her happy or at least happier than I've seen her in a long time."

"But?" Daryl asked.

"I want Mom to do what she loves and be level. Write, teach...that stuff. She hasn't had the chance to work on her novel lately and I know it's killing her. The Mom I remember before Richard is back because of you guys. She wasn't looking backwards as much or worried. If you can be the men she needs and my dad, then I'm all for this... situation."

"You're okay with me being married to Liam?"

Todd rolled his eyes. "Then be life partners with Mom. I don't know. Whatever."

"Is that you giving us your blessing?" He faced Todd. "I need to be sure."

"Yeah." Todd grinned. "Like I'm going to turn down two father figures? Yeah, no. Have I mentioned Homecoming is the day before Halloween?"

Ah, there's the teenager I expected. Daryl sighed. Some of the fury was gone. He could handle life again. He chuckled. "You know how to take the edge off."

"See? I told you I'm still a kid." Todd clapped Daryl on the shoulder. "We'd better check on Mom and Liam. I bet they wonder where we are."

"They know we're bonding." He followed Todd back to the trailer and inside. He wouldn't deny still being shaken, but he could face life with Liam, Sarah and Todd in his corner.

Chapter Thirteen

Daryl had thought the space in the trailer was a bit cramped with just him in it, but with the others...he couldn't wait to get the hell out of New England.

Sarah and Liam sat together on the couch. Tears streamed down her cheeks and Liam held her. The television was on, but the sound had been turned low. Daryl glanced over at the screen. The reporter recounted the shooting and incident. He focused on the man talking about the situation. "Did he just say Richard is dead?"

"Dead?" Todd staggered over to the couch. "What? How?"

"The bastard killed himself. He stole a gun from the cops and committed suicide in the holding cell." Liam shook his head. "They aren't sure how he managed to lift the gun, but he's gone."

Sarah gasped. "Oh my God. Look." She pointed to the screen. "Mischa."

Daryl eased onto the couch and huddled beside Sarah. He couldn't believe his eyes. Mischa's mugshot graced the screen. "Using fake identification and alleged conspiring to commit fraud as well as bribery. She's a real peach."

"According to the news app, she's also accused of the murder of Summit County's Judge Matthews, aiding her fugitive brother and using false identification to pose as a professor at the college," Liam said. "The kicker is Kenton has no record of her, or her alias Mischelle Del Brown, working for the college. She's not even licensed as an educator in the state of Ohio."

"Holy shit." Daryl switched his gaze between Sarah's,

Liam's and Todd's. "She and Richard were…are siblings?"

"Sounds like." Liam shrugged. "She's being held without bail because they think she's a flight risk."

"Then it's over." Daryl scooted around in his seat to face Liam and Sarah. "It's not totally done, but we just got a huge break."

Sarah nodded and Liam didn't say anything.

Daryl blew out a long breath. Joy he'd been holding back bubbled in his heart. So many things came to mind, especially the words he'd practiced in front of the mirror on a nightly basis. He should keep quiet, but fuck it. He needed to get the speech out. "We've waited long enough. Sarah, I don't want to be without you and now that I know about Todd, I don't want to put any more distance between me and my son. I love you and Liam. Todd, too. Let's make this family permanent."

Her eyes widened and her lips parted. "Daryl?"

"Be reasonable. Be safe. I don't care. You walked away from me once and I'm still kicking myself for not fighting for you. I'm not letting that happen again. My life is right because I've got you and Liam and Todd in it." Daryl gripped the back of the couch. His heart beat and his skin heated. His stomach churned again. Fear and nervous energy zapped in his brain.

Liam half-shrugged. "Hon, he's right. We belong together as our own oddball family."

She paled and sagged in her seat. "Todd?"

"I gave Daryl my blessing. Liam's got it, too." Todd grinned. "I'm happy for the Richard chapter to be closed and this one is ready to get going."

"You're not supposed to be so mature in all of this." She wiped her hands over her cheeks and sighed. "I feel triple teamed." She paused. "I like my house and my job. I like Kenton. It's not perfect, but it's home."

"Who says we have to leave Kenton?" Daryl asked. He'd assumed she'd argue. Hell, he'd made plans without asking her. "I'd like to live here. I want you to work, too. Write, teach…whatever makes you happy."

Sarah shook her head. "I'm not sure. This is… I'm worried you're saying this because of what happened. It's not what you want, but because you feel you have to. I'm okay. Crisis averted, more or less, and we'll be fine. I won't keep you from Todd."

Fucking hell. Daryl gritted his teeth. He wasn't sure how else to convince her, but he had the sickening feeling she was pushing him away again.

"Hold up, sweetheart." Liam tipped her chin. "The beauty of being semi-famous is that we don't have to live in California. Frankly, I don't want to. I like Kenton, too. We've got an agent who can keep us in the loop and friends who make independent movies. Somehow, we'll find work. As for Daryl, he's right. We want to be where you are. No one is pushing me and I can say the same for him. The crisis didn't bring this on. Our feelings for you did."

"See?" Daryl caressed her back. "I'm not letting any of you go. I'll do whatever it takes to keep you in my life."

"What about my house?" She stared at Daryl. "I can't just abandon it. I like it there."

"We don't have to sort out the house details right now. If we find a house we like—all of us—then there's that possibility. If we don't, then we're fine. We can always sell the other half of the duplex to Addie and Ham. I bet they'd love having the whole thing. Whatever it takes, we'll do it."

"I agree." Liam palmed her thigh. "Promise."

"This is crazy." Sarah fluttered her hands. "Crazy. Why? I'm in love with the both of you. I've lost my mind. The guy I once thought I loved is dead. The one I never stopped loving came back and he brought a husband. My head is swimming. I don't know what to think. Part of me wants to jump into the deep end, but the rest isn't sure."

The joy in his heart spread through his body. She loved him. The feelings hadn't died or gone away. "Nah, you're not crazy. You've got our hearts in your hands and you're overwhelmed." Daryl grasped her hand and Liam's in his.

"We love you, too."

"What do you think, Sarah?" Liam asked. "We're good together."

She flexed her fingers and sighed. "Let's do it."

"Is that a yes?" Daryl's breath lodged in his throat. "Babe?"

"Yeah." She shook her head. "Yes."

Todd laughed. "Parents are so lame."

"Yeah, well…we're yours." Daryl winked at his son. For the first time since they'd all come together, he believed in them being a family unit. He'd give his life for Todd, Sarah and Liam without a second thought.

"And you're all I've got. Dorks." Todd shoved his hands into his pockets. "Serious dorks."

Daryl's heart leapt. Sarah loved him. Liam loved the both of them and now they were a triad. He had a great kid and the danger was mostly gone. With Sarah and Liam in his corner, he could tackle anything. They'd deal with the ups and downs of life together.

* * * *

Two months later

Sarah stared out at the bustling New York skyline. Had someone told her back in October she'd be spending her Christmas Eve anywhere but Ohio and with Daryl and Liam, she would've laughed. She rubbed her chilled arms and watched the snow fall. She couldn't remember the last time there had been actual snow on Christmas Eve. Usually the weather hit a warm streak right before the holiday or there wasn't enough precipitation to create snow.

"Daryl should be about done with his interview." Liam touched her elbow. "Like the view?"

"I do." She leaned into him. Dressing up for the gala downstairs then listening to Daryl chatter on about the movie wore on her nerves. She wasn't the glamour type. Liam, though, worked the tuxedo so well. When he removed his jacket and draped it around her shoulders, she fell even more for him. She wished Daryl was done with his obligations at the gala and television broadcast. But no. Not yet. The remainder of the show flickered on the television, but she paid it little mind. She preferred the quiet of the suite and watching the show from a distance over being right on set.

"We shouldn't have left the party so early." Liam held her and rested his chin on her shoulder. "I know he was working, but it felt like we were a secret. I'm tired of not being able to be myself."

"I don't know. I'm not wild about the cameras." After Richard's passing and the initial interest in Mischa's case, the media had hounded Sarah. Once they'd found out Daryl and Liam were spending time at her house, the tabloids had shown up. "I'm tired of being found and photographed. I'd rather just be with my family and since this is Christmas, it's time for us to come together. I'm happy to spend it with you, Daryl, Todd and the rest of my family—not the rest of the world." Her only wish that Christmas had been for Mischa to be held in jail and for life to go back to semi-normal. The court documents stated Mischa would be held until her court date about nine months away. As for life... just being with her men and son was enough.

"Daryl isn't here and neither is Todd." He kissed her neck. "Todd won't be back to our suite until one."

She knew. She'd been the one who'd given him permission to hang out next door with Alyssa, Addie and Ham. A whimper bubbled in her throat. She needed private time with her men. "Daryl will be back." She swayed into Liam, then snapped her attention to the television. "I could swear I heard him say your name."

"You did?" With Sarah in his embrace, Liam turned to the massive screen. "Are you sure?"

"I think that's what I heard." She focused on Daryl.

A blonde woman in a tight red Santa dress sat on Daryl's left while an older gentleman was on the right. The man spoke about the television movie, working in the cold and the excitement of appearing opposite Daryl. The blonde grinned, then turned to Daryl.

"So, what are your plans for Christmas?" she asked. "It'll be the big day in less than two hours."

Daryl shook his head. He seemed interested but annoyed. Sarah glanced over at Liam, but said nothing.

"I'm heading home to my husband and our partner, then spoiling my son." Daryl grinned. "I'm dying to get going. Trust me. We can't be done fast enough."

Sarah covered her mouth with her hand. She'd heard Daryl right. He'd mentioned all of them.

"No way," Liam blurted. "He didn't."

"Yeah. He did." She squeezed him tightly. "Wow."

The blonde's lips parted and she fumbled. "You mean, your wife and son? Right?"

"No. I meant what I said. I'm heading to my suite with my husband, Liam Turner — you've talked to him, if I recall." Daryl folded his hands on his lap. "He was here over the summer."

"Liam Turner?" she managed. "Yes. He was." Her eyes widened to the size of dinner plates.

"We've been married for more than six years," Daryl said. "Now our partner, Sarah Morrison, is here with my son."

"Oh, you adopted." The blonde smiled and seemed to regain her confidence. "Well, happy holidays and merry Christmas."

The show switched to a commercial for soap and Liam chuckled. "Looks like the cats are out of the bag."

"Yep." She laughed. "He made a mess of his explanation. I'm betting he'll be expected to field questions about it for the next year."

"Probably, but he won't care. The secret is finally out." Liam sighed. "We're all out."

"You're not having second thoughts?" She palmed his cheek. "Not worried it'll fall apart now that everyone knows?"

He kissed her and patted her ass. "I'm not worried about a thing. I'm glad we found each other. Life happened in a funky way, but it was all for a reason. We needed to go down this road to appreciate the now."

"Philosophical. I like it." She remained in Liam's embrace. "I'm glad. I like where I'm at."

"Me, too." Liam nodded toward the door. "Speaking of being glad, the man of the moment is here."

Daryl swept into the suite. He groaned and kicked out of his shoes. "I assume you saw the interview?" A wide smile spread across his face. "She's still stunned. Blew through the promo for the movie and everything."

"She did?" Liam asked.

"Oh yeah." Daryl removed his jacket. "I'm sorry you left and I couldn't go with you. Trust me, I wanted out of there." He crossed the room to where they stood. "How long until Todd comes back?"

"A couple of hours. Addie promised to keep him busy over there until one so we could have some private time." Sarah grasped Daryl's hand. "Call it our Christmas present from her and Ham."

"I love it." Daryl kissed her, then Liam. "You're not secrets any longer. I was so tired of not talking about you." He turned to Liam. "No regrets?"

"Not a one." Liam winked at him. He then focused on Sarah. "So…what are we supposed to do during this time that's our Christmas gift?"

"I've got some ideas." She pulled away from them long enough to turn the television off, then tugged her men to the bedroom. They could have so much fun in the space of two hours.

Along the way, Daryl removed his jacket and shoes. Liam twiddled with his cummerbund and bowtie. "I hate these ridiculous suits," Liam grumbled. "Too complicated."

"But you look so hot." She untied the satin bow. "You weren't voted one of the hottest bachelors in Hollywood for nothing."

"I'm not a bachelor," Liam corrected. "They were wrong." He unbuttoned his shirt. "On both accounts."

"I agree with Sarah. The tux certainly makes the man and you're one fine specimen of sexy."

She unbuttoned Liam's shirt. Most of the time when she slept with her men, they ran the show. This time, she wanted to be in charge. "You're both handsome and even more so together. Show me. I'm your audience." She unzipped her dress and stepped out of the garment. The ribbing on the bustier dug into her waist, but she wanted to be dressed while they weren't. She left the dress slung over the armchair in the bedroom then crawled onto the bed and crossed her ankles. "I see the passion in your eyes. Burn for me."

Liam nodded once then shrugged out of his shirt. Within moments, he stood before her in nothing more than a smile. Her mouth watered and she longed to run her fingers over the taut muscles of his abs.

Daryl groaned. Soon, he divested himself of his clothing. He snagged Liam in an embrace. Both men kissed and touched all over each other's body.

Sarah pressed her lips together and slid her hand over her breast. She tweaked her nipple, needing the pain to spur her pleasure. Her panties stuck to her pussy. She eased her palm into her underwear and between the lips of her cunt.

"Oh fuck." Daryl raked his nails down Liam's chest. "Look."

Liam glanced at her and his smile widened. "Nice." He dropped to his knees and buried his face in Daryl's groin. He dragged his tongue along the underside of Daryl's dick.

"Suck on him," she coaxed. She scraped her fingernail over her clit. The rush of desire filled her veins. She moved the cup of her bustier down to expose her breast. The chilly air kissed her skin. She sucked in a ragged breath and watched Liam bob his head. Part of her wanted to join them. The rest of her enjoyed the show.

Daryl pumped his hips and threaded his fingers into

Liam's hair. He stole glances over at Sarah between thrusts. His nipples beaded and his skin flushed. He tipped his head back. "Fucking hell. I'm close." His movements turned jerky, then his pace increased. He shoved his dick deeper into Liam's mouth.

"Stop," Sarah said. This wasn't how she wanted him to come.

"Can't. Gotta ride this out." Daryl closed his eyes and continued to thrust. "Jesus. Love this…oh shit."

"Stop. I want to watch him fuck you." She removed her hands from her panties. "Daryl." She wanted her orgasm ignited by their display of passion for each other.

"With a boner of steel?" Daryl gasped. "I'm going to come."

"No you're not." She crawled down the bed and rested her hand on Liam's shoulder. "Grab the lube."

Liam relinquished his hold on Daryl's cock then sat back on his heels and wiped his mouth. "Yes, ma'am." He scrambled over to the suitcase and rummaged for the required item.

"I want you to fuck him." Sarah patted the bed. "And I'm going to watch."

A wicked glint shimmered in Liam's eye. He popped the cap on the bottle. She watched in awe as he stroked himself then coated his fingers in the clear fluid. Daryl and Liam had put so much attention on putting her in the middle, but she rather liked playing the voyeur.

Daryl caressed his dick. "Shit. I'm not going to last." He leaned over the end of the bed and flattened his palms on the blankets. Pre-cum shone on the blunt head of his erection. "Sarah."

"I'm going to watch and enjoy the show." She stayed on the bed, but stretched out beside him. She propped herself up on her elbow.

"I'm going to blow." Daryl crooked his finger. "Let me lick your pussy then. I'm hungry."

She shook her head. "Not until he's in you."

Liam knelt behind Daryl, out of her line of view. She couldn't see what he did, but she could hear the noises— Liam's tongue on Daryl's skin, the slap of Liam's hand on his husband's ass and each grunt emulating from Daryl.

"Fucking hell." Daryl rocked forward and tensed. His forehead crinkled and he closed his eyes. "Feels so good." He rested his head on her thigh. "More."

Sarah worked her panties down her legs until she removed the undergarment, then resumed rubbing her clit. With the bustier cup still down, she lay on the bed and tweaked her nipple. Heat rose within her and her nerve endings sizzled. Watching Daryl writhe turned her on. She slid her middle finger into her pussy then smeared her cream over her labia.

"Damn it," Liam said. "I love what I'm seeing."

When she opened her eyes, she met Liam's gaze. He'd taken his place behind Daryl and grasped his husband's hips. Raw need built in Daryl's eyes. He opened his mouth but no sound came out.

"I like it, too." She tucked her knees to her chest and toyed with the tiny bundle of nerves at the apex of her cunt. Her legs trembled and she arched her back. A whimper escaped from her throat.

"Put him out of his misery—and mine, too." Liam nodded once. "Come on, dirty girl."

She'd let them flail long enough. Time to give them the last piece they needed. Sarah scooted into place beneath Daryl. "Fuck me while he fucks you."

"One hot machine." Daryl kissed her. "Anything for you." He slid his cock into her pussy, stretching her to the limit.

She grunted. Holy shit, he made her feel so full. She tightened her knees around him. Liam caressed her calves. Excitement built within her. Each time Liam pushed into Daryl, Daryl sank into her. Within seconds, they'd found a steady rhythm and seemed to move as one entity. Daryl kissed her at the apex of each thrust.

Her mind swam. Being with them now was like old times with Daryl alone—but better.

"God, this is hot." Liam moved faster, colliding with Daryl. "Ah…"

Daryl's eyes widened. "Fuck," he said, drawing the word out. "Love this."

Little by little, the orgasm swelled in her. She clutched Liam's hands and arched her hips to meet Daryl's thrusts. The breath wrenched from her chest and she could've sworn she'd been licked by flames from within. She loved being with both men and appreciated how they knew all the ways to pleasure each other. The heat in her body soared and she gasped.

"Fucking, fuck." Liam tipped his head back and growled. The sound echoed in the room. "Coming." He shivered and gripped her hand.

"Me. Too." Daryl buried his face against her neck and his cock throbbed in her cunt. He said something else, but she couldn't understand the muffled sound.

Sarah stopped fighting the orgasm and embraced the languid, melty feeling in her limbs. She moaned.

"Sweetest sound in the world." Liam sighed. "Damn."

Daryl turned his head, but remained stretched out on top of her. "Love it when you fill my ass just as much as I love being in charge." He kissed Sarah. "I love your naughty streak. Imagine you bossing us around."

"I know what I like—seeing you two together." Sarah settled against the sheets.

Liam wound his arms around Daryl and tugged him to his chest. Without a word, he turned Daryl's head enough to meet him for a kiss. He palmed Daryl's throat. The move—oddly possessive but sweet—intrigued her. Passion radiated off both men and she thanked God she had the good fortune to be included in their relationship.

Liam sighed then let go of Daryl. He backed away from the bed. "I don't know if my legs will hold me up." He collapsed beside Sarah on the bed. "Good sex will do that, though. Make you weak in the knees."

Daryl braced himself on his forearms and stayed on top of

her. She should encourage him to move, but she liked being surrounded by her men. Daryl pulled out then flopped onto the blankets on her other side. "The room isn't supposed to be spinning, is it?"

"If you have good sex it will." Liam draped his arm across her belly. "Was it…good?"

"Of course." She kissed him and slid her palm over his cheek. "I'll never get enough of either of you."

Liam grinned then propped himself up on his elbow. "Good. Um…Daryl? Ready?"

"You want round two so soon?" she blurted. They had quick recovery time, but this was crazy.

"In a little while, but not yet." Daryl left the bed and strode nude to the suitcase. "Since it's officially Christmas Day, we want to give you your gift right now." His ass waggled as he dug through the mass of clothes. "Shit. Where is it?"

"You could lose an elephant in there." Liam rolled his eyes. "Did you pack it?"

"Yeah, I tucked it in here, but you're right. I brought too much crap." Daryl stood and cracked his back. "Found it." He made his way back to the bed. "Sarah, close your eyes and hold out your hands."

She bit back a groan and did as they'd asked her to do. The anticipation of the gift—something big? Small? Crazy expensive?—worried her. Daryl placed the item in her palm.

"Open," he whispered.

When she opened her eyes, she gasped. The red paper and bow sparkled on a small package. Her hands trembled as she tugged the bow free. Once she removed the paper, she recognized the box. "Jewelry?" she blurted. She opened the box and her breath lodged in her throat. She'd never seen such large diamonds in her life.

"Like that?" Daryl rested his arm around her. "Four diamonds. One for each of us."

"We can't get married," Liam said. "But we can claim you as ours. This way everyone knows who you belong to and who loves you more than anything."

Daryl slipped the ring free from the white satin and slipped it onto her finger. "We've got an actor friend who does union ceremonies. Will you be our partner for good? I'm not hiding who I am or who I love." He put his wedding ring on, then offered up Liam's. "Babe?"

"Finally." Liam eased the band over his knuckle. "I've wanted this since we exchanged vows."

"The one we chose for you goes with the ones we have," Daryl said. "We're unconventional and I love it. I wouldn't ask for anything or anyone else."

She stared at the stones in the platinum setting. Liam and Daryl had her heart already. They lived with her and Todd. But now they wanted to make the triad permanent. How could she tell them no? Easy—she didn't want to. "When do you think he'd do the ceremony?" Her eyes watered and she blinked back tears. "We belong together and I can't see any reason to break up a good thing. I love you both."

"Merry Christmas," Liam said. He kissed her cheek. "Love you and Daryl."

"I love you, too." Daryl rubbed the top of her hand with the pad of his index finger. "Merry Christmas, my loves."

Liam sat up and moved the blankets out of the way. "We do have fifteen minutes until Todd returns. How about a quick round two to seal the deal? She mentioned it. I'm just running with the idea."

"Um...yes?" Daryl nibbled on her neck and palmed Liam's cock. "I'll do whatever you want and go wherever you tell me to go to make you happy."

Sarah laughed. Her life would never be boring with two actors in her bed. She'd always wondered if the relationship with Daryl could have a second act. Now she knew. Like Liam had said, things happened for a reason and she'd gone through the different trials in order to love the life she'd forged with Liam and Daryl. She had them and their love. No matter what, she'd never let go.

More books from
Pride Publishing

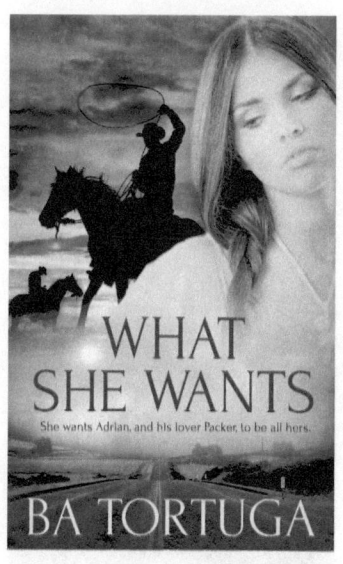

Calleigh and Adrian might have an open relationship, but she's tired of staying home. She wants Adrian, and his lover, Packer, to be all hers.

Part of the Totally 5 Star collection

An ordinary girl catapulted into an extraordinary world meets two even more extraordinary men — but what will she do when she discovers their sexy secret?

Book one in the Love & Rivalry series

The competition is on when two sexy players set their sights on one woman who has no intention of being anyone's prize. Will the ultimate challenge be true love?

SANCTUARY
CALL FOR BLOOD

AURELIA T. EVANS

Book three in the Sanctuary series

*Something draws the supernatural to her sanctuary, but
what keeps drawing her to them?*

About the Author

Megan Slayer

When she's not writing the stories in her head, Megan Slayer can be found luxuriating in her hot tub with her two vampire Cabana boys, Luke and Jeremy. She has the tendency to run a tad too far with her muse, so she has to hide in the head of her alter ego, but the boys don't seem to mind.

When she's not obsessing over her whip collection, she can be found picking up her kidlet from school. She enjoys writing in all genres, but writing about men in love suits her fancy best. The cabana boys are willing to serve, unless she needs them. She *always* need them. So be nice to Javier or he will bite--on command. She also writes under the name of Wendi Zwaduk

Megan Slayer loves to hear from readers. You can find contact information, website details and an author profile page at https://www.pride-publishing.com/